The Buddha, Geoff and Me

D0415121

Dedicated to the memories of Jan Hillgruber,
Dick Causton and Charlie Darlington

The Buddha, Geoff and Me

A Modern Story

Edward Canfor-Dumas

RIDER

LONDON · SYDNEY · AUCKLAND · JOHANNESBURG

The author would like to thank the following for permission to use
copyright material: Faber and Faber and Harcourt Inc. for lines from
'Little Gidding' in *Four Quartets* by T.S. Eliot; Daisaku Ikeda for material
from *A Lasting Peace* (New York: Weatherhill, Inc., 1981) p.133-134; the
Random House Group Ltd for the extract from *Man's Search for Meaning*
by Viktor Frankl, published by Rider.

First published in 2005 by Rider,
an imprint of Ebury Publishing, Random House,
20 Vauxhall Bridge Road, London SW1V 2SA

Addresses for companies within The Random House Group Limited
can be found at:
www.randomhouse.co.uk/offices.htm

The Random House Group Limited Reg. No. 954009

The Random House Group Limited supports The Forest Stewardship
Council (FSC), the leading international forest certification organisation.
All our titles that are printed on Greenpeace approved FSC certified paper
carry the FSC logo. Our paper procurement policy can be found at:
www.rbooks.co.uk/environment

Mixed Sources
Product group from well-managed
forests and other controlled sources
www.fsc.org Cert no. TT-COC-2139
© 1996 Forest Stewardship Council

Printed and bound in Great Britain by CPI Cox & Wyman, Reading, RG1 8EX

A CIP catalogue record for this book is available from the British Library

ISBN 9781844135684

Chapter One

Nothing prepares you for the moment when you meet the person who's going to change your life. I'm not talking here about meeting someone and falling in love and deciding to start a family and all that. I'm talking about meeting a person who alters, deep down, the way you look at life, and sets you off on a totally unexpected path.

Geoff was the bloke who changed my life. I wasn't looking to change. I wasn't looking for a new direction. I wasn't looking for anything. Except a drink.

It had been a terrible day. In fact, it had been a terrible week. On Monday I'd broken up with Angie, my girlfriend of two-and-a-half years. Or, to be more accurate, she'd dumped me, citing 'irreconcilable differences' – the main one being between me and the wealthy, good-looking, kind and sensitive man she wanted to spend her life with. It went downhill from there.

At that time – this was the summer of 2000, soon after the dot-com bubble had burst – I was working for a struggling business ezine, ItsTheBusiness.com, based in sunny Holloway. Internet start-ups were falling like skittles all around us but somehow we were managing to cling on. Officially, my job was to copy-edit articles and proof-read

1

the text before it went onto our website. Unofficially, my job was to rewrite all the rubbish we got sent to make it halfway readable, then take the flak from outraged contributors who resented even a comma of their masterpieces being changed. This despite the fact that most of them wouldn't know a comma from a hole in the head.

These weren't professional writers. Oh no. Martin, our editor, had dreamt up a bright wheeze: our 'niche marketing ploy' would be that the ezine was written exclusively 'by people in business, for people in business'. In their own words. Even if most of them never held a pen except to sign a leaving-card. Risky, some might say, but certainly cheap. It was on the basis of such logic that he'd persuaded various rich mates to stump up the cash to fund the site.

In reality, ItsTheBusiness.com was little more than a form of vanity publishing, and for me, one long headache. The current pain was coming from a linoleum manufacturer from West Bromwich who was threatening to sue us for misrepresentation. Martin, bless him, was pointing the finger at me, saying it was all my fault – I'd 'mashed' this bloke's article beyond recognition. Which had made me lose my rag, there'd been this big dust-up, I'd said things I shouldn't have said – I believe the words 'tight-fisted git' passed my lips. And now here I was on an official warning and heading for The Three Crowns with Steve (classified advertising) for an outraged lunchtime drink.

I really ripped into Martin over my first pint. He wasn't just a shit for blaming me, when I was only carrying out his instructions; he was a cowardly shit. He didn't have the guts to admit to his rich friends that he was losing all their money on an idea that just wasn't working. To my mind, if he had any bottle, he'd put up his hand and confess before everything disappeared down the plug-hole. But he

2

wouldn't, of course. Too much loss of face. Plus he'd be out of a job.

'Sounds like you'd all be.'

I hadn't noticed Geoff when I'd come in. I was too steamed up, I guess. He was sitting at the end of the bar, reading a paper and smoking a roll-up. Balding, about fifty, with a little pot-belly, a bit tanned and weather-beaten. Nothing remarkable to look at; nothing remarkable about him at all, in fact.

'Yeah, I suppose that's half the problem, mate,' I said, and turned back to Steve, who decided that this was the moment to visit the Gents.

'Sorry, I couldn't help overhearing.' Geoff smiled.

'That's all right.' I finished my pint and ordered another half – didn't want to roll back pissed and give Martin more ammunition against me.

At which point Steve banged out of the Gents, looking green. 'Christ, the stink in there! I'll have to wait till we get back to work.'

The landlady looked sheepish. Tree roots had damaged a pipe, she explained. She'd called various drainage companies but the earliest someone could come was the day after tomorrow. There was nothing to be done, unless . . . She looked pleadingly at Geoff. He pulled a face.

'You've got to get it fixed, Shirley. And properly, you know.'

'Yes, yes, I know. And I will. But just for now, Geoff – would you?'

Geoff looked at her, sighed, put his paper down and disappeared through a door behind the bar.

'He's fantastic,' the landlady enthused. 'Nothing fazes him at all.'

Geoff reappeared, holding a length of garden hose. 'I'm going to need a volunteer,' he said.

3

Steve and I looked at each other. No way. But there were only us and a couple of young girls in there, plus this old bloke with a dog, both dozing in the corner.

'Don't worry – it's only to turn on a tap.'

Steve shook his head, immovable.

'You, then. Come on.' Geoff nodded to me and went into the Gents.

I looked at Steve.

'Take a deep breath,' he advised.

I did, and followed Geoff.

The hum was disgusting, but not half as disgusting as what came next. The Gents was cramped, Victorian, lined with dirty white tiles and badly in need of a makeover – the sort of place you really don't want to spend more time in than you have to. Geoff had rolled up his sleeves and was wrestling with a metal inspection plate in the middle of the floor.

'Fix that on the tap, would you?'

He gave me one end of the hosepipe, which I secured onto the cold tap that fed the cracked hand-basin in the corner. I looked round – and the sight turned my stomach.

Geoff had got the inspection plate off, revealing a square pit in the floor – full of sewage. Piss and shit and water. Bits of floating toilet paper. A condom. But more than that, he was down on his knees, taking his watch off and putting it in his pocket. Then he picked up the other end of the hosepipe and stuffed it deep into the pit. His arm went with it, past the elbow.

'Turn it on full,' he ordered.

I turned the tap – and the level of sewage in the hole started to rise. I glanced anxiously at Geoff, ready to turn off the water, but his gaze was fixed. The sewage continued to rise, threatening to spill over the floor. There was a gurgle and a loud burp. A large bubble broke the surface.

4

But still the sewage rose. Geoff turned his face from the hole, trying to breathe some less fetid air. He jabbed the hose deeper.

'More,' he barked, his whole arm in now, right up to the armpit.

I tried to turn the tap. 'It's on full,' I said, my throat tightening. My beer was starting to churn back up my throat. And still the sewage rose.

Geoff grunted, grimacing at the smell, working away at the blockage. Grunt, jab. Grunt, jab. Then he smiled. 'Got it,' he said. And as if by magic, the level started to drop, gradually at first, then more rapidly, as he moved the hose around in the pit, using the force of water to clear a larger and larger gap in the blocked pipe at the bottom. Suddenly, with a deep sucking sound, the pit was empty. Geoff pulled his arm clear, took the hose in the other hand, and washed down his dirty arm in the stream of clean water. 'Thanks,' he said with a smile. 'You can get back to your beer now.'

I fled back to the bar, dazed at what I'd seen. The simple, no-nonsense . . . heroism isn't the right word. Balls. The simple balls of what Geoff had done knocked me out. I was still going on about it to Steve when Geoff joined us a few minutes later. He picked up his pint and drained it.

'You *have* washed that arm, I hope?' I asked him. 'With soap.'

He pulled back his sleeve, twisting his arm this way and that. 'Clean as a baby's bottom,' he grinned.

'Didn't it bother you? Sticking it into all that shit?'

He shrugged. 'Had to be done, didn't it?'

'Not by you.'

'No. But then Shirley's looking at – what? – another two days with that stench, minimum. *If* the geezers turn up when they say they will. She'd lose business, wouldn't she? I mean, I wouldn't come back till it was fixed. Would you?'

Steve and I shook our heads.

'Well then – if I'd left it, what would that say about me, eh?'

'That you're normal?'

He laughed. 'What – you mean gutless?'

I nodded.

He laughed again. 'The thing is, though, if you don't sort out a problem when you can, chances are something worse is going to happen further down the line. A bit like your situation at work, sounds to me.'

Steve and I glanced at each other.

'Anyway.' Geoff picked up his tobacco tin. 'Got to be going. Thanks for the help.' And with a nod to Shirley, he was gone.

There was silence for a moment. The old bloke and his dog were still both asleep. The girls had left. I turned to Shirley. 'Who was that?' I asked.

'Oh, that's Geoff.' She smiled. 'Our local Buddha.'

***

Geoff was on my mind a lot over the next week, especially that little remark about my situation at work being like the shit-hole in the pub. I'm not sure if that's exactly what he'd meant, but it's how I took it. Certainly there was a big, bad smell around the office. Everyone knew what I'd said to Martin, and how I was on an official warning. We gave each other as wide a berth as two people can in a limited space – one large room with half a dozen smaller offices partitioned off around the edges, all constantly clacking with keyboards. Whenever we did have to speak one-to-one we were terse, blank, businesslike. Which was fine, except we both knew everyone else was on tenterhooks, watching and waiting for the next explosion. It was a strain all round, to be honest. But as for plunging my arm in to

6

sort it out, I really didn't know what to do. I mean, I know calling Martin a git wasn't exactly clever, but he was totally out of order for blaming me over Mr Brummie Lino Man. Things did get a bit better when he decided not to sue us after all – he didn't really have any grounds. But he cancelled his subscription and vowed to report us to the CBI, the DTI and every local Chamber of Commerce in the West Midlands. All my fault, according to Martin.

I'd gone back to The Three Crowns once or twice during this time, hoping to bump into Geoff again. There was something about him that made me feel he might be able to shine some light on my situation. But Shirley said he only popped in occasionally, and hardly ever at lunchtime. I tried to pump her for information about him, but she didn't really know much, only that he was a Buddhist – hence the nickname – and was basically a nice bloke; interesting to talk to, a good listener. And he was very practical, she said, down-to-earth – and she wasn't just talking about drains, which finally she'd got properly sorted.

But she had her doubts about whether he really was a Buddhist, because he smoked and drank and she'd served him a meat pie once; and one time he'd really lost his rag and swore at some bloke during an argument. She didn't know what it was about, 'But that can't be right, can it? I mean, they're supposed to be all peaceful, aren't they, Buddhists?' I said I thought they were and made my exit. I was disappointed not to have found him, to tell the truth.

Then, a couple of days later, by sheer fluke, I bumped into him coming out of the newsagent just as I was heading for the Tube after work. 'Ah, the human Dyno-Rod,' I exclaimed, genuinely pleased to see him.

He looked blank for a moment, then the penny dropped. 'Oh yes, my gorgeous young assistant. How's it going?'

And I don't know why, but as I started to tell him, in an offhand sort of way, about how work wasn't getting any better, and how this permafrost had deepened between me and Martin, and how tense I seemed to be the whole time, and isolated, and overworked and unappreciated and ground down and nothing was going right for me at the moment, what with Angie leaving and everything and . . . well, suddenly I found myself getting all choked, on the point of tears almost. It was like a dam burst or something, not like me at all.

Geoff obviously realised I wasn't in the best of shape and asked if I fancied a beer.

I thought for about a nano-second and said, 'Yeah. All right.' So off we went to the pub. And that, looking back, was the turning-point.

***

'The thing about problems, Ed,' he said, as we tucked into our first pint, 'is that they're not really the problem.'

'Eh?'

Geoff grinned. 'What I mean is, they're not what actually cause us grief. It's *us* that causes us grief.'

I didn't follow.

'Basically, everything comes down to the way we look at things; how we think and feel about life in general, and about ourselves. And then what we do about it.'

'OK . . .' I didn't totally agree but give the bloke some space – he'd only just started.

'Let's say you're feeling down. You've got no faith in yourself, nothing seems to be going right, you feel you're going to be stuck for ever. What I'd call a low life state. Ring any bells?'

'Loud and clear.'

'Well, in that life state, when a problem hits you, chances

8

are it's going to bring out all your negative feelings about yourself – right? "Oh no, not again. Why does this always happen to me?" Etcetera, etcetera.'

I nodded. 'Story of my life.'

'Right. And feeling like that only makes things worse. You think you'll never solve the situation, so right away you're on a loser.'

I nodded again – bang on.

'But it's not the problem that's the problem,' said Geoff, 'it's how you see it, how you react.'

'Hmm . . . All right.'

'Because if you have basic confidence in yourself – what I'd call a higher life state – the same problem might make you wound up for a bit, or hacked off or confused; but underneath you'll know that even if it's difficult, somehow, in the end, you'll find a way through – right? And if you have a very high life state, you'll actually welcome the problem.'

I laughed – this I couldn't swallow.

'Yes,' Geoff insisted, 'because you'll see it as a challenge. In fact, I reckon in a very high life condition you'll even go looking for trouble, because you know that's exactly what you need to make life interesting. So the real question isn't, "What's your problem?" It's, "What's your life state?" And how can you raise it?'

'Well, that's bollocks,' I said, as he took a slug of beer. 'No one wants problems. I mean, obviously, if one comes along you've got to deal with it. But to go looking for trouble – that's crazy.'

Geoff put his pint down. I was getting the feeling he liked a good argument. 'OK, what about Dyno-Rod? They love blocked drains, don't they? They advertise for blocked drains, just so they can come along and unblock them.'

'Only because you pay them. They're not like you,

sticking their arms in shit just for the thrill of it. They're doing it for money.'

'All right, then – mountaineers. The harder the climb, the better they like it. And the bigger the buzz they get from reaching the top. Or surfers. A champion surfer sees a huge wave as a great ride. To you and me it's a wall of death.'

I wasn't having this. 'Look,' I said, swallowing another mouthful of beer, 'what you're talking about is things people choose to do, for fun or for cash. What I'm talking about is problems you don't want, like me losing my girlfriend, or getting cancer, or unemployment, or having a car crash, or losing your home, or your family falling apart, or your dad becoming an alcoholic or whatever. You know, the horrible stuff. The stuff you wouldn't wish on anyone.'

'Not even your boss?'

I thought for a second. 'Well, there are exceptions, obviously.'

Geoff smiled, then took another sip of his pint, thoughtful. 'The point is, Ed, the horrible stuff's all part of life. You can't hide from it. Even if you've lived a charmed life for years, what's to say that you're not going to get sick tomorrow? Or lose your job because of something outside your control? Or that someone you love won't suddenly die?'

I must have looked a bit depressed at this because he added quickly, 'I don't mean you specifically, but anyone. Life's unpredictable. It's always changing and stuff is always going to happen. So unless we develop some kind of inner strength, when the bad stuff happens we're just going to be overwhelmed, aren't we?'

'OK.' I was prepared to concede him that. 'But you still don't go looking for it, do you? Unless you're a bleeding masochist.'

'Well, some people do. Doctors and nurses, counsellors. They go right to where there's pain because they know they can help there. And they get satisfaction from it. Which means their life state's already quite high.'

I couldn't answer this. He just didn't seem to get what I was saying. But what was I saying? I didn't know – only that there was something in me that didn't want to accept what I was hearing.

Geoff ploughed on. 'There's a bloke I know, an undertaker, who's in this special team that jets off round the world whenever there's a plane crash somewhere. It's his job to recover the dead bodies and body parts, identify them, and then return them to the relatives so they can give them a decent funeral. Now, that's a pretty bloody gruesome job as far as I'm concerned, much worse than sticking my arm down some blocked pipe. But this bloke sees it as a privilege. The grief, the tragedy cuts him up, sure. But he knows the fact someone cares enough to do that job brings incredible comfort to the relatives. For them the loss is horrendous. But he helps to make it better for them, and so he feels better, too.'

'And your point is?'

'I've told you. Problems are just facts. It's our attitude to them that makes us suffer – or not. And that depends on our state of life.'

He could see I still wasn't buying.

'OK, put it this way. If we feel bigger than the problem, we cope. If we feel smaller than it, we suffer. A lot of the time problems just show us our weakness and that's what we can't handle. So we get unhappy.'

'Right. So if I'm miserable it's because I'm a sad, weak bastard?'

'That's about it.'

'Cheers.'

11

Geoff laughed. 'Don't worry, we're all in the same boat. And you can do something about it.'

'That's a comfort. How?'

'Well, your life state's not fixed. It changes moment to moment. So the question, for me, is how can I keep it as high as possible? Like, if I'm knackered, just the thought of what I have to face the next day can make me depressed. But after a sleep, next morning it doesn't seem half as bad. The facts haven't changed – I have.'

'So it's all down to getting an early night, then?'

Geoff didn't rise to the bait. 'Getting enough sleep is important, yes – but there's a bit more to it than that.'

'Really?' I couldn't keep the sarcasm out of my voice.

Geoff couldn't help noticing. 'Look, Ed, you're going through a hard time, right?'

I nodded.

'And I'm trying to explain something that might help you. I know because I've been there, done it, got the T-shirt. But if you're not interested, it's no skin off my nose. I'll drink up, shake hands and say good luck to you, mate.'

'No, no – I am interested.' I was being honest here. 'It's just a habit of mine, you know, sarcasm.'

Geoff weighed me up.

'Please, go on. And I'll keep my sceptical side under control.'

'You can be as sceptical as you like, Ed. But if you just want to take the piss . . .'

'All right, I'm sorry. Please, I want to hear more.' Blimey – touchy or what?

Geoff looked at me, decided and continued. 'Well, I reckon everything comes down to three things: wisdom, courage and compassion. If you can build up those in yourself you can use any problem to create something better, like a weight-lifter uses heavier and heavier weights to get stronger and stronger.'

I tried hard to keep the scepticism off my face – and out of my voice. 'Fine. But who does that – apart from weight-lifters?'

'All sportsmen, for a start. Take a champion golfer. He knows he has to beat all the best people around to become the champion, right? So if he loses, what's the real problem? Not his opponent or the golf course or the fact it pissed down all afternoon – it's him. He just wasn't good enough on the day. So if he wants to win next time round he's got to work on his swing, his club selection, his approach play, his putting, his mental attitude, whatever. Same with us. If we want to become truly happy, we should look at problems like that – as training to make us fit for life.'

I looked at him, amazed. 'Well, that is just . . . bollocks.'

'That's the second time you've said that.'

'Yes,' I said. 'Because . . . because it is. People just aren't like that.'

'Yeah – most of us. But some people are. And everybody can be. Well, I reckon they can, anyway. It's amazing what people can do – if they have to. Because *everyone* has wisdom, courage and compassion inside them. They just don't know how to bring them out, that's all, or make them stronger. Which is where problems come in.'

This time I couldn't help my scepticism showing. 'This is Buddhism, is it? 'Cos Shirley said you were a Buddhist.'

'Yep. We call using problems in a positive way "turning poison into medicine".' He sipped at his pint. 'But that's not exclusive to Buddhism. To me, it just makes sense, because if shit happens anyway, the quicker you can turn it into compost the better.'

My heart sank.

Geoff must have noticed. 'What?'

'Dunno,' I muttered. 'There's just something about positive people that always makes me feel depressed.'

Geoff laughed.

'Seriously. It's like they've taken some happy pill that makes them not quite human. "You've got cancer? Never mind! Time to ask those big questions you've always been avoiding and become a better person. Or find God – better still!" Makes me want to thump them, actually.'

Geoff looked rueful. 'I know what you mean. But if it helps, being positive doesn't come naturally to me either.'

'You force yourself?'

'Not exactly. But I have to work at it. I mean, I'm a bit of an Eeyore at heart, really. I expect things to go wrong or fail. And they do a lot of the time, so I'm proved right. Except I've also got a bit of Tigger in me, and Tigger's always up for it, isn't he? The eternal optimist. So there's this constant battle, and over the years I've learned it's better to encourage Tigger and tell Eeyore to sod off, because if he wins then I'll probably do nothing, or fail – and I'll have been proved right all over again. But what's the result? Failure. And who wants that?'

This was interesting. 'You're saying expecting to win or fail is just habit?'

'Pretty much. And it makes a big difference to whether you win or fail. Doesn't guarantee it, of course. Sometimes you win or lose whatever you expect. But in the long run, I see people get on in life because of their basic attitude, their habit of thinking – especially with problems. It's like being fit. Doesn't guarantee you're going to win the race, but it gives you a damn sight more chance than if you're wheezing after ten yards. The only catch is that getting fit and staying fit takes effort, so you've got to make a habit there, too.'

'Bloody hell. Sounds too much like hard work to me.'

'Well, if you want to stay a weak, sad, miserable bastard, be my guest. Just do nothing.'

I looked him straight in the eye, and he looked straight back. Why was I letting this almost total stranger insult me? I don't know. Perhaps because I was so weak, sad and miserable that I didn't even have the strength to lamp him one. Or perhaps because I had this sneaky feeling that what he was saying sounded . . . true? Ish.

'All right,' I said tersely. 'Go on.'

Geoff continued. 'Well, if you think about it we're creatures of habit all round. Like – I bet you have regular meetings at your work, with the same people.'

'Of course.'

'In the same room?'

'Usually.'

'Right. Well, I'll lay odds that everyone sits in the same place every time.'

I thought about it, then nodded.

'Now, why is that, do you suppose?'

I shrugged.

'Habit. When we first decide where to sit, we'll choose where we're most comfortable. This person will always sit facing the door, that person near the radiator or window. Or near the boss or as far from him as possible, or next to a mate, or whatever. Then, unless we've made a serious boo-boo – like, we realise it's way too hot next to the radiator – we won't change. We've found a comfort zone and we'll stay there. Plus, we'll be comforted by the fact that everyone else stays put, too. You try sitting somewhere different at your next meeting and see what reaction you get when the others come in.'

'I will.'

'Good. Careful, though.' Geoff wagged a finger. 'Years ago, when I was a builder—'

15

'You were a builder?'

'Was – yes. Anyway—'

'What do you do now?'

'It's not relevant to this story.'

'Oh.'

'I'll tell you in a bit. Anyway, I was doing a job at this factory, building a wall. First day, come tea break, I go to the canteen and sit at one of the tables. A couple of minutes later this bloke comes up to me and jerks his thumb towards another table. "Oi," he says. "That's my seat." I look round and there are empty tables all over the place. He obviously sees what's going through my mind because he says, "I been here thirty years and I always sit there." Well, you sad sod, I think, and move away, because it obviously means a lot more to him than me.'

I shook my head in disbelief.

'True story. The point is, we all create these habits, and they can end up trapping us. And the most powerful habit of all is how we think, because that controls how we act. We shoot ourselves in the foot by saying we can't do this, we can't do that; that something's impossible. Maybe we're scared of how we'll look if we fall flat on our face, or maybe we failed before and lost heart and don't want to try again – when, actually, if we made just a bit more effort or developed some kind of skill, or got the right advice or help, or just stuck at it for a bit longer, we'd definitely succeed. I mean, look at all the people in history who've been written off but won in the end just because they didn't give up: Robert the Bruce, Nelson Mandela, Churchill, God knows how many scientists and artists. That's my motto, in fact: "Perseverance Wins".'

'So what about all those people who persevered and lost?'

'Like?'

16

I thought for a moment. 'Hitler. He didn't give up and look what happened to him.'

Geoff sighed. 'If you think negatively, Ed, you can always come up with a negative example.'

'I'm just challenging your motto, that's all. Or do I have to accept everything you say?'

'Would make life a lot easier if you did.'

We both smiled.

'All right,' he went on, 'I should have said something about doing good. "Perseverance for the sake of good wins." Except it doesn't have the same punch, does it?'

'No,' I agreed. 'But I don't know if that's true, either.'

'OK. Let's just leave it for now, then. But my point is I've tried to train myself not to just accept my "natural" i.e. negative way of looking at my problems. I've learned a new habit, which is: show a bit of courage and expect to solve them. That way, I keep my life state up and generally find a way through. And my negativity doesn't drain away all my life force just when I need it. Same again?'

He pointed at my almost empty glass.

I nodded – 'Cheers' – and he went to the bar. I went to the Gents.

There was a lot to ponder as I sprinkled the porcelain. Problems are good. What matters is life state. What we need is wisdom, courage and compassion. Hmm. But that thing about meetings was true. We did always sit in the same places. I liked to be on the corner, far away from Martin. Even so, I couldn't see how I could use any of what Geoff had said to sort things out at work – let alone get Angie back. But as I turned to wash my hands I caught sight of the inspection cover in the floor and had a vivid flash of him down on his knees. No way could I be made to believe he'd actually been enjoying himself down there, however much he'd trained himself to think positively.

17

'I wasn't enjoying myself,' he protested as we started on our second pint. 'I was just doing what had to be done.'

'All right,' I said. 'I'll grant you that there are some people in this world who get a buzz out of doing good for others, who go to war zones, famines, help the sick and the dying – the whole Mother Teresa bit. And I even accept there are some people who might personally like problems.'

'Challenges,' Geoff corrected. 'If you think you can solve a problem it's a challenge, a test of your strength.'

'All right – challenges.' Said through gritted teeth. 'Anyway, the bottom line, Geoff, is I'm not like that. For me problems are just a pain in the arse and I'd rather not have them.'

'Fine,' he said, and sipped his beer.

I waited.

He put his glass down and looked at me. 'Well?'

'Well what?'

'Have they gone? Your problems?'

I sighed – of course not.

Geoff raised his glass to me with a grin – and I wound up for my killer question.

'OK. Let's suppose everything you say is true: we've got all these bad habits in how we look at things and so on. The question is: how do you stop it? Because I can't even stop biting my nails, let alone the whole way I think.'

Geoff was unfazed. 'Well, the first thing is: remember you've got a choice. When you feel you can't handle something, you can either *choose* to feel miserable and helpless, or maybe put your life in someone else's hands to sort out – if they can be bothered. Or you can decide to take charge, take full responsibility for whatever's happening, even if none of it seems to be your fault, and decide to turn poison into medicine.'

'Yes, but *how* – practically? Like with me and Angie, or Mart the fart.'

'Well, I'd use my Buddhist practice.'

I groaned. 'Religion.'

'Is that a problem?'

'Too bloody right. I can't stand religion.'

'Where have I heard that before?' He smiled ruefully. 'Well, some people prefer to call Buddhism a life philosophy, if that helps.'

'Might do – if you can put it into practice without the religious bit.'

'You can try.'

'All right, just tell me about that, then. Because I had enough religion stuffed down my throat as a kid to put me off for life. Junk – all of it. And dangerous. I mean, look at the damage it's done: religious wars, massacres, persecution. So – no religion. Just practical, down-to-earth, hands-on, useful advice about how to get my girlfriend back and things sorted at work. OK?'

'OK. But if you change your mind at all . . .'

I shook my head, decided.

Geoff took it on the chin. 'Fine. But – bloody hell.'

'What?'

'Sorry, it's going to have to wait. I was due somewhere else five minutes ago.'

Now it was my turn to be disappointed. But I played it cool – 'No problem' – as Geoff swiftly downed his pint. We agreed a time and a place to meet again, then he stuck out his hand.

'Till next time.' We shook on it, and then he was gone.

It's strange, but as I sat there finishing my drink I felt like something good had happened. I couldn't put my finger on exactly what at first. Then I realised it was something I hadn't felt in a long while. Hope. I don't know how, but

19

this bloke had made me feel positive even though I didn't really agree with him. I was already looking forward to seeing him again. There was something he'd mentioned I wanted to ask him about: life force. He said pessimism sucked it away. But what was it? And other questions were already starting to come, like what he did for a living – he'd never told me. But they'd have to wait.

Still, looking back now, I'd say that was definitely the day my life started to change.

Chapter Two

At the time, of course, I didn't see it like that. I was just getting some free life advice from someone who might be able to help. I felt good, up. But then the doubts started to creep in.

I didn't know anything about this bloke. He might be trying to suck me into some weird religious cult. He might fancy me. He might even be planning to find out my darkest secrets and then – gulp – blackmail me. Not that I had any secrets, apart from clicking on the occasional porn site at work. And cheating in my GCSE Physics. But still, I started to regret being so open with him. And when I thought back to almost blubbing over him in the street, such a hot flush of embarrassment washed over me that I actually broke into a sweat. Steve was passing my desk at the time and noticed, which made it worse. A lot worse.

'You all right, mate?' he enquired, with genuine concern.

'Early menopause,' I quipped, rapidly tugging at the front of my shirt to create a cooling breeze between material and skin.

Steve stared, as if expecting me to spontaneously combust.

'I've just got a very low boiling-point,' I assured him, the

21

sweat starting to drip into my eyes. 'Nothing to worry about.'

Steve didn't budge, fascinated. 'Bloody hell, looks like you're melting.'

'Ha!' I tried to laugh. 'Feels like it, too. 'Scuse me.'

I got up and dived for the loo, where I drenched my face in cold water and gradually returned to room temperature. What the hell was going on? All I could think while drying myself off was I must be cracking up, having a nervous breakdown. First swearing at Martin, then getting choked up in the street, now this . . . I'd lost control over my core self or something. I looked in the mirror. Thirty-one and already the grey was showing through the black. Bloody hell. And Angie had said I was putting on weight. I sighed. It was true. Too much beer.

Looks were the last of my worries, though. My real worry was Martin. I was convinced he was planning a 'reorganisation' – i.e. a clear-out. Subscriptions and advertising had dropped off and he was spending more and more time huddled in meetings with people we didn't know – people in suits, people he wouldn't identify . . .

Then, suddenly, it was D-Day – my meeting with Geoff – and the clock was steadily edging towards H-Hour. Decision time. I toyed with not going, but that seemed a bit juvenile: I mean, he hadn't actually done anything to deserve being stood up. And why was I getting cold feet anyway? What was I scared of? I thought about it for a while, and the answer came. It was the fact that a complete stranger was offering to help me – for what? I weighed the options again: religious conversion, gay sex, blackmail. And decided to meet him.

What swung it for me was the chair test – you know, the one about people always sitting in the same place at meetings. I tried it out that afternoon at our weekly 'editorial conference'. I arrived a bit early and sat in Julie's seat, opposite the window – and right next to Martin. When the others drifted in there wasn't a word about it but everyone seemed surprised, and Julie looked frankly pissed off to be relegated to my place on the corner. And Martin – well, he was distinctly uneasy. You could see the wheels going round in his head: 'What is Ed up to?' He was so nervous that whenever he spoke to me he leaned right away, as if he expected me to lunge forward any moment and bite him.

The funny thing was, I actually felt more powerful, as if this single action had shifted the initiative my way a bit. Not that Martin would answer any of my probing questions about the future of the company. But I thought that if such a small change could affect the whole atmosphere of a meeting, or at least how I felt about it, then maybe it was worth hearing a bit more of what Geoff had to say.

So – meet him, I told myself, but be on your guard. Because you can never be too careful taking gifts from strangers.

***

'I almost didn't come,' I confessed, as I put our pints down on the table. We were in a different pub, The Swan – long and narrow, with faded carpets and a noisy slot machine in the corner.

'Why's that then? Cheers.'

'I thought you might be trying to trap me into some weird cult.'

Geoff gave the long satisfied sigh of a man whose thirst has just been slaked and put down his glass. 'Well, if it makes you feel any better, Ed, I almost didn't come either.'

'Oh?'

'Yeah. I thought, what do I want to spend time with this loser for? I mean, life's too short. I got things to do, people to see . . .' He smiled cheerfully.

I decided not to take offence. 'Exactly.'

'But I can't help it; it's my bodhisattva nature.' He took out his tobacco tin to roll a cigarette.

'Your . . .?'

'Bodhisattva nature. The part of my life that just insists on doing good. We've all got it – even you.'

'Oh yeah?'

'Yes. Only in some people it's more developed than others. And in some people it's hardly developed at all.'

'Like Hitler.'

'You've got a thing about Hitler, haven't you?'

'Have I?'

'You mentioned him last time.'

I thought for a moment. I had. 'I suppose that's because he sums up, you know, the worst-case scenario for a human being.'

Geoff licked the strip of gum on his cigarette paper. 'Even a heartless villain loves his wife and children. He too has a portion of the bodhisattva world within him.'

'Eh?'

'Buddhist quotation. It's talking about all the different states of life everyone has – suffering, anger, joy, greed, instincts, humanity, etcetera, etcetera – including bodhisattva. Which means even your Hitlers can be kind sometimes, to some people.'

'Eva Braun.'

'Among others. And even your saints can sometimes act like real bastards.'

'For example?'

'I'm being metaphorical.'

'Ah.'

24

'Though I think St Paul could have a bit of a rough tongue at times. Anyway, Buddhism says everyone has a positive and a negative side. So the question is, which side wins? Or wins most often.'

'Well, that's common sense, isn't it?'

'Buddhism is common sense. Common sense plus.'

'Plus what?'

'Plus the spiritual bit you're not interested in.'

'Right. So here's to common sense.' I raised my glass, he raised his, we clinked, we drinked. More lip-smacking.

'But don't you think it's interesting we both felt negative about tonight?' Geoff had a cunning look on his face.

'You mean you really didn't want to come?'

'No.'

I felt a bit deflated. So much for him fancying me.

'But that's because the positive and negative go totally hand in hand. There's a saying: "Good by the inch invites evil by the yard." Which means the positive stirs up the negative. Us meeting was positive, so there had to be negative reaction somewhere.'

'Hang on. What's so positive about us meeting? It's just two blokes having a drink.'

'On one level, yeah, sure. But you want to move your life forward, right? Which is positive. I want to help you do that, which is also positive. So there has to be a negative reaction somewhere. That's part of the law of life.'

I didn't totally buy this, but let it pass – for now. 'I'll take your word for it.'

'Very wise – you're learning.' He chuckled. 'Anyway, the fact is, the stronger the positive, the stronger the negative resistance. Like exercise.' He took a drag on his roll-up. 'I know it's good for me, and every now and then I think, Lose some weight, you fat bastard. So I pull on my shorts and running-shoes and start pounding the pavement. But

25

after a couple of runs I look out the window and see it's a bit wet and think, Nah – next time. And next time it's maybe a bit too hot. And next time it clashes with football on the telly. And eventually I think, Sod this for a game of soldiers, and give up. In fact one time, before I was a Buddhist, I joined this peace group – you know, anti-war, anti-violence, all pacifists. And they hated each other. Always at each other's throats. Couldn't agree about anything. I couldn't understand it at the time but now – well, it seems inevitable.'

'Why?'

'They were trying to make a really positive cause, so they were hit really hard by negativity – backbiting, disunity, always rowing.'

I didn't like the implications of this. 'So you're saying any good thing anyone ever tries to do is going to get beaten by negativity?'

'Not beaten by it – hit by it. Because once you know it's going to strike, or you can recognise it when it does strike, you can take steps to get through it. It's like a plane going down the runway. It goes faster and faster and the resistance against it builds up. If it keeps going it'll take off. It actually needs resistance to fly. But if it slows down, sure, the resistance slackens off – but it stays on the ground.'

'So if I want to fly I've got to keep going?'

'Through your negativity, yeah. In fact, after a time you'll come to see the resistance is positive, because it shows you you're trying to do something or change something really important. That peace group fell apart because of their negativity. If they'd known about this principle they'd have realised that it only came up because they were on the right track – and maybe they'd have continued through it.'

I scratched my head. 'This is another of your "bad is

26

good" scenarios, isn't it? Like your "pro...
idea.'

Geoff laughed. 'That's not what I'd call it. But you tell me if we don't often get the strongest resistance with what we want most. Like this actress friend of mine. Gets terrible nerves before an audition if she wants the job, but if she doesn't give a toss about it she's cool as a cucumber. And when did you last call Angie, by the way?'

'What?' This was a sudden change of subject. He was looking at me innocently. 'Not since we split up.'

'You've wanted to?'

'Course.'

'But something inside stops you.'

'I just know it won't do any good.'

'You know – or you're afraid it won't?'

I was about to answer when I stopped. Was I afraid? Blimey – I was. Afraid of getting a final, total, no-way-back rejection.

Geoff pressed on. 'If you want to be happy, fulfilled, whatever you want to call it, you've got to beat what Buddhists call your "fundamental darkness", your internal negativity. But first you've got to recognise how it shows up in your life.'

'Hello darkness, my old friend?'

'That's the one. Because it can be pretty bleeding devious – you know, subtle. Like, I'm fairly laid back, which can be positive – problems don't rile me generally. But that means often I can't be arsed to do much about them. That's part of my fundamental darkness.'

A couple of girls had come in – a blonde and a brunette, both lookers – and gone up to the bar. They glanced down the room, checking out the talent – and looked straight through me. I sighed, depressed. Getting a replacement for Angie – if that were possible – wasn't just a matter of

...ight. Now I had to deal ...ness too.

... a bit like the church to me,' I ...ion back to Geoff. 'Make a long list ...rmine to be a better person ...'

He ground the damp stub of his fag into the ...hat's dualism. You've got to forget that.'

There aren't two boxes: right, wrong; good, bad; you, me.

'No?'

'No. There's *funi* – two but not two, not two but two. Which means things are separate; but from another viewpoint they're also one. So your faults can also be your strengths. What's positive can be negative, and vice versa.'

'*Funi*?'

'Yeah. Buddhism. For example, are you stubborn at all?'

'Can be.' One reason Angie walked.

'Well then, if you're stubborn about something and you turn out to be right you're resolute, confident, determined, dogged, tenacious. But if you're wrong, you're pig-headed, arrogant, inflexible, obstinate, and any other negative word you can think of. The same trait can be a plus or a minus, depending on the situation.'

I frowned. 'OK. But how do you know when that trait is positive or negative, if it's part of your character? I mean, how can *you* tell if you're being laid back or just bone idle?'

'Well, that's just it, because often what starts out as positive turns negative and—'

'Vice versa.' I was getting the hang of this upside-down logic.

'By George, he's got it!'

I grinned.

'So, if there's a problem and I don't take action and

28

everything works out OK, I was probably right not to. But if it all goes pear-shaped probably I should have stirred myself.'

'Fine. But how do you know?'

'By the result – sooner or later.'

'Yes, but that's hindsight. How do you know if being stubborn or laid back is the right thing at the time?'

'"Know thyself." You've got to look in the mirror – which is where my practice comes in, the religious bit. It forces me to be totally honest with myself.'

'And without religion?'

'Well, I guess you have to train yourself to ask yourself hard questions – you know, relentlessly – and sift the answers for any bullshit. Or get a really good mate to tell you.'

Hmm. All sounded a bit theoretical to me. And my really good mate was Angie. Was. 'All right,' I said, 'here's a real situation. Martin picks on me. He's always criticising me. Nothing I do is right. I try to do it his way, it doesn't work, there's a cock-up and I get the blame. Like with the Lino Man. And that really pisses me off. So, should I not be pissed off, just put up with it? Where's the positive, where's the negative? And – $64,000 question – how do I change it?'

'Hmm.' Geoff swirled the last inch of his beer around in his glass, thinking. 'The unreasonable-boss-worker-as-innocent-victim scenario.'

'That's it.'

'And what pisses you off is he's unfair.'

'Totally.'

He sniffed. 'How do you think he sees the situation?'

'He's seeing his business dream go down the toilet and won't accept responsibility for it. So he's looking to offload it onto someone else – *moi*.'

'Whoa, you switched viewpoints there, Ed. Him seeing his business dream go down the toilet – that's his POV. You judging he's not accepting responsibility – that's yours.'

'Well, he's not.'

'You might be right. But how does *he* see things – and you?'

I looked at him blankly.

'Go back to him watching his dream go down the toilet.'

I frowned, trying to understand.

'Put yourself in his shoes. He's got this dream, he's borrowed a lot of money from his mates, it's not working out – so . . . ?'

I began dimly to see where he was going. 'So . . . he's under a lot of pressure, I suppose. Stress.'

'Thinking straight?'

I barked a laugh.

'Scared?'

'Probably.'

'Right. So how does he see you?'

'He doesn't like me.'

'Because?'

I'd never really thought.

'I mean, you seem a nice enough bloke to me. Why not to Martin?'

'Dunno. We just don't get on.'

'Do you like him?'

'I think he's a prat. And a coward.'

'Uh-huh. And do you think he might possibly have sensed that – before you actually told him to his face?'

'Are you saying it's my fault he picks on me?' For some reason I was starting to get irritated.

'I'm just saying it's human nature to try to protect yourself when people show up your faults – especially if you're trying to hide them from yourself.'

'Pah.' I picked up my pint and drank.

'Why are you angry?'

'I'm not,' I lied. 'I just don't think it's my job to flatter the ego of the jerk who's my boss.'

'I never said you should. But you *are* angry.'

'Because it's psycho-babble, Geoff. Sorry.' I drank again.

He wasn't the least bit discouraged. 'I'm just pointing out a basic fact, Ed, which you're showing right now. Most people, as soon as they think they're being criticised, become defensive, prickly, stop listening, or withdraw. So does Martin. He thinks you've seen through him. And every time he sees you he feels threatened.'

'You can say that again.' I told him about the chair test at the meeting that afternoon, and about Martin leaning away from me as far as he could.

'You sound like you enjoyed it.'

'I did.' I grinned.

Geoff started rolling another ciggie, thoughtful.

'What?'

'Well, what does that say about you?'

'What do you mean?' I said – defensive, prickly . . .

Geoff chose to go deaf on me. 'The question, as I see it, isn't: "Are you right? Have you analysed things correctly?" You probably have. Martin's making duff judgements. My question is: "So what conclusion do you draw?" He's got to be chucked out? You've got to get him to chuck you out, so you get the severance money? Or you've got to help him to turn the company round?'

'Look, Geoff , whenever I make a suggestion he turns it down.'

'Probably because he hears it as even more criticism.'

I sighed. He was like a dog with a bone over this.

'Because he doesn't trust you.'

'Why shouldn't he trust me?'

31

'You drink at lunchtime, for a start. Plus you don't sound committed.'

'Committed! On what he pays me?'

'Fine. But that's your fundamental darkness.' He was looking at me steadily. I really didn't get it, and he could see. 'Because your environment at work is fundamentally negative, you've decided to be negative too. The negativity there draws out the negativity in you, but you feel justified, which adds to the overall—'

'Negativity.'

'Yes. And so it goes on – a classic vicious circle. Buddhism calls it the oneness of life and its environment: your life's reflected in the environment, and your environment's reflected in you. *Funi.*'

I could feel myself drowning in the awful sense that he might be right. I kicked hard for the surface, for what I knew. 'But the guy is a twenty-four-carat, A1 prat.'

'Maybe. But that's his problem. Your problem is how to make the best of your situation. Is thinking he's a prat, and treating him like a prat, actually making things better?'

I was silent.

'What if you used a bit of wisdom, courage and compassion on the situation? What do you think might happen?'

'I've no idea.' I was sulking now.

Geoff noticed. 'Another one?' He was pointing to my empty glass.

I hesitated. I wasn't sure if I wanted any more of this. It was all starting to feel a bit . . . heavy. 'Oh, all right,' I said.

He picked up the glasses and went to the bar. I thought about Martin – and wisdom and courage and compassion. I had this black feeling Geoff was going to suggest I grovel to him; and that was something I absolutely would *not*

32

do. The girls had bought their drinks and camped themselves at a table nearby. I threw them a friendly smile. 'All right?'

'We're waiting for someone,' the blonde said, hard-faced.

I nodded – of course they bloody were – and turned away. Geoff coming back with two brimming pints was a welcome distraction. Round Two.

'So what do you reckon to a little WCC then?'

I looked blank.

'Wisdom, courage and compassion.'

I picked up my pint, silent.

'If it's any help,' he said, 'compassion is supposed to be the mother of wisdom.'

'Really?'

'That's what they say.'

'Oh. Well, you know what I say, Geoff? I say if anyone should be applying WCC or whatever, it's him, not me. He's The Boss, and I'm just carrying out his orders. It's him who's making the cock-up, not me – day in, day out. And it's him you should be talking to.'

He grabbed the finger I was jabbing at him and smiled. 'Want to hear a really basic Buddhist principle?'

'No.'

He raised an eyebrow.

I sighed. 'What?'

'Look at your hand.' He let go of my finger.

I looked.

'Your index finger's pointing at me, right?'

I nodded.

'And your thumb's on top. But where are the other three fingers pointing?'

I looked again. They were pointing at my chest.

'Whenever you point, three fingers point back at you –

which means blaming and criticism's fine, but taking responsibility takes three times more guts.'

'Here we go.'

'What?'

'You're going to tell me to grovel.'

'Not at all. I was going to ask if you'd heard of Mahatma Gandhi.'

'Of course. Led the independence movement that kicked the British out of India in 1947.'

'Right. Well, he came up with this great statement: "Become the change you want to see." In the Buddhism I practise it's called "human revolution", but it comes to the same thing. You change your situation by first changing *your* attitudes, not other people. Most of the time we want to rearrange the environment – especially people around us – to fit our way of thinking. But most of the time the environment doesn't want to change. This principle says that if you change, your environment must change to reflect that.'

'Why must it?'

Geoff sucked the air through his teeth. 'Big question that, Ed. Very. We'd have to get into deep, deep philosophy to unpack it.'

'I'm not going anywhere.'

'I am. And anyway, after a couple of beers I'll probably get lost. I will explain it some other time, just not now.'

I looked disappointed.

'Anyway, the point is – if you want to see change in your surroundings, the people around you, work on yourself. Because you're the one person you definitely can influence.'

'You think?'

'I've seen it again and again. And in people a lot worse off than you are.'

Ah – this reminded me. 'What do you do again? You know, your job?'

'I . . .' Geoff hesitated, choosing his words carefully. 'I help people see things more clearly.'

'An optician?'

He smiled.

'Or some sort of consultant?'

'No.'

'Life coach?'

He shook his head.

'OK then, *where* do you work?'

'All over the place. At all levels.' He smiled, enjoying himself.

'You know, you're sounding very evasive, Geoff. You're going to tell me you're a ghost next, or maybe the spirit of the Buddha reincarnated into this human form.'

He laughed. I waited. He stayed silent.

I leaned forward, staring at him hard. 'You did say last time you'd tell me what you did for a living.'

'And I will, I promise you. When you're ready.'

When I'm ready? What was this?

'I really don't think you'd understand at this point.'

I took a deep breath.

'Trust me, Ed – please? If anything I tell you or any advice I give turns out to be a crock of crap, you can just walk away.'

***

That night, at home in my sad little one-bedroom flat, I felt truly depressed. The first time I'd left Geoff I'd felt hope. Now it was despair. I couldn't get out of my head the picture of me standing in front of Martin's desk and stammering out what a bad boy I'd been but

35

now I'd seen the error of my ways and wanted to turn over a new leaf and . . . I kept getting to this point and gagging.

Geoff had a point, though. Being right – and everyone there agreed with me about Martin – wasn't getting me anywhere. But how the hell could I change the way I think? 'Think about it,' Geoff had said, and I'd almost thumped him. Here I was, though, lying in the dark, staring at the ceiling and trying to do just that – think.

Nothing.

Then, for some reason, the letters WCC popped into my head – wisdom, courage and compassion. Then 'Compassion is the mother of wisdom.' Fine. But what the hell did it *mean*?

I pondered. If you feel sorry for someone, you . . . er . . . No, it's more than that. Compassion means . . . it means . . . caring. About someone. About what they're going through. Their ups and downs. Their happiness. But that was just the point. I didn't care about Martin. In fact, I didn't care about anyone except Angie and . . . I stopped. An awful truth had hit me. All I cared about was Angie and myself. My parents were both dead. I had a brother I never spoke to – we drifted apart years ago. I had a few friends but we weren't really close. It was just Angie and me; or rather, it had been. And how much did I really care about her anyway? How much did I want her just because she made me feel good? Did I *really* care about her happiness? When we'd been together I just assumed she was happy with me because I was happy with her. Until she'd got all needy and started to complain about me not doing anything for her or paying her any attention or blah blah blah. I'd batted it away as just more female nagging – then she left. So did that mean that truly, deep down, all I really cared about was myself? The more I thought about it the

36

more convinced I became: I was a totally selfish, shallow, worthless . . . piece of shite.

I turned the light on, jumped out of bed and grabbed pen and paper. Then I sat down at the table and started writing a list. There were two columns: 'Tomorrow I Will' and 'Tomorrow I Will Not'. Top of the first column was 'Make a fresh start with Martin'.

***

I got to the office just after 8.30. I knew he'd been coming in earlier and earlier as things had been getting worse, and I wanted to catch him for a good heart-to-heart before the others arrived. I didn't know if it was wise, or compassionate, but from where I stood it definitely needed courage. To eat humble pie in front of your worst enemy . . . But I was determined to do this. Something had to change, and after my realisation the night before I knew it had to be me. I was locked inside my own little world of me, me, me, and I was suffocating.

Martin was alone in his office when I arrived, reading through a long fax. I knocked on the door and he looked at me with dull eyes. But with no surprise, which was a surprise to me – he knew I normally didn't get in till almost ten. Still, I was decided. I entered.

'Not disturbing you, am I?'

He shook his head.

I sat down opposite him and took a deep breath. 'Look, Martin, I know things haven't been good between us recently. Well, never, to be honest. We, er, see things very differently at times. But I just want to say that I do appreciate the efforts you've made for the company – I mean, if it wasn't for you we wouldn't be here. And I appreciate all you're doing to get us through this rough patch, business-wise. So I just want to say that from now on, mate, I'm on your side and I'll do whatever I can to help you. OK?'

He looked at me, stupefied. I gave a quick, embarrassed smile. And then his chin started to quiver. His lip trembled. And suddenly, he burst into tears.

'We've just gone bust,' he said.

Chapter Three

My first reaction was shock – then anger. Not with Martin, but myself. How could I not have seen this coming? All the signs were there, but I'd been so wrapped up in self-pity and Geoff's bloody Buddhism that they'd totally passed me by. I should have just left, got out months ago when I'd first realised Martin was a total dick-head. I mean, how would a bloke like him ever run a business successfully? Instead, I'd hung in there, hoping things would improve, despite all the evidence to the contrary. And last night – ha! There I'd been, beating myself up for being too self-centred, when if I'd been *more* self-centred – and smarter – I'd have looked after myself a bit more and worried about Martin a lot less.

This was the gist of my tirade down the phone to Geoff later that morning. Things had moved fast after Martin dropped his bombshell. Even before everyone got in the bailiffs arrived and literally chucked us onto the street – turns out Martin was weeks behind on the rent. They padlocked the doors and that was that. We milled about for a while, wondering – fat chance – if we'd be paid what was owed us, while Martin scurried off to the bank 'to sort things out'. He'd been hit by a sudden burst of wild

39

optimism – which just convinced us he really was completely round the twist.

We never saw him again – not as employees, anyway, because he did reappear unexpectedly in my life some time later. But more of that anon.

It was way too early for the pub, so we couldn't even drown our sorrows. Instead, everyone just sloped off home, or popped into town for a bit of retail therapy. But I was too wound up to go back to my little cell. I'd spent half the night working myself up for a major life change, remember? So I paced around for a bit like one of those lions in the zoo, then found myself on the pay phone in a local coffee shop berating Geoff. He was very calm – which maddened me even more.

'I don't know what you're complaining about,' he said. 'You wanted a life change and now you've got it.'

'Not like this,' I protested. 'I'm out of a job, out of pocket, owed a stack of money . . .'

'You'll be all right,' Geoff purred. I could almost hear a smile in his voice. 'As one door closes—'

'Another's slammed in your face!'

There was a brief silence on the line; then: 'Never heard of the Chinese for "crisis"?'

'No,' I barked. I was not in the mood for more bloody philosophy.

'They write it with two characters. One means "danger", the other "opportunity". So this situation could go either way.'

'How?'

'Depends on the choices you make.'

'Such as?' I knew he wasn't to blame for my predicament, but somehow I felt cheated that all the positive thinking I'd done at his urging had come to zilch.

'I don't know,' he said.

'Oh, great,' I sneered. 'So much for wisdom, courage and compassion.'

'OK. You can either feel sorry for yourself and do something stupid – like beating up Martin—'

'He's done a runner.'

'Ah. Or you can see this as the chance for a total rethink – and let's face it, you might never have done that if you'd stuck with him.'

'But only yesterday you were telling me to make a real commitment!'

'That was yesterday. Things change. You've got to be flexible.' Bloody hell. 'And anyway, I never told you to do anything. I just make suggestions. You can take them or leave them.'

I sighed. I felt too battered and pissed off to get into this discussion. 'All right then, O wise one, so what do you *suggest* I do now?'

***

And so it was I found myself, about an hour later, standing outside a small and dreary-looking employment agency in Baker Street. Personal Personnel was owned by a friend, Geoff said, who'd be able to fix me up with a new job.

'How about a new life?' I sighed.

'Well, that too maybe – if you ask nicely.'

The window was full of cards for 'W/P Operators! Top rates!' and 'Exec PAs – start now!' Not exactly what I was looking for. And I felt an instinctive distrust of anyone so liberal with the exclamation mark. With heavy heart I pushed open the door and went in, leaving the rumble of traffic behind me. A black woman in her late thirties was pinning more enthusiastic job cards onto a board on one of the walls. She was curvy, with a thick head of glossy black hair – obviously a wig – a black business suit, long

41

painted nails and big false eyelashes. She looked like she was auditioning for The Supremes.

'Yes?' A Londoner. For some reason I was expecting Caribbean.

'Geoff sent me. Told me to ask for Dora.'

'Ed?'

I tried to smile.

'Suddenly available?'

'That's me.'

'Yes, he called me about you. Well, sit down and let's see what we can do.'

She gave me a registration form, and bustled about pinning up job cards and watering her collection of aloe vera plants while I filled in my personal details. Then she sat down and studied what I'd written.

'No religion?' She looked up at me.

'Is that a requirement?'

'I just thought you might be a Buddhist.'

'No, I met Geoff in a . . .' I was going to say 'pub' but suddenly decided it made me sound a bit alcoholic. 'In a social way.'

'Down the pub, you mean?'

I hesitated, rumbled.

Dora gave a throaty chuckle. 'Yes, likes a drink, does Geoff. So what are you looking for?' she asked. 'More computers, the Internet?'

'I'm not sure, really. Geoff thought this might be a chance for a radical change.'

'Right. So what would be your ideal job, if you could choose anything in the world?'

The answer needed no thought. 'Bestselling author.'

'Ah.' She flipped open a box of job cards on her desk and riffled through them with practised fingers. 'We had one of those last week but – oh dear.' She sighed. 'It's gone. Sorry.'

42

I smiled. 'That's OK. I appreciate that openings like that are pretty thin on the ground.'

She snapped the box shut. 'But it's good. At least you know where you want to go.'

'Even if it is impossible.'

'Why should it be impossible? The world's full of writers.'

'Mmm. But I don't have any talent.'

'Bah – talent, schmalent. The important thing's not talent, it's *ichinen*.'

'Itchy . . . ?'

'*Ichinen*. It's Japanese. Means determination – sort of. It's what's in your life moment by moment, pushing you this way or that. So if you've got a strong *ichinen* to be a writer, you'll do whatever it takes to become one. But if your *ichinen*'s weak, well, it'll just stay a daydream.'

'OK. But you've still got to have talent.'

'And what's that?'

'Talent?'

She nodded.

'Well, it's – you know – being good at something. Naturally good.'

'And you haven't got any?'

'No.'

'OK, you're never going to achieve your ambition, then. So what are you going to do instead?' She smiled enquiringly.

I frowned. I didn't like the way this interview was going.

'You just told me what you want is impossible,' said Dora, 'so I'm offering to help you choose second-best.'

'Aren't you supposed to encourage me?'

'No skin off my nose if you live the rest of your life frustrated and unfulfilled,' she said.

I studied her hard, trying to figure out if she was joking. She seemed pretty serious.

'Look,' she said, 'I've got a niece who plays the violin. Only nine but plays like an angel. Sounded terrible when she started – like cats fighting. But she wanted to play. Every morning, first thing she does when she gets up is grab her violin and bow and . . .' She mimed playing. 'Now, is that talent? Hard work? Desire?' She shook her head. '*Ichinen*. Covers the lot.'

'Fine. But it's still a fact that some people are more naturally gifted than others.'

'So? Doesn't mean they end up the best. In fact, with some people, being good at something means they don't really value it.'

'Plus your niece doesn't have to make a living.'

She sighed. 'OK. You're not going to be a writer. So let's find something you can regret doing for the rest of your life.'

'All I'm saying, Dora,' I said, and frankly I was starting to get a bit hacked off with her, 'is there are practical obstacles to achieving what I want to achieve, and having to make a living's one of them.'

'And all I'm saying, Ed, is you seem to have made up your mind already to let these obstacles defeat you.'

'I'm being realistic, that's all.'

'I'd say you're being pessimistic. Reality's what you make – through how you think, what you say, what you do. So if you keep telling yourself you can't do x, y and z – well, you won't. And your future's going to be made by someone else with stronger *ichinen*.'

I sighed. This was pretty much what Geoff had told me, but the moment I decided to do something positive the wheels came off.

Dora must have sensed where I was because her tone softened. 'Look, Ed, I don't know much about you, apart from what Geoff's told me—'

44

'Which is what?'

'Only that you've been having a hard time lately. But I think he's right. You've got this chance to redraw your map – you know, to start a journey to somewhere you really want to go. So why not make a plan and get on with it?'

'The journey of a thousand miles begins with a single step?'

'Yes. And if you really want to go to Russia, go to Russia. Don't say it's too far without even trying and just make a day-trip to Calais.'

'Are you saying you can help me become a bestselling writer?'

'Darling, I'm helping you already!' She slapped my arm and burst out laughing.

I couldn't help smiling. 'Do you know anything about writing?'

'No.'

'Ah.' At least she was frank.

'But I do know about different jobs, careers, how to get on in work. A lot applies across the board, believe me.'

'Even with something creative?'

'It's not just "creative" jobs that are creative, you know.'

'I meant artistic.'

'You want to be a bestselling writer *and* artistic?' She sucked air through her teeth. 'Tough.'

'That's my Russia.'

'Siberia, more like. But OK – if that's where you want to go. Where are you now?'

'Baker Street.'

'In your writing?'

'Nowhere. I've got an unfinished novel in my drawer, ideas for a screenplay . . .'

'Nothing published?'

'Not since college, no.'

'Right. So you want to be an A writer but currently you're a D.'

'Am I?'

'It's just my way of looking at what people want to do – artistic stuff, running your own business; anything that could be a hobby at one end or a real money-spinner at the other.'

'Sounds interesting.'

'It is. I am.' That chuckle again. It was quite sexy, to be honest.

'Go on,' I said. *Concentrate.*

'Well, the first thing is, you can be happy and fulfilled at any level – A, B, C or D. It's up to you. The pain only comes if you're at one level and want to be at a different one.'

'For example . . . ?'

'Well, a D writer – and I'll use writing, but you could be a dancer, painter, knit jumpers, mend cars, whatever.'

'Writing's fine.'

'OK. So a D writer has total freedom. He can write exactly what he wants – anything. Only problem is he's not paid for it. Basically, it's a hobby. From time to time he might sell something but that's not really why he does it. He writes for himself, and perhaps a few people around him.'

'Like poets.'

'If you say so. Anyway, he might fantasise about success, but he's sent stuff to publishers or film companies or whatever and been rejected and given up. Or maybe they've asked for changes and he's said no because he doesn't want to "compromise his vision". Or maybe it just never crosses his mind that what he's written could ever reach a wider audience, that anyone would want it.'

'Sounds familiar – especially the rejection bit.'

She smiled sympathetically. 'Now, your C writer does get paid, but he has practically no freedom. He writes what he's told to by whoever's paying him – like a company brochure, say, or a press release, or a lot of journalism; something that has to fit a very specific function. The C writer is hired because technically he can do it – on time, the right length, hitting all the points. No freedom or creativity – or not much – and there's not much of his personality in there, but at least he gets paid for it. Can even make a good living at it.'

'Hmm. Does rewriting articles about lino count?'

'That's your C writer.'

'Or hack, as we call him. OK. What's a B writer, then?'

'He's got a lot more freedom and is offered better paid work, and it's probably more interesting too. But he's still working to someone else's rules.'

'Such as?'

'Well, someone writing for a TV soap. He's given the characters and situation, maybe even the plot, but he has to take all the ingredients and create an entertaining episode from them.'

'So he's basically a souped-up version of C, a super-hack.'

'Your words, Ed. He's still very skilled and can make a lot of money.'

'Sorry. I have this tendency to be a bit judgemental.'

Dora just smiled.

'And the A writer . . . ?'

'Same as the D writer – except he gets paid top dollar. He writes exactly what he wants, when he wants, but people are itching to get their hands on what he comes up with. And he has the pick of any work that's on offer.'

'He's a bit of a star, in other words.'

Dora nodded.

'So why wouldn't everyone want that? Why would a C or B writer want to stay at their level?'

'Because different levels bring different challenges. People expect more of an A writer, so he can feel pressured to keep coming up with great material, which can be very stressful. Especially if you don't know quite how you hit the jackpot in the first place.'

'The follow-up syndrome.'

'Yes. C and B writers might have more modest ambitions and settle for less, but can feel happier working within their limitations.'

Hmm. All very interesting, but I wasn't sure exactly where it was taking me. 'Well, let's say I want to be an A writer. I still need a job – now.'

'Of course you do, darling, and I'll find you one. But I need to help you make a map first, so this job helps you get where you want to go – OK?'

'If you can, that'd be great.' She was beginning to grow on me.

'Did Geoff tell you about *kyo chee gyo ee* at all?'

'Kyo . . . ?'

'Obviously not. How about value creation?'

I shook my head.

She pursed her lips, clearly rolling up her mental sleeves. 'Well, then – we'd better get to work.'

***

I sipped the mug of weak coffee Dora had plonked in front of me as she cleared a space on her desk, and pulled a clean sheet of paper from a pile in her in-tray.

'Not too strong?'

'It's fine,' I lied, through my grimace.

'Good. So – *kyo chee gyo ee*. *Kyo* is your goal. *Chee* is your wisdom. *Gyo* is the action you take. And *ee* is your resulting status. This,' she announced grandly, 'is how to achieve all your goals in life.' And she wrote it down:

48

KYO – Goal
CHI – Wisdom
GYO – Action
I – Status

'Is this Buddhism?' I asked, realising I'd spelled it wrong in my head.

'Everything's Buddhism, darling.'

'You know what I mean.'

'Well, I learned it from a Buddhist – I think it's a variation on a very deep Buddhist principle. But I just use it 'cos it works.'

'That's good enough for me,' I said. 'Go on.'

'So, the starting point is setting your goal – where you want to go, what you want to achieve.'

'To be an A writer.'

'No.'

'Eh?'

'Common mistake. You're confusing *kyo* and *i* – your goal and the status you get from reaching your goal. Being and doing.'

'I don't understand.'

'Your goal is something outside yourself, something you achieve through *doing*. Your status comes from doing it.'

I furrowed my brows, still struggling.

'It's like saying, "I want to be a traveller," rather than "I want to travel."'

'What difference does it make?'

'It helps you focus on something concrete – and doable. Like, you want to go to Russia? OK, but where in Russia? You look at a map and pick a place. That's your goal. In going there you become a traveller – that's your status. Doing leads to being.'

'I see.' I wasn't sure I did completely, but I was curious where this was heading.

'So what do you have to *do*, as your goal, to *be* a bestselling writer?'

'Write.'

'What?'

'A bestselling book?'

'Good.' She smiled, pleased that I'd got it. Except I hadn't.

'Is that it?'

'No. But it's the start.'

I was lost. 'Well, I'm sorry, Dora, but to me this all sounds like stating the bleeding obvious.'

'Then why didn't you?'

I opened my mouth. And closed it. And opened it again. Nothing came out.

Dora just smiled. 'It sounds like a small thing, Ed, but the difference is massive. If you focus on *kyo*, your goal, all the time you're thinking about "out there" – how you're going to get to your destination. But if you focus on *i*, your status, all the time you're basically thinking about – worrying about – yourself. And if your self-image and what you want to be are miles apart – well, that can be very painful, paralysing even.'

I nodded bleakly. She'd got my number, all right.

She looked at me sympathetically. 'Don't worry, we all suffer from it. In fact, I think it's why sportsmen – even champions – can choke at big moments. They suddenly switch focus from the game itself to what it could mean if they won or lost this point, or missed this kick or whatever.'

I thought about this for a moment. 'OK. It makes sense but I still don't see how it helps me write a bestselling book.'

'Right.' It was Dora's turn to furrow her brow. 'Well, I suppose I start by asking, what makes a bestselling book?'

'If I knew that, Dora, I'd have written it years ago.'

'Think of it like any other product.'

'But it isn't. It's . . . different.'

'How?'

Another silence. I was stumped again.

'Why do people buy anything, Ed?'

'Advertising.'

She shook her head. 'I'd say it's because it meets a need of some kind – physically or mentally; spiritually even. Any successful product does that, for a lot of people, and better than its rivals. Even books.'

'But a lot of successful products – and books – are almost by accident.' I felt I had to argue with her; she was making it sound too easy.

'That's right, because often the creator won't know how many people have the same need as him or her.'

I pulled a face, still unconvinced.

'All right – this is a true story. A man I know is very successful, all because he wanted a good night's sleep.'

'Go on, then.' I sighed. I leaned back in my chair and made myself ready for the amazing tale I expected to unfold, à la Geoff. For some reason, these Buddhists just loved telling stories.

'Well, his wife has a baby and is trying to wean him onto a bottle. But the baby's having none of it. So one night, when this kid's bawling his head off after another go at giving him a bottle, Dad decides to stop moaning about not getting enough sleep and investigate the problem. He looks at the design of the teat and realises that baby's just not getting enough milk. The harder he sucks, the more blocked the holes become. But you can't tell a baby to suck less hard, can you? Especially when it's hungry. So Dad sets about designing a different teat; in fact, a whole different bottle, because when he does some research he finds out that baby bottles are based on the shape of beer bottles, because originally mothers would just fill up empty beer bottles with milk, improvise a teat and stick it in their babies' mouths. So Dad designs his bottle fatter and squatter – easier for the baby to hold – and designs a teat based on his wife's, you know . . .'

'Nipple. It's all right, Dora – I am familiar with the word.'

She laughed and pressed on. 'Anyway, he does that because he wants his baby to be comfortable with something he knows.'

I nodded.

'And, most important of all, instead of putting pinholes in the end, like all the other teats, he puts a small slit in it. If you twist it vertically and the baby sucks on it, it opens up and he gets a lot of milk; but if you twist it horizontally it won't open up so much. So you can actually control how much your baby is getting, and how fast.'

'Clever.'

'Yes. But the point I'm making is he did all this to get some sleep, and for his baby to get a good feed. And in doing it he realised that a lot of other people had the same need; millions of people around the world, in fact, because that's where his bottle's now sold. He didn't do any of this because he wanted to become a rich, successful business-man. He did it to meet a need.'

'Right. So all I've got to do is write a book that meets an absolutely basic need and I'll have a massive hit on my hands?'

'Exactly. And in reaching your goal – *kyo* – you become a bestselling author – *i*.'

'Well, I'd better get going then. Thanks.' I started to get

52

to my feet, impatient with the utter banality of what I'd heard.

Dora looked concerned. 'Don't you want to know about *chi* and *gyo*; wisdom and action?'

I hesitated, then sat down again – if only because I owed it to Geoff not to walk out on his friend.

Dora smiled, thinking I'd just been joking. 'Right. So you've identified your goal – and put status to the back of your mind. Now you've got to work out how to get to where you want to go. Seeing that your baby's bottle is no good is one thing; working out how to improve it is something else. That's where your wisdom comes in: you've got to rack your brain to figure out how to reach your goal. And action is just what you do to get there, based on your wisdom. Trial and error, a bit at a time.'

'The problem, Dora,' I said, trying to keep the irritation out of my voice, 'is you make it sound so simple – and it's not.'

'It is simple. But simple doesn't mean easy. Climbing Everest is simple – you just keep going up. But it's also difficult, so a lot of people don't even try. Or give up when it gets too hard.'

'Perseverance wins?'

'Exactly!' She sounded positively triumphant, as if the penny had dropped with a particularly thick pupil.

'It's what Geoff said.'

'Well, he ain't wrong.'

The door opened and a young woman came in. 'Hello. I look job.'

An Eastern European – and my cue to escape. I got to my feet again. 'All right. Let me think about it.'

Dora's face fell. 'Are you going?'

'Er, yes, sorry. I've just remembered I'm meeting someone.'

'What about the job?'

'Well, I'll be too busy with my bestseller for that. But thanks again for all your help.'

'The key,' she said, ignoring my sarcasm, 'is fixing your goal in your heart.' And she pressed the *kyo chi gyo i* paper into my hand.

'Got it,' I said – and walked out.

***

It was evening and I was back in my flat. There was nothing on telly, and I was sitting staring at my late-night list of determinations and Dora's piece of paper. I was trying to work out why I'd started to feel so hostile towards her. She was only trying to help me. It was the same with Geoff. After a time I had just started to feel irritated by him. Perhaps I simply didn't want to be helped. Perhaps I was one of those strange people who supposedly want to fail, and unconsciously sabotage anything positive that comes their way. Like this thing I'd read somewhere that said, 'it's not our darkness that scares us, it's our light' – whatever that means. Or perhaps I was so out of touch with what I felt and needed that I was destined to be alone and miserable and unfulfilled . . . for ever.

Then it hit me. I had started to feel negative when Geoff or Dora tried to encourage me because, deep down, I simply didn't believe them. If getting on in life was that bloody simple why hadn't I worked it out? The more they explained things, and told me this principle and that, the more my heart sank. It all made sense and sounded fine – until some little voice piped up in my head and told me it was all just words. I stared at Dora's paper. The secret to success had to be more complicated than a four-word formula, whether it was *kyo chi gyo i* or anything else. No – it was not for me.

But why not? If it worked for them, why not me?

I searched for an answer, trying to be as honest with myself as I could. And almost at once a thought started to emerge from the murk of my subconscious. An unpleasant thought. But instead of pushing it back down again I let it rise to the surface – and speak.

'Because you're a failure,' it said. 'And you know it. Even this morning, when you went in to turn over a new leaf with Martin, you knew it wouldn't come to anything. Because nothing ever does. Like your writing. Ha – what a joke. The reason you can't write is that you haven't got anything to say. You can't meet your own needs, let alone anyone else's. Genius might be one per cent inspiration and ninety-nine per cent perspiration, but you haven't even got that one per cent. Face it: you're so ordinary, so average, that all you can expect, all you actually deserve, is an ordinary, average life. Dull? Yes – but that's reality. And who are you to believe any different?'

The phone rang – Geoff. I could hear music in the background, voices. Life.

'Hi. I was just wondering how you got on with Dora.'

Hmm. Did he know? 'Fine. She taught me all about *kyo chi gyo i*.'

'Ah. How about a job?'

'Erm . . . work in progress, you know.'

'You all right? You sound a bit down, mate.'

'Just tired. Been a stressful day.'

'I bet. Well, if you fancy a jar sometime give us a bell and we'll fix something up.'

'OK – cheers. And thanks for calling.'

I put the phone down. Alone again – except for My Evil Friend.

'Of course he knew. She probably called him the moment you walked out and they giggled and tut-tutted

55

about you on the phone. Well, stuff them. Religious nutters, peddling quick fixes you know are never going to work. Life's hard, Ed. Failing's the norm. Only the lucky few ever make it, and not many of them are actually happy. Because you know the old saying: "Money doesn't make you happy, but at least you can be miserable in comfort." Except you're not even going to be rich. You're—'

'SHUT UP!'

I actually shouted. Out loud. Which quite startled me. Christ, I thought, I really am going mad. But at least it did shut him up. I grabbed the phone before he could start again.

'Geoff? It's Ed. I think I fancy that jar right now.'

***

My mother used to say there are only two types of people in the world. No, not people-who-say-there-are-only-two-types-of-people-in-the-world and people who don't. Her pair was 'drains and radiators': people who drain away your energy, and people who give you theirs. If that's true then Geoff was definitely one of life's radiators. He listened to me moan on for a good fifteen minutes, just sipping his beer and lighting and relighting his roll-up. Then, when I'd exhausted my whinge, he smiled wryly.

'My Evil Friend . . . Mmm, I know him well – the bastard. He's found your weak spot and knows exactly when to press it.'

I nodded bleakly.

'Only I don't know where you got this idea that I'm peddling a quick fix. I told you as soon as you tried to change things your negativity would jump up and try to stop you – and it has. It's a battle.'

'Well, I expect My Evil Friend wiped my memory banks so I'd forget at the crucial moment.' I was only half joking.

Geoff nodded. 'Cunning bleeder.' He thought for a moment. 'Tea-cup – that's what you need.'

'Eh?'

'Thinking Correctly Under Pressure – TCUP. Sportsmen use it to stay focused when the heat's on.'

'Ah. So how do I develop it?'

'Practice. Anticipation. Preparation. Because your Evil Friend's right – life is hard. Bad stuff happens. So expect it, be prepared for it. Then you'll be better able to deal with it when it shows up.'

'How could I expect Martin to go bust?'

'Come on, Ed. You said yourself there'd been signs.'

I sighed, still depressed. 'OK. But how do I deal with MEF? He's there constantly, criticising, putting me down, making cynical remarks . . .'

'It's your life state, mate. I told you the second time I met you: if your life condition's low all this negative stuff just appears, like the rocks at low tide. They're always there, but when the tide's in – when your life condition is high – they disappear. You literally rise above it all.'

I looked at him. 'So how do I raise my life state?'

'I told you that, and all. I do it through my Buddhist practice. But you don't want to know about that, do you?' He looked at me searchingly.

'I am not becoming a Buddhist, Geoff – sorry.'

I must have sounded more aggressive than I intended, because he held up his hands in surrender – or was it defence? 'OK, fine.' He took refuge in his beer for a bit, thinking. 'It seems to me that whatever MEF says, you need a result. You've got to win somewhere, to feel what it's like again, and build on that. Build your confidence. Like years ago, when I was at rock bottom, I challenged a parking ticket and was let off. It was only a little thing, but it felt good – you know, winning. And it reminded me that I could actually make something positive happen.'

'So what do you suggest?'

'I think what Dora said about *kyo chi gyo i* is right. You do need to set your goal, and have the balls to make it big and bold and something that means something to you. Your golden vision. Because in the end, going for it is what's going to give your life purpose, meaning. But—'

'I felt there was a "but" coming.'

'It's not a bad "but" – don't worry.'

I waited, sceptical.

'I was going to say, but you need a series of little goals on the way; sort of staging-posts so the journey becomes more doable. It's like that riddle: how do you eat an elephant?'

I waited. 'Well?'

'One bite at a time.'

I laughed.

'So, first step,' said Geoff, 'is you go back to Dora and get a job. Not just any old job. It's got to be exactly what you need for your life at this moment.'

'I can't.'

'Why not?'

'I walked out on her. It's embarrassing.'

Geoff smiled. 'There's a Buddhist saying, Ed.'

I groaned.

'If you can't cross a ditch ten feet wide, how are you going to cross a ditch that's twenty or thirty feet wide?'

'And in English . . .?'

'Are you seriously going to let a little embarrassment stand between you and ultimate fulfilment?'

Put like that, how could I refuse?

Chapter Four

Morning saw me heading back to Baker Street. The Tube was packed but I didn't care. I was on a mission – to get my life going, give it a kick, move it in the direction I wanted to go. Geoff was right: people who know what they want don't give a toss what others think. They just put their heads down and get on with it. So what if they're called ruthless or ambitious? That's just the weak whinging. 'Show me a good loser and I'll show you a loser.' Nice one.

Soon I was sitting opposite Dora, mapping my future. She'd waved away my apology with a hoot of laughter – 'Don't worry about it, darling. I just wish more men in my life would come back!' – and got straight down to the task in hand.

'So,' she said, 'you know what your goal is—'

'Write a bestseller.'

'OK. But you need to work out how to get there and still pay the mortgage, keep the lights switched on—'

'Eat.'

'Vital. And have a bit of fun every now and then.'

'That'd be nice.'

She smiled.

59

'Geoff said I need a job that's perfect for my life right now, as a stepping-stone to where I want to go.'

'OK. Well, I think there are three elements to any job: beauty, gain and good.'

'More Buddhism?' I was beginning to suspect it everywhere.

'No,' she said.

'Ah.' I was surprised.

'Though the principle was developed by a Buddhist.'

I smiled. There we are then. 'And what principle's that?'

'Value creation.'

'Which is . . .?'

'Basically, that everything's neutral and only gets a value – positive or negative – through how we relate to it. And these values are beauty, gain and good.'

'Explain.'

'Right. Say you've got the world's largest diamond. Is it valuable? Yes, if you can sell it; but if you can't, what's its value?'

'Unless you just like looking at it.'

'Which still means its value depends on how you relate to it. Beauty is how much you like something, the pleasure you get from it. Gain is the benefit you get from it, which would be the money, of course, if you could sell it. And good is how much it does for everyone's happiness and well-being.'

I digested this for a moment. 'You're saying we give value to things?'

'Almost. The value's *created* through our relationship to that thing, our attitude.'

'And this relates to work?'

'It relates to everything, darling.' Dora smiled. 'The more value we create, especially for other people, the happier we are.'

60

'OK. But work . . .?'

'Beauty is how much you like a job. Gain is mainly how much you get paid for it, though you could get other benefits too, like experience. And good is what it contributes to society. And different jobs have different amounts of beauty, gain and good for different people.'

'For example?'

'Advertising might give you a lot of gain but some people say it doesn't do much good.'

'It helps the economy.'

'Which is what other people say – especially if they're in advertising. Anyway, at the other end of the scale, nursing does a lot of good but doesn't give you a lot of gain.'

'Meaning it doesn't pay much.'

'Right. Though you might benefit a lot from learning about human nature or stuff like that. And beauty's in the eye of the beholder – how much you like the job's down to you, and can change. You might love being in advertising, love the salary, then start to wonder if you're actually doing any good and go and become a nurse.'

'Or you might start out all idealistic and work as a nurse, then get hacked off at having no money and go into advertising.'

'Exactly. And often people stay in jobs they really don't like because either the money's so good, or they think they're doing something really worthwhile. But the point is people are always juggling beauty, gain and good in their work, even if they don't see it in these terms.'

Hmm. Did this fit my time at ItsTheBusiness?

Dora guessed my thoughts. 'Make any sense? With your old job, for example?'

'Well . . . beauty? Definitely not. I pretty much loathed every minute.'

'Anything you didn't loathe?'

61

'Some of the people. And there was a kind of grim satisfaction, I suppose, in turning something unreadable into a half-decent article.'

'Gain?'

'Not a lot. Definitely not enough for the stress involved.'

'OK. And good?'

'Not that I could see. No one ever read it.'

'Right. So a pretty low score on all three.'

'Yep. Bum job all round.'

'Whereas writing a bestseller . . . ?'

'Well, lots of gain, obviously. Lots of good – because if it sells a lot I'll be meeting a lot of need in a lot of people, right?'

'In some way, yes. And beauty? Will you actually enjoy the writing? All those hours alone, slaving over a hot keyboard . . .'

Good question. 'Dunno – till I try it.'

Dora studied me thoughtfully, as if uncertainty was tattooed across my forehead. 'Does it help, thinking about work in this way?'

'Sort of. But until I apply it to this perfect job you're going to find me . . .'

She laughed – 'Point taken' – and unpeeled a fresh sheet of paper from her stack.

***

Half an hour later, after a rigorous application of beauty, gain and good to my life and skills, Dora came up with the perfect next step for me: business writing.

'I just did that,' I groaned.

'I'm not talking about the Internet,' Dora enthused. 'Businesses have all sorts of things that need writing – brochures, marketing material, newsletters, company magazines; lots of stuff. You could work in a PR department somewhere, or even a PR company.'

I pulled a face. 'But I don't like business.'

Dora frowned. 'Look, Ed,' she said sternly, 'right now gain is your number one need, not beauty. You've got to pay the bills, right?'

I sighed.

'Plus, one thing leads to another. There are all sorts of openings you'll only ever hear about if you're working somewhere.'

'Feels like a step back, that's all.'

'Well, you can look at it that way,' she said briskly. 'Or you can see it as the first step towards your ultimate goal.'

'How?'

'Something a wise friend of mine once advised me: "You can only take a step forward if the place where you're standing now is solid." Which means you have to advance from a secure base. And I've seen a lot of people fail because they didn't do this. They started businesses or new careers with too little money, or experience, or knowledge, or a wobbly income – or even no income at all. And always, unless they were really lucky, they fell on their faces. This basic thing that was missing at the beginning held them back more and more as time went on. So don't under-estimate the importance of gain, is all I'm saying. Because as long as what you want to do, your *kyo*, is in here' – she patted her shapely chest – 'more and more you'll find yourself moving into the position where you can actually do it.'

I hesitated. 'Can I think about it?'

'Course you can, darling. It's your life.' She smiled.

***

I did think about it. For the rest of that day, in fact. And the more I turned it over in my mind, the more I warmed to it.

I began to see myself as the hero of my own story, about to set off on my very own adventure, to meet and slay dragons, overcome perils, and emerge triumphant at the end. If this *kyo chi gyo i* stuff was true, all I had to do was what Dora and Geoff said: fix on to my *kyo* like the Pole Star and it would guide me inexorably, unwaveringly, to my destination. Eventually. Plus – and I have to admit that this was a big factor – with the dot-com bubble well and truly burst more and more people were saying a recession was coming. Now was not the time to be out of a job.

I called Dora before the close of business with my decision: I'd like her to try to set up some interviews.

'Darling, I already have!' she enthused. The first was for the following morning . . .

***

Geoff told me more about value creation that evening. We were supposed to be going to the pub – inevitably – but when he'd rung the doorbell I was halfway through a large Scotch and Coke and offered him one. I'd bought a bottle of Famous Grouse to help me cope with the challenge of unemployment and this seemed a good time to lean on it for support. That drink led to another, and another, then to ordering an Indian takeaway. So now I was sprawled on the sofa, replete and half-cut, while he was sunk deep in the armchair, politely ignoring the mess that I called my sitting-room and talking about this Japanese bloke, Makiguchi.

'He developed the theory of value creation during the 1920s and 1930s because he didn't agree with philosophers who said the highest values in life are truth, beauty and good, since truth isn't a value.'

'Eh?'

'Makiguchi reckoned truth's absolute and value's

64

relative. Truth describes something exactly as it is, and value basically describes how we feel about it.'

'For example?'

'Right. You see a horse. You say, "This is a horse." That's truth.'

'If it is a horse.'

'Obviously. Whereas, if you say, "I like that horse," that's value; it's about your relationship to it. So Makiguchi swapped gain or benefit for truth, because he saw that as being the value missing from the list. "This is a horse," equals truth. "I like this horse," equals beauty. "I can ride this horse," equals gain or benefit. And "We can use horses to plough with," equals good.'

I burped loudly. ''Scuse me. Too much Coke.' I cleared my throat. 'So what's the big deal?'

'Well, according to Makiguchi, mixing up truth and value leads to all sorts of muddle.'

'Such as?'

'The idea that truth equals good.'

'Doesn't it?' I could feel one of those Buddhist 'black-is-white, up-is-down' moments approaching. Geoff leaned forward in his chair.

'The Nazis knock on the door of the house where Anne Frank's hiding. "Seen any Jews around here?" they ask. The house owner shakes his head and the Nazis move on. Truth's not always good, and doesn't always create value. It depends on the situation.'

'That's a pretty dangerous line,' I countered. 'It's saying you can always lie if you reckon it's to your advantage.'

'Well, a lot of people do. But society won't agree with this sort of lying unless it benefits the greater good – though different societies often don't agree about what that is either.'

'Slower . . .'

'Right. A Nazi general's spying for the Allies. To his side he's a lying traitor, to the Allies he's a hero. The fact that he's spying is "truth"; how he's seen by each side is "value".'

'All right – I get that. But I still don't see the big deal.'

'It helps make communicating a lot clearer if we know: are we talking truth, or value?'

'As in . . .?'

Geoff twisted a stray hair of tobacco from the end of his newly rolled cigarette, then suddenly looked up at me. 'Sorry, I didn't ask. Is it OK?' He waved the roll-up.

'Fine,' I said. 'The cleaner's coming in tomorrow.'

'You have a cleaner?' Geoff sounded surprised.

'Does it look like it?' I waved a hand at the pile of several days' empty takeaway cartons, the unwashed plates and coffee mugs, the newspapers strewn everywhere. 'It's all gone to pot a bit since Angie went, I'm afraid.'

Geoff nodded sympathetically, then lit his roll-up. 'Where was I?' he said, blowing out a plume of smoke.

'Er . . .' Too many Scotch and Cokes.

Geoff remembered. 'Truth and value. Right – take religion. A lot of people say different religions are always arguing and contradicting each other, and if only they could agree perhaps we'd have a bit of peace on Earth – yes?'

'Amen.'

'While a lot of other people say they're all basically the same, and are just stating the same thing in different ways; they're different paths leading to the same goal, etcetera etcetera.'

'They *are* the same – all as bad as each other.'

'Right. Well, this is your basic truth-value split. The arguments tend to be about truth: about which religion has got the best take on life and death and all that. And the agreements tend to be about value: how beauty, gain and

66

good are taught by different religions. So you can have Buddhism and Christianity totally divided over whether or not there's a God – truth – but still—'

'Hang on. Are you saying Buddhism doesn't believe in God?'

'Yes.'

'I never knew that.'

'You do now. Anyway—'

'Funny sort of religion.'

'Well, actually, I suppose it depends what you mean by God. If you mean an old bloke with a beard up in the sky running everything – then definitely not.'

'I don't think anyone believes that any more – do they?'

Geoff thought for a moment. 'Dunno. But even if you mean God as some sort of all-knowing intelligence, Buddhism disagrees with that too. And it doesn't think there's a divine plan that's slowly unfolding or anything like that either. But even if Christianity and Buddhism disagree about something as fundamental as God, they can still agree totally that human behaviour should be based on compassion and respect, i.e. about "value". In fact, from what I can see, religions more and more are agreeing to disagree about truth – most of which can't be proved anyway – and concentrating on value to find common ground.' He looked at me to check I'd understood, then re-lit the roll-up, which had gone out while he was talking.

But I was still digesting his remark about Buddhism and God. 'Can you have a religion that doesn't believe in God?' I was confused.

'Buddhism,' Geoff said simply.

'Except a lot of people say it's not a religion, don't they?' I was beginning to remember.

'Only because some people can only think about religion in terms of a god or gods.'

'You said yourself you can call it a life philosophy.'

'And you can, if you want. But apart from not having a god, on all other counts it qualifies as a religion. Sorry.' He'd seen the disappointed look on my face. 'There's a practice, scriptures, doctrines – the works. And endless internal splits.' He laughed and took a slug of his drink.

'About?'

'The nature of enlightenment.'

'Sounds interesting. Care to enlighten me?'

Geoff groaned. 'Can we save it for another time? It's a long conversation.'

'I'm not going anywhere,' I said. I fancied another drink – or three.

'Well, you should be,' said Geoff. 'Bed. You've got a job interview tomorrow.'

***

I'd fought off the idea of having another drink – alone – and was just brushing my teeth, ready for bed, when the doorbell rang. Must be Geoff, I thought. Must have forgotten something. Unless it was . . . No, not Angie. She wouldn't turn up unannounced. Except she *was* sometimes quite unpredictable – like if she'd had a glass of wine too many.

I quickly rinsed my mouth out, tousled my hair, and hurried down to the front door – my flat's at the top of the house. I took a deep breath, yanked open the door with a nonchalant air – and got a total surprise. On the doorstep was the last person I expected to see again: Martin.

Chapter Five

You know what never fails to amaze me? People. You think you've got them pinned down, sorted, because 'they're always like that' – greedy, or selfish, or selfless; you name it. You label them, put them in a box – and then, bugger me if they don't go and do something totally out of character. Mild-mannered Mr X murders his wife because she puts his socks in the wrong drawer. Mousey Miss Y runs off and marries an African chieftain she met on holiday. The miserly old git in No. 15 dies and leaves a million quid to charity. And Martin – Martin who strutted and barked his way around the office, who always knew best, who never listened to a bleeding word I said . . . Martin turns up on my doorstep in the middle of the night and asks for my help.

'Because you did offer to help, didn't you?'

Talk about nerve. The bloke owed me a month's money, had given me grief for over a year, had put me on a formal warning – and here he was asking for my help! I pointed out, coolly, that the offer was made when I still had a job; and I was about to go inside and slam the door on him when I saw the crushed look on his face, and his slumped shoulders and sagging head and – well, I amazed myself and asked him to come in for a drink.

69

Mistake. Christ, what a bloody whinger. OK, so he was facing personal ruin and homelessness: he'd remortgaged his posh Docklands flat to invest in the company, and was almost certainly going to lose it. But the way he went on! And like none of it was his fault! It was all I could do not to hit him. But I didn't. Instead – and this is the freaky part – after a time I started to tell him some of the stuff that Geoff and Dora had told me. I didn't say it was Buddhism, of course; he was even more cynical than me. But I talked about taking responsibility and three fingers pointing back at you whenever you point the finger of blame, and 'danger-opportunity' and problems helping us grow and all the rest of it. Well, as much as I could remember, because things got a bit hazy as we worked our way steadily through the rest of the Famous Grouse.

But the amazing thing was – and I know it's the third time I've been amazed since the beginning of the chapter, but I was . . . well, pretty bloody amazed by the turn of events. Anyway, the thing was, by the time Martin left – at past 1 a.m. – it was like I was his best friend!

'God, you've really helped me,' he blubbed, and gave me a big, emotional hug. 'The whole time I've thought you were a complete bastard, and there's been all this . . . this . . . insight, just bursting to get out.'

He thought *I* was a complete bastard? Huh. But all I said was, 'Yeah, well – you know . . .' with a modest, drunken shrug.

'Still, too late now,' said Martin. 'For ItsTheBusiness anyway. But thank you, thank you.' And with another brief hug he was gone.

Hooray. I staggered into my bedroom, collapsed onto the bed and passed out.

***

70

First thing next morning was my interview with Writers Inc. I'd planned to bounce in bright-eyed and eager. Instead I had just about the worst hangover I can remember. My head thumped, my stomach heaved and my guts churned as I declined a black coffee with a weak smile and tried to focus on the gorgeous female interviewing me: mid-thirties, smart, full and very kissable lips . . . Fortunately, while fantasising about the sexual tigress that obviously prowled beneath her crisp, businesslike exterior, I heard myself talking about creating value; about how much satisfaction I'd get out of helping different companies achieve their goals, and Writers Inc. achieve its goal, and how eventually that would help me achieve mine.

'And what's that?' she asked.

'Well,' I said with a shy smile, 'I hope one day to write something that will really – you know – move people.'

I don't know if that's what swung it, or the guff about value creation, but there was a phone message waiting for me when I got back home: When could I start?

Bingo! Result! Hole-in-one! I was so excited – and relieved – I forgot about taking my nausea straight back to bed and rang Dora with the good news.

'Well, of course you got it,' she said. 'I chanted for you.'

Uh-huh. 'So I had nothing to do with it then?'

She laughed. 'It was all you. But every little bit helps, eh?'

'Every little bit of what?'

'Good vibrations, positive thinking, prayers – whatever you want to call it.'

'Right . . .'

'Anyway, I'm really happy it's worked out for you, Ed. Anything else I can help with, just call.'

I pointed out that I wouldn't be needing an employment agency for some time, at which she laughed again – 'Let's hope not!' – and rang off. Hmm. Did she know something I didn't?

I rang Geoff too, on his mobile, and he also seemed genuinely pleased. 'How about I buy you dinner soon?' I said, wanting to show my gratitude.

'Fine by me,' he agreed. We set a date and I was about to ring off when a thought struck me.

'You didn't chant for me as well, did you?'

'*Mais bien sûr, mon frère.*'

'In French?'

Geoff laughed. 'It works in all languages.'

'Well, whatever you did, I owe you.' I made a mental note to ask him more about this chanting palaver over our meal, but I had to cancel him before the week was over: Writers Inc. expected me actually to work for my money, all hours . . .

***

I didn't mind having to blow him out, to be honest, because things were going really well. OK, I was taking work home, but Writers Inc. were a professional outfit and I could see a tangible result: smart, well-produced, corporate literature. As long as I hit my deadlines and delivered what the client wanted all was hunky-dory. Then there was the benefit of Cathy, my boss – she of the kissable lips. She was cool, but friendly and reasonable, a real change from Martin. She was also unattached, as far as I could tell, and obviously secretly fancied me but was playing the long game. Fair enough: I could wait. I was still nursing a broken heart from Angie, after all. But in time I expected my subtle charm to work its magic and her to succumb to the inevitable: a drink together, a film maybe, dinner – then bed. I simply had to apply myself to work and be patient . . . But then came The Carpet Tile Incident.

It started harmlessly enough, with a visit to the company on a trading estate just off the North Circular in Wembley. They wanted a video made about their super-deluxe carpet tile, and Cathy had entrusted me with my first script as a step up from the brochure work I'd been doing. I'd only been there a month and already I was in film!

The showroom looked like a dance-floor, surrounded on three sides by tiered seating. The fourth side was given over to a selection of industrial floor-cleaning machines: washers, scrubbers, polishers. I was shown to a ringside seat by Brian, the sales director, along with half a dozen others – potential customers, he murmured as I sat down. Then he straightened up and addressed us with a beaming smile. 'Thank you very much for coming, everyone. Now please, just relax – and enjoy.'

Enter Wilf – fiftyish, thinning, wiry, with a Zapata moustache. He sized us up and started his patter in broad Cockney. 'Anyone 'ere like 'oovering?'

No one moved.

'No? I love it. But then, I'm very strange.'

He reached for a bag of flour on a nearby table and sprinkled a good handful onto the dance-floor, now seen for what it was – a collection of the company's carpet tiles. 'Most people hate it. My wife does. But even the people who don't, don't really know 'ow to 'oover.' He grabbed a domestic appliance waiting patiently at the side, pulled it onto the dance-floor and turned it on. ''Ow many Mrs Mops you seen doing this?' He pushed the cleaner head hard into the carpet tiles, over the sprinkled flour. Very little was sucked up. 'Sad, really. 'Cos it's not the vacuum that cleans, you see – it's the updraught. So you've got to make a space for that to work, see? On the *back* stroke.' He pulled the head towards him and – presto – the flour disappeared. I was mildly impressed. I'd remember the

73

lesson – if I ever found myself anywhere near a vacuum cleaner.

'But you didn't come all this way to learn that,' Wilf said, noting my immobile features. 'No, you come for something more spectacular.' He crossed again to the table and opened an egg-box. He took out two eggs, checked them briefly, then lobbed them over his shoulder. They splattered dramatically on the carpet tiles. I raised an eyebrow and Wilf reached for the margarine tub. 'Marge?' he enquired.

We all nodded.

He scraped out a large lump and dropped it onto the floor, then picked up a tin of engine oil and poured. Thick, black liquid joined the egg and margarine mix. 'What else? Something that really stains.'

'Toner,' Brian offered 'You know, from a photocopier.'

'Nice,' said Wilf with an evil smile, and tipped it onto the mess on the floor. He thought for a moment. 'I know –'ow about some Tippex? Bugger to clean, that is.' He grabbed a small bottle from his table and tipped out its contents. 'Anything else? You, sir.' He was looking at me.

'Pasta sauce?'

'Ah.' He looked disappointed. 'Very staining, but we're right out of it. 'Ow about beetroot juice?'

I nodded.

He smiled, and added the purple liquid from a bottle of pickled beetroot to the mess on the floor. 'But, of course, it's no fun unless it's really ground in, is it?' And with that, he got down on hands and knees with a palette knife and started to knead and mix the ingredients into a foul, sticky, impossible goo. He smeared it with a theatrical flourish across the carpet tiles, then scanned his rapt audience. 'And now,' he declared, 'to clean it up. If we can.' His eyes twinkled.

He began to scrape off the goo with the same palette knife, attacking the carpet with the vigour of a convict scratching through the concrete of his prison cell. The carpet pile was made of some virtually indestructible fibre, he explained, and was cunningly designed to reject dirt. 'It'll take practically any punishment you can dish out,' he grunted, stabbing the floor to make the point, then got to his feet to survey his handiwork. A big, black mark still stained the carpet.

'Phase Two,' he announced, dragging a state-of-the-art industrial cleaner onto centre stage. He hit the start button and the machine – clearly his pride and joy – jumped into life, eager for action. Wilf glided it over the offending area with practised ease. 'Flood and scrub, that's the secret,' he shouted over the whirr and suck of the machine. And, blow me, in no time the carpet looked bright, spanking new. We clapped, impressed, as Wilf took a bow, then straightened up. 'So,' he declared, 'anyone still think 'oovering's for wimps?'

I hurried back to Writers Inc. armed with carpet tile literature and a clear idea for the video. All we need do, I thought, was film Wilf's demo, top and tail it with some technical blurb, and Bob's your uncle.

I never got that far. Cathy was waiting for me as I walked in. 'My office,' she hissed and turned on her heel.

People glanced up from their desks as I followed her, then slid their eyes away. What was going on?

Cathy came right out with it as soon as we reached her office. 'They don't want to do the video.'

'What? Why?'

'You tell me.'

Her voice was heavy with accusation, but I was genuinely baffled.

'Some offensive remark you made, apparently. About black cleaners.'

Eh? I desperately scanned my memory of the visit. All I could think of was telling Brian how Wilf's love of cleaning reminded me of this Ghanaian bloke I met once, who confessed his secret ambition was to buy a top-of-the-range cleaning, polishing and buffing machine and make Accra airport really sparkle. Seriously. But he couldn't have taken offence at that – could he?

'And what conclusion did you draw?' Cathy's tone was icy.

'Conclusion?'

Cathy nodded.

I thought again. 'Er . . . well, only that perhaps what some people say is true: you know, that for every job, however dirty, there's always someone, somewhere willing to do it.'

'Meaning black people are suited to dirty jobs?'

Clang. The penny dropped – and alarm bells rang. 'No, no, not at all. I just meant that – you know – it takes all sorts.'

Cathy stared at me, unmoved. 'No, I don't know, Ed. All I know is that whatever you meant you've lost us a ten grand production fee and a client – neither of which we can afford in this climate. Another screw-up like that, and you're out.'

***

'Totally bloody unfair! Some suit misinterprets a completely innocent remark and suddenly my job's on the line! Bloody hell!'

Geoff gave a deep sigh. 'It's karma, mate,' he said, slicing into his Quattro Formaggio. We were in a busy pizzeria, eating the 'celebratory' meal I'd promised him a couple of weeks earlier, and I'd just vented my spleen – all over him.

76

'I don't care what it is. It's still not bloody fair!' I finished my lager and ordered another to help me cool down.

'Depends how you look at it,' Geoff mumbled through his pizza.

I shot him an angry glance. 'I do hope you're not going to say it's all my fault.'

'Fault? Well . . .' And he rocked his head this way and that, as if literally turning the thought over in his mind.

'Look, Geoff,' I said, jabbing my knife at him, 'the last thing I need right now is you telling me I did something wrong. Because I didn't.'

'I'm not saying you did. But I can offer you a different way to look at things, if you like. Might help you turn the situation round.'

'How?' I spat out the word, in no mood to be pacified.

'Well,' said Geoff, 'there seems to be a pattern here. I mean, what is it with you and flooring?'

'Eh?'

'Wasn't it a lino company who gave you all that grief in your last job?'

'Coincidence.'

'No such thing in Buddhism.'

'Oh yeah?' Here we go again – upside-down world.

'Mmm. Buddhism says everything works according to cause and effect. Coincidence is just an effect where we can't see the connecting cause. But perhaps this isn't the best time to talk about it, seeing as how you're so steamed up.' And he bit off a long string of melted cheese.

'I want to talk about it. That's why we're having this meal. And I'm not steamed up.'

'Just doing a good impression of someone who is?'

I scowled, but before I could answer the waiter brought my lager. I drank a third straight off and felt better at once. I looked Geoff in the eye. 'You were saying?'

77

He put down his knife and fork and studied me for a moment, chewing. 'OK,' he said. 'But I warn you – cause and effect and karma is something a lot of people have issues with. It can make them quite . . . emotional.'

'Why?'

'Because we live in a culture, a philosophy, that can only take so much responsibility.' And he pointed that stubby finger at me again – showing the three pointing back at his chest.

'All right,' I said. 'I promise not to get emotional. Continue.'

'Well,' said Geoff, sawing away at his pizza, 'karma's like a bank balance of cause and effect that you carry round with you everywhere. Everything you've ever thought, or felt, or said, or done is imprinted deep in your life. It shapes you – how you think and feel, what you say and do – and it's the sum total of all those causes that's brought you to this moment. So it's not a static bank balance; it's like your basic tendency in life, too. And it shapes your future.'

'How?'

'You know the story of the baby circus elephant?'

I shook my head.

'Well, one day mummy circus elephant has a little baby, and the moment it's suckled it has a metal chain clamped to one of its feet, with the other end bolted to a metal stake in the ground to stop it running off. So every time it moves away the chain yanks it back. And it grows up like this. What it doesn't realise is that as it grows bigger it also gets stronger, so by the time it's an adult it could easily break the chain and run off to freedom. But by now it's stopped even trying and so stays put.'

'It's been conditioned.'

'Exactly. And that's karma. The elephant's born into a

situation and grows up conditioned by it. We're all like that in a way. We get into habits of how we think and act in different situations and with different people. If we meet the sort of person we like we'll be open and friendly and they'll probably be friendly in return, and we'll carry that positive experience forward. But if it's the sort of person we don't like we'll be less friendly, which they'll pick up on and reflect back to us, and we'll come away thinking, What a miserable sod. Our earlier thought's confirmed by our experience and carried into the future, but it's the earlier thought that's largely produced that outcome in the first place. So karma repeats itself, and usually gets stronger as time goes on.'

'Right. So you're saying what – somehow I've got this deep unconscious hatred of flooring manufacturers, which they pick up on and turn against me?'

'Maybe.' I bridled – and Geoff grinned. 'All I'm saying is twice now you've been in a work situation, dealing with a particular type of company, and twice it's produced grief – for you.'

'OK. But in a nutshell, it's my fault.'

'Fault's a loaded word, Ed, very judgemental. But the cause was definitely in your life, else it wouldn't have happened to you.'

I took a deep, long breath, held it for a count of five, then slowly exhaled. I looked up from my pizza and gave Geoff the pleasantest smile I could manage. 'The only problem is the cause and effect don't match. I said something totally innocent, which *they* misinterpreted, and now it's got blown out of all proportion. So how do you explain that?'

Geoff didn't even break stride. 'Well, first, I expect they picked up on something in you they didn't like. A bit of contempt, maybe, or arrogance?'

'No.' Meaning yes, probably, but I wouldn't admit it at this stage, even to myself.

'And second, cause and effect isn't just limited to what we can see or remember. It's eternal.'

'Ah.' This was safer ground. Less personal, more open for a counter-attack. 'So this is the whole Buddhist reincarnation thing, eh? The sales director's an enemy from a previous life and he's been waiting all this time just to get back at me.'

'Could be,' Geoff said cheerfully, biting into another slice of pizza.

I shook my head. This was all so barmy I didn't know where to start demolishing it, or even if it was worth the bother.

Geoff studied me, chomping. 'You think it's all bollocks, don't you?'

I nodded regretfully.

'Yeah, well, I did say people found it difficult, especially in the West. Not in India, though, or large parts of the East. In fact, probably around half the world believes in karma in one way or another.'

'More fool them. Sorry, Geoff – no offence. But that just goes to show what a load of claptrap religion is. I mean, karma teaches that if you're born sick or poor you're being punished for stuff you did in a previous life – right?'

'Not punished. You're suffering – or enjoying, because there's good karma, too – the results of your own actions. If you get cancer after smoking all your life no one's punishing you. You're just getting the effect of causes you've made over years of smoking.'

'OK, except not everyone who smokes gets cancer. Like my gran. She was on twenty Embassy a day till she was over eighty.'

'Karma's not like a slot machine, Ed: you do "this" and

"that" happens. It's more like this huge, complex web of cause and effect and most of it we just don't know – *can't* know. But the heart of it is about taking total responsibility – for everything in our past, present and future. And not blaming something or someone else for whatever happens to us.'

I shook my head. 'I'm sorry, Geoff, but this is such rubbish.'

Geoff smiled and took a sip of lager. 'OK, so why do you think people are born so unequal? Rich, poor, healthy, sick, some in the developing world, others in the West . . .'

'Easy. The physical stuff's genetics. And the rest, like where you're born, is just luck.'

'And if the same parents, with the same genes, have one clever, healthy kid and another one who's not so bright and with a terrible disease?'

'Luck again. There's the same gene pool, but it's luck which ones get attached to each child.'

'No God anywhere?'

I just laughed.

'Or the stars, astrology?'

'Well, that's been proved a load of bunk. You get ten astrologers together and give them the same info and they come up with ten different sets of predictions.'

'OK,' said Geoff. 'So basically you agree with cause and effect for what you can see and explain, like genetics. But it's down to luck, or chance or randomness – whatever you want to call it – for what you can't explain?'

Was this what I thought? I'd never really boiled it down before. But it seemed a fair summary. 'Yes,' I said. 'Basically. I mean, say we're both crossing the road and you get hit by a car.'

'Cheers.'

'You're welcome. Anyway, obviously you can explain some of it through cause and effect. You can trace back from the moment the car hit you to the bloke starting his journey and what he did before that etcetera, etcetera. But you can't explain *why* the car hit you and not me. That's just bad luck.'

'Or because you're telling the story.'

I grinned.

Geoff waved the waiter over and ordered more lager, then turned his attention back to me. 'OK. So how do I deal with my bad luck? Assuming I'm still breathing.'

'What – you mean mentally?'

'Yeah. How do I make sense of it? Just shrug and say shit happens?'

Mmm. Tough one. 'Could do,' I said, 'though obviously it's going to be harder the worse you're damaged. But that's the same whatever you believe, isn't it? I mean, Christians are always wondering why God lets bad stuff happen if He's supposed to be so merciful and loving. Whereas if any real father neglected his kids like He does he'd be locked up.'

'How's that?'

'Think about it. He's all-knowing and all-powerful, yet He lets his children – us – stumble around, fighting and causing mayhem and getting sick and injured and dying horrible deaths . . .' I shook my head – another absurdity. 'In the real world the social services would have them off Him in a flash.'

Geoff smiled. 'Maybe,' he said. 'But I have a problem with your view. Mixing cause and effect and chance doesn't make sense.'

'Why not?'

'There's no logic to it. How can cause and effect work at some points and not others? If we're both crossing the road and I get knocked down but not you, to my mind it's because somewhere, somehow there's a reason, some cause I've made.'

'OK,' I said, 'maybe if I could map all the causes ever made since the beginning of time I'd be able to work out if it's safe for either of us to cross the road. But I can't. So as far as I'm concerned, it's chance.'

'But that's just the point,' said Geoff – and he was starting to get wound up himself now. 'It's because we can't work everything out that we fill in the blank with God or luck or – with me – karma. And I choose to believe in karma because as far as I'm concerned it makes most sense, *plus* it doesn't take away my power.'

'What?' This really did not make sense.

'If you believe your fate's in the hands of God, or chance, in the end you can't do anything about it. You're powerless. You can pray and beg, and hope He's listening and comes to the rescue – but it's His decision. And luck? What can you do there? Carry a rabbit's foot? Go to a fortune-teller? Chuck pennies in a wishing-well?' He was really fired up now, like this was a hot topic for him. 'Again, you're giving your life to some external force and just hoping things will turn out the way you want them. But if you believe in karma, that you made all the causes for this situation you're in, then you can make new causes to get out of that situation. The problem's made by you, so the solution can be, too.'

'Even if you don't know what you've done?'

'Yes.'

'How?'

'As I said, through taking total responsibility and not blaming other people.'

I leaned back and blew my cheeks out. This was too much. 'So you always blame yourself, the victim?'

'I keep telling you: it's not about blame,' said Geoff. 'It's about being convinced you can change things.'

'Sounds more like the recipe for a guilt trip to me. "I must have done all this terrible stuff in the past, woe is me, that's why my life's so fucked up!" ' And I mimed a bit of self-flagellation.

Geoff smiled. 'There's a famous Buddhist story about two brothers, Asanga and Vasubandhu. Asanga's older, Vas is younger, and they're both experts in Buddhism. But they don't agree. Asanga reckons the Buddha's later teachings are superior to his earlier ones, while Vas thinks the opposite; and he goes round giving lectures and writing articles slagging off the later stuff.'

'Like Bob Dylan – the early albums are great, but after about 1980 . . .'

Geoff laughed. 'Very similar. Anyway, one day Asanga decides to have a serious talk with his younger brother, and Vas realises he's made a big mistake – the later teachings are obviously better. And he feels terrible. He's led all these people astray, told them the wrong thing. In fact, he feels so bad he decides to cut out his tongue and chop off his hand.'

'Bit extreme.'

'Exactly what his brother said. Instead of punishing yourself, Asanga told him, you should use your tongue and that hand to spread the later teachings, and put right what you've done wrong. Which is what Vas then did.'

'Nice story. And the point is . . .?'

'Guilt's a form of self-punishment. But instead of concentrating on *effect* – i.e. looking backwards at what you might have done wrong in the past – Buddhism says you should concentrate on *cause*. You look from this moment forwards, and decide what it is you need to do *now* to take you where you want to be in the future. So you can right wrongs, challenge injustice, improve your present situation. But you still have to take total responsibility for it, because that puts the ultimate power in your hands.'

I thought about this. It seemed a nice theory, but . . . 'That's fine,' I said, 'if you know what you've done – like Vas. But if you don't know, or it's from a previous life . . .'

Geoff shook his head. 'Still works,' he insisted.

'How?'

'Because if you take full responsibility you're in charge. You're not waiting for other people to change, because chances are they won't, and you'll be waiting for ever. The only person you can really change is yourself. But the beauty is ' – he leaned forward and dropped his voice – 'if you change, they will too.' He straightened up, triumphant.

Again, I was nonplussed. 'Why?'

'The oneness of life and its environment. I mentioned it before.'

'Did you?'

He nodded. 'Basically, it says your environment's a total reflection of your life – your karma if you like. Everything that goes on in here ' – he tapped his forehead, then his chest –'is your inner self. And everything that goes on out there ' – he waved his fork at the restaurant – 'is your outer self. They're a perfect fit. So if you change the inside, the outside's got to change.'

'Why?'

'Because it *has* to.' He saw my furrowed brow. 'You'll have to trust me on this, Ed, because I think they're closing. And anyway, you've got enough to take in for one night.'

He was right there – my head was spinning. Though that could have been the lager. 'But I still don't see how it's going to change my situation at work – which is what you said.'

85

'I know. So what we need to do before they chuck us out is make a plan of action . . .'

***

Which is what we did. And which is why I called work first thing next morning to say I'd be in late. And why I took a cab round the North Circular to the carpet tile people and talked my way past reception and into an unscheduled meeting with Brian the sales director. Who was very surprised to see me – not to say embarrassed and uncomfortable, because he obviously expected me to make a scene or something. And was then gobsmacked when I offered a full and sincere apology for any offence I'd caused the previous day – and it was sincere, not just a good act. 'It wasn't my intention to put black people down in any way,' I said. 'But I can see how my words could have been interpreted like that and I realise now that I should have expressed myself more carefully and, frankly, with a lot more sensitivity.'

There was a long moment of silence as Brian processed my contrition. 'Well, thank you for that,' he said, finally, clearly unsure how to proceed. At which point I said I understood completely if he chose not to use us for the video, but would he at least allow us to pitch him our idea? He pulled his head back sharply, as if I were asking to marry his only daughter, but just said he'd have to think about it. So I left – though not before shaking his hand.

Heading back to Writers Inc. I really didn't know if I'd done the right thing. And when I arrived back I was even more worried: Cathy wanted to see me in her office the moment I got in.

'Brian's been on the phone,' she said coolly when I presented myself.

The knot in my stomach tightened. 'Ah,' I said. 'And?'

'He was very surprised by your visit and wanted to know if I'd sent you.' She clearly didn't approve.

'I thought I'd see if I could retrieve the situation . . .' Mad, obviously. I waited for the blow to fall.

'Hmm.' She gazed at me thoughtfully. 'Well, I don't know exactly what you said but we're back on board.'

'Really?' The knot vanished.

'He's allowing us to pitch – partly because the other ideas he's seen are total crap, and partly because he was "impressed by your honesty", apparently, and the fact that you'd gone to apologise in person.'

'Ah,' I said again. 'Good.'

'Yes,' said Cathy. 'But we still haven't got the job yet. So . . .?' She looked towards the door. I took the hint and scurried away to write up my idea. It was like the sun had been turned on again.

***

Geoff was really chuffed, too, when I gave him the news. And again a couple of days later when I phoned to tell him we'd got the job. 'Just do your best,' he said. 'Give it a hundred per cent.' Which I did. I wrote and rewrote the script eight times during the next week, accepting each change without a murmur, even the dumb ones, until finally Brian was happy, the director was happy, Cathy was happy. Filming was going to be over three days the following week, and I was on a bit of a high, to tell the truth. Perhaps novel-writing wasn't where my true talent lay. Perhaps it was film, screenplays, drama. I had a vision of The Call coming from Hollywood and jetting out, Club Class. Sure, they'd put me through the creative mill, and I'd be unhappy with the changes they'd want; but in the end they'd wave large wads of cash in my face and, after a period of agonised soul-searching . . . I was wrestling with whether or not I'd accept their filthy lucre when Cathy called me into her office for a chat.

'Hi, Ed,' she said with a friendly smile as I walked in. 'Sit down.'

I sat. This was the warmest she'd been towards me since before The Carpet Tile Incident. What could it mean? Promotion? More money? Whatever it was, the signs were good.

'Ed, I've been very impressed with your work on the video.' Cathy smiled again.

'Thank you. I enjoyed it.'

'In fact, I've been pretty impressed all round – that recent little wobble aside.'

I tried to look suitably humble.

'So it's all the more difficult to tell you that I'm going to have to let you go.'

Wham. Just like that. My mouth fell open.

'The problem is, since the dot-com bubble burst – well, basically, the money's been drying up. Everyone's slashing their budgets and the first thing to go tends to be marketing. Not logical but there you are.'

'But – but why me, if my work's been —?'

'Last in, first out. I'm sorry, but it's the fairest way.'

Talk about a body-blow. I reeled out of her office as if I'd been whacked with a hammer. After all the extra hours I'd put in. After all those pathetic, niggling script changes I'd made with a cheerful grin fixed permanently to my face. After . . . But somehow I didn't have the energy to be angry. The sun had been turned off and I was back in the pit. The black, bottomless pit of despair. Pop went Hollywood. Pop went The Bestseller. Pop went my future. And out of the darkness slid My Evil Friend, smirking. 'I was right, wasn't I?' he whispered. 'You'll never amount to anything. Not in a million years. Never.'

Chapter Six

One day you're up, the next down; the next down further than that. And before you know it you're living permanently in the dull, grey murk that stretches unbroken across the British sky for three-quarters of the year. So it was for me. As I worked out my notice at Writers Inc. my spirits sank lower and lower – just about in line with the Footsie Index, which was dropping faster than a liftful of miners. I felt doomed to misfortune, despite Geoff's best attempts to encourage me.

'Let's say you're flying a plane,' he said, 'from London to Paris, and let's say it's an hour due south as the crow flies.'

'Let's not.'

He ignored me. 'You take off and set your course, and after an hour look out of the window for Paris. What do you reckon the chances are it's going to be there?'

I shrugged. I didn't fly and I didn't care.

'Slim,' he said. 'Because you forgot the wind.'

'Silly me.'

'A tailwind and you've passed it. A crosswind and you're east or west of it. And a headwind – you're not there yet.'

I sighed. 'Your point being . . .?'

'Karma's like that. You can't see it, just the effect of it. Some people seem to get where they want to go very fast,

89

without effort almost, because they've got a tailwind – good fortune. Other people get sidetracked or blown off course – that's a crosswind. And a lot of people really struggle and don't seem to make much progress at all, because their karma's a headwind.'

'Great. I've got a headwind. So what's the answer?'

'Bigger plane, stronger engines.'

'Which means, translated?'

'More effort, more determination.'

I sighed again. 'What's the point? I've crashed on take-off.'

'No you haven't,' said Geoff. 'It's just a bit of turbulence, that's all.'

'The market's in free fall, Geoff, and so am I.'

He shook his head stubbornly. 'Only if you let yourself. How's your list going, by the way?'

'What list?'

'Your daily dos and don'ts.'

'Oh. Well, I only did it the once – when I decided to support Martin. And look what happened there.'

'Perseverance, sunshine.'

I smiled cheerlessly. 'It's no good if you're fated to lose. Though God knows what I must have done to cause a sodding economic slump.'

Geoff shook his head. 'This isn't personal, Ed. This is collective karma.'

'Uh-huh.' I thought Buddhism might just have an answer.

'Yeah, the stuff we share as a society – you know, like being born at the same time in the same place, going through wars and climate change together, booms and busts. The big stuff.'

'Then why aren't you going through it?'

'Who says I'm not?'

'Are you?'

'Yes, as it happens. It affects my clients so it affects me, too.'

'Clients?'

'The people who pay me.'

'And you do what again?' He still hadn't told me.

'All in good time.'

I looked quizzically at him but he just smiled inscrutably. I couldn't be bothered to pursue it. If he wanted to play international man of mystery, let him. 'You don't look like it's affecting you,' I said.

'Not suffering enough, you mean?'

I nodded.

'Well, the money's not exactly pouring in, if that makes you feel any better.'

I nodded again.

Geoff laughed. 'You really are a miserable bugger. Don't know why I bother with you.'

'Must be your . . . you know, the altruistic bit.'

'My bodhisattva nature.'

'That's the one.'

'Right – which you're testing to destruction.'

It was my turn to smile.

***

I think he got fed up trying to encourage me because he sent me off to have another chat with Dora. I wanted her to find me another job, but she seemed more interested in giving me another seminar on karma.

'It's like sending letters to yourself,' she said.

'What?' I was sitting opposite her at her desk. Today she was sans shiny black wig and showing tightly cropped brown curls; but she still wore the same polished nails and big eyelashes.

91

'Your past causes are like letters you've sent yourself but forgotten about. And then they're delivered, one after another – that's the effects coming back to you. The nice ones are lovely surprises, but the nasty ones are a real shock, because you don't remember writing them. So you sit down and write some nasty letters back – but they're still addressed to you. And so they get delivered at some point in the future, and so it goes on.'

'I need a job, Dora,' I said patiently.

'Of course you do, darling.' She smiled. 'But the point is to write different letters, i.e. make different causes. "If you want to know what you've done in the past, look at the effects you're getting now. And if you want to know what you'll experience in the future, look at the causes you're making now." Buddhist quote.'

'A job, Dora. J-O-B, job.'

She sighed. 'You and the world, Ed.' She smacked her left hand on a bulging file of registration forms. 'But employers hiring . . . ?' Her right hand lifted a slim folder and let it fall with a gentle slap on the desk. 'In fact, if things don't pick up in the next few weeks *I* might have to take early retirement.' And she chuckled. *Chuckled.*

'Doesn't it bother you?' I asked – because her sangfroid certainly bothered me.

'Oh, it won't come to that.' She smiled.

'How do you know?'

'I don't.'

'But if it does?'

'Well, danger-opportunity . . . ?'

And I swear her eyes actually shone.

***

Which was all very well, but other people being unnaturally positive at the prospect of disaster was no use to me. I had my own danger-opportunity – aka crisis – to worry about. I left Writers Inc. on the last Friday of the month with no fanfare and only enough money to live on for about four weeks – five, maybe, if I cut out the booze. But God, booze was the only faint glimmer I saw in the gloom stretching ahead of me. No booze, no sex – what else was there? I decided to take it a day at a time and only go onto emergency rations if – well, there was an emergency.

The first week wasn't too bad. Causes – that was the key, according to Geoff and Dora. As long as I kept making Causes I was bound to get an Effect; several, if I was lucky – or rather, 'fortunate', as they both insisted on correcting me.

So that first week I faithfully drew up a list of dos and don'ts each night, and spent as much of the next day as I could making Causes. I signed on at every employment agency I could find, scoured the jobs in the local and national press, and contacted friends and acquaintances vaguely connected with the Internet, or business writing, or the wacky world of corporate video – because didn't I now have a credit to my name? I made so many Causes I felt quite proud of myself. And I actually got some encouraging Effects in return.

'Really interesting cv, Ed. Leave it with us and we'll get back to you . . .'

'It's a bit quiet at the moment, Ed, but as soon as things pick up . . .'

'Once we've heard about this mega-project we're pitching for, Ed, we'll be in touch – definitely . . .'

And so on. Nothing solid, but I started to feel more cheerful. Perhaps this cause and effect thing might work after all. So cheerful, in fact, that I decided to start writing The Bestseller. Why not? I had time on my hands, plus all the Buddhist theory: *kyo chi gyo i*, value creation, *ichinen*, positive thinking . . . I just had to apply it and – lo! – things would come to pass.

But what to write? Write about what you know, they always say. So I decided to tell a story about this bloke who loses his job and his girlfriend and fights really, really hard to turn things round, but can't quite . . . so sinks lower and lower . . . and lower . . . until – bloody hell – he commits suicide! No, rewind that bit. Until, just when he's about lose everything, he . . . he . . . what?

'I know,' I told myself, 'just start and let the story come. Let it unfold as the characters spring to life and tell *you* the story. After all, you're not God. You're just the scribe who records the reality of your characters' lives.' So I fired up the computer and started tapping away. If this wasn't a massive bloody Cause I didn't know what was. Russia here I come. All I had to do was keep going. But that's the hard bit.

By the end of the first week I'd written almost *five thousand* words. By the end of the second I could hardly prise myself out of bed.

What happened? Well, it was like there was a hole in my petrol tank and all my fuel just seeped away. One minute I was going like the clappers, the next I was stranded permanently on the hard shoulder.

'Hell state,' said Geoff decisively. He was on the doorstep, looking concerned. 'I heard it in your voice last night when I phoned, and I thought there's only one thing for it: this man needs a job.'

'You woke me up to tell me that?' I was wearing only my cotton kimono dressing-gown and a three-day-old beard, and I was starting to shiver.

'No, I mean *any* job,' he went on. 'You hang round in this flat much longer and soon the neighbours will start

94

wondering about the smell. They'll knock down the door and find you covered in flies on the kitchen floor.'

'I'm supposed to be the one with the imagination, remember?' I said. Except I wasn't, which was the problem. My characters stubbornly refused to spring to life, like a couple of sulky teenagers rooted to a sofa. That's what had brought on the depression: The Bestseller was totally stuck.

'Let me buy you a beer and see if we can fix you up with something,' Geoff offered.

'Bit early, isn't it?' I said. 'The pubs aren't open for hours.'

Geoff gave me a pitying look. 'Ed, it's nearly lunchtime.' He showed me his watch: 12.45.

I was confused. I'd looked at my clock when the doorbell rang and it had said 9.20. Then I remembered: it had stopped a couple of days ago and I hadn't got round to buying a new battery for it.

'Couldn't be arsed, hmm?' Geoff said.

'No, it's not that. It's just . . . you know.' But it was that. I couldn't be arsed to do anything. My opus had ground to a halt and so had my life. All my Causes had produced nothing, and each list of daily determinations made me more dejected – because deep down I didn't believe I'd be able to make any of it happen. My reality was no job, no girlfriend, no money. And no real prospects, either.

'Sleeping a lot, are you?' asked Geoff.

I nodded.

'Finding it hard to get up?'

I nodded again.

'No appetite?'

I shook my head sadly. 'For anything.' I sighed.

Geoff smiled. 'Come on. Get out of your Madame Butterfly costume and let's try to stoke up some life force in you.'

95

That phrase again – life force. I'd been meaning to ask him about it, except I hadn't quite got round to it. Like everything else.

***

My local is one of those unpretentious Irish pubs dedicated to hard, no-nonsense drinking, mainly of Guinness. Cavernous and colourless, with a faded carpet pockmarked with cigarette burns and hardened chewing-gum, it's dominated by enormous wall mirrors that reflect an atmosphere of joyless intoxication. At the bar two puffy-eyed alkies were already hard at it, sinking their third – or was it their fourth? – pint of the black stuff. The perfect environment for a chat about depression.

'To life force,' I said, raising my glass. 'Whatever it is.'

'It's energy,' said Geoff, tucking into a pie and beans. 'Except it's deeper than that. It's . . .' He finished his mouthful, trying to find the right words. 'Probably the best way to explain is through a thing called the Three Truths.'

'Another principle?' I asked. 'Only I'm losing track, to be honest.'

'Oh, this is an easy one to remember,' said Geoff, and he started to draw lines in the creamy head of his Guinness.

'What's that?' I asked.

Geoff looked at his handiwork. There were three lines meeting in the middle, like the old 'Ban the Bomb' symbol, dividing the head into three equal sections. Geoff seemed satisfied. 'So,' he said, 'the Three Truths says there are three basic aspects to life – the physical.' He pointed at the upper left section. 'The mental and/or spiritual.' He pointed at the upper right section. 'Though that's not spiritual as in religion or ghosts or anything like that, but in terms of your spirit, how you feel.'

'OK.'

96

'And then there's this third aspect called the essential, which is a bit hard to pin down.' He pointed at the third section, at the bottom. 'So one way to look at it is to call it life force – the essence of your life at that moment, which reveals itself in these other two aspects of your life, the physical and the mental.'

Some of this sounded familiar. 'I thought your life moment by moment was *ichinen*.'

'It is.' Geoff seemed surprised.

'I have been listening, you know.'

'Glad to hear it. But you can look at it as different ways of describing the same thing. Anyway, the point about life force is it changes according to your life state, your life condition. You remember I told you about that? When I explained about being a bodhisattva.'

'Vaguely.'

'Well, right now, as I said, you're in a life state we call Hell. Some religions say it's a nasty place you go to be punished when you die for all the bad stuff you've done, and early types of Buddhism say that too. But more advanced Buddhism says actually Hell's inside you. It's the life condition of suffering. And you, my son, are displaying the classic symptoms.' He stuffed another forkful of beans into his mouth.

'Thank you, doctor.'

'So if you're in Hell here,' he mumbled, pointing to the bottom section of the head, 'in the essential bit, it's got to show up in the physical and mental bits.' He swallowed. 'So, on the physical side you lack energy, appetite, you sleep a lot, you're lethargic, everything seems a real effort.'

'Yep.'

'While on the mental side you're unmotivated, nothing excites you, you lack hope or ambition and you tell yourself there's no point doing anything because you're only going to fail. Time crawls, and you're spending a lot of it with your Evil Friend, who's always telling you you're no good, and nothing else is, either. He's not great company, but about the best you can do right now because, basically, your life's shrunk to this.' He held up thumb and forefinger, about an inch apart.

'That much?'

He nodded. ''Fraid so. Everything's negative, nothing's positive, and you feel like shit. You're trapped, constricted. In Hell.'

'Only one thing for it, then,' I said. 'Cheers.' I picked up my glass and drained it. 'Another one?'

Geoff gazed at me thoughtfully. 'You drinking much?'

I pulled a face. 'So-so.'

'Is it helping?'

'Immensely.' I grinned, getting to my feet to go to the bar.

'Really?' He sounded anxious.

'Don't worry,' I said. 'I'm not becoming an alcoholic.' Which I believed – even though part of my difficulty getting up in the morning wasn't entirely unrelated to the string of large Scotch and Cokes I'd been sinking each night.

Geoff didn't look reassured. 'The problem is, trying to get out of Hell through booze, or drugs, or anything that will give you some sort of quick relief . . .' He shook his head. ''Cos when it wears off where are you? Back where you started. Or worse.'

I followed his look over to the bar. The two alkies were starting to sway slightly, their mouths glued to fresh pints of Guinness as if they were eating them. I frowned and sat down again.

'Bloody hell, Geoff. You're the one who dragged me down here.'

'I know. I wanted to get you out.'

'Why?'

'When I called last night you didn't just sound down, you sounded pissed.'

'So? I'm over twenty-one.'

'Don't get defensive. I'm worried about you, that's all.'

'Well, you needn't be. I'm OK.'

'OK in Hell?'

I was silent; he had me.

'I've been there,' said Geoff. 'The slippery slope. Took me a long time to see Heaven and Hell as just different sides of the same coin.'

'Heaven? What's that got to do with it?'

'Heaven isn't up there, you know,' he said, jabbing his finger at the ceiling, 'any more than Hell's down there.' He jabbed it at the floor. 'They're just names for different life states. Heaven's rapture, the buzz you get from something – like sex 'n' drugs 'n' rock 'n' roll. And booze. But "heaven is the devil's nest". Meaning there's a chute from there straight to Hell.'

'Eh? I thought they're supposed to be opposites.'

'In Christianity, yes, but Buddhism is all about how things link up, how life actually works. So, on the one hand, Heaven feels very different from Hell. It's nice, the sun shines, you've got energy – life force – and basically everything in the garden's rosy. Until you try to hold onto it, because it can't last – like bubbles in champagne. You drink – it's nice. You keep on drinking – you wake up with a hangover. Heaven' – he held out his hand, palm up – 'Hell.' He turned it over.

'OK,' I conceded. 'But I'm suffering basically because I lost my job.'

Geoff grimaced, as if he'd just sucked a lemon. 'Well, even there, strictly speaking you're looking at the same thing.'

'How?' I really didn't get it.

'Because Heaven – or rapture, which is another name for it – is also what we feel when we get something we want, like your job at Writers Inc. But because it's bound up in that thing, it disappears as soon as that thing disappears.'

'Eh?' I still couldn't see the connection.

'You were down in the dumps before you got it, then up when you had it, then down when you hit the carpet tile problem, then up when you turned that round, then down when you got the shove – and so it goes on.'

Not for the first time I looked at him as if he were a complete idiot. 'But that's life, Geoff,' I said. 'You know – happy, sad, up, down. It's normal, what normal people go through.'

'I know,' he said. 'And Buddhism is about learning how life works so you can make choices that don't cause so much bloody grief – for yourself or other people.'

'I'm not causing grief for other people,' I said defensively.

'No,' he said, 'but you need to build up some inner strength so you're not so knocked about by the ups and downs. "A truly wise man" – and this is a quote – "A truly wise man will not be carried away by any of the eight winds: prosperity, decline, disgrace, honour, praise, censure, suffering and pleasure. He is neither elated by prosperity nor grieved by decline."'

'But that's impossible,' I said. 'You'd have to be a robot.'

'It doesn't say you shouldn't be affected by the eight winds – that *is* impossible. It just says you shouldn't be carried away by them – you know, go to extremes.'

'Hmm,' I grunted. It all sounded wonderful – in theory – but totally impractical. 'OK, that's fine,' I said, 'but the problem is I can't control how I feel. It's not in my hands.

I mean, last week I felt . . . good. I was doing lots of things, making lots of causes—'

'Great.'

'Writing. But I just ran out of steam. I hit a block and I can't seem to get round it. Then up pops you know who—'

'MEF?'

I nodded. 'And before I know it I'm facing the same block but feeling ten times worse.'

'That's why I chant,' said Geoff simply. 'I can top up my life force at will.'

We looked at each other, both knowing that this was the fork in the road. I don't know why, but every time Geoff – or Dora – mentioned chanting I just switched off. It was like I could go every step of the way with him, because so much of what he said sounded like good sense; it had a sort of logic to it. But then suddenly it went all weird and religious and I just didn't want to know. But I didn't want to offend him again – I had few enough friends as it was. So all I said was, 'How's that then?'

'Because, believe it or not, chanting strengthens this life condition everyone has called Buddhahood.'

I didn't believe it, but what the heck – let the guy finish.

'It's the "wisdom, courage and compassion" life condition. And as it gets stronger, bit by bit, all your other life conditions sort of settle into their proper place, and you get a bit of balance. You're not so up and down. And you can draw on this extra strength to get you through things, over hurdles – whatever.'

'Sounds great – for you.'

'Well, it's there if you want it, too.'

I shook my head with a polite smile.

Geoff sighed ruefully. 'Very frustrating,' he said.

'What is?'

'Knowing you've got something that can really help someone and they're just not interested.'

'I told you, Geoff: I'm not looking for a religion. If I was I'm sure it would be Buddhism, but I'm not. OK?'

'Fine.'

'I like the theory, the principles – but praying or chanting or anything like that . . . ?' I shook my head firmly.

'OK, message received.'

I was genuinely intrigued by the philosophy, though. It made sense of a lot of things – as far as I could accept it. 'So, these life conditions,' I said. 'There's Hell, Heaven, Buddhahood – and you mentioned anger, didn't you?'

Geoff perked up. 'Yes,' he said. 'There are ten altogether: the Ten Worlds. They're called that because early Buddhism said they were literally different worlds you were born into when you were reincarnated, depending on the causes you made in each lifetime. But later Buddhism taught they're all states everyone goes through in their individual lives.'

'So what are they? Hell . . .'

'Yes, which is suffering; Hunger, which is where you're driven by your desires but never satisfied, even when you get what you want – you've got to move on to something new; Animality, where you're dominated by your animal instincts – for food, sleep, sex, survival.'

'Sounds familiar.'

'We all have it, because we are animals. And stupidity's also part of Animality, because you live in the here and now and don't think about the consequences of your actions. It's the law of the jungle – you know, might is right, pecking orders, hierarchy, that sort of thing.'

'Martin. Always looking for the short-term fix. Plus he bullied us.'

'Yep, a lot of Animality in business. Dog eat dog.'

'And cat. And members of staff. Next?'

'Anger, which isn't so much losing your temper as always thinking you're the best or always right, and trying to prove it by putting other people down or judging them. So you feel you're always in competition with them, or you're always getting into rows and arguments.'

'How's that different from the last one, the law of the jungle?'

'Animals don't have egos, just urges.' He nodded towards the alkies at the bar, who were into yet another pint and well on the way to getting seriously blotto.

'That's Animality?'

'Looks like it to me. Can't see further than their next pint.'

Hmm – interesting.

'Plus a person who's got strong Anger is always sensitive to criticism himself, because deep down he lacks confidence. So he tends to get his attack in first – you know, as the best form of defence.'

This sounded a bit near the knuckle. Moving swiftly on. 'So that's four. Five?'

'Humanity, aka Tranquillity, which is basically being calm, decent, reasonable – human. Or perhaps humane might be a better word for it.'

'Like you.'

'Nice of you to say so, Ed. But it can also mean being bone idle – which I can be. Or not wanting to rock the boat. And it's easy to upset, like Heaven. You need peace and quiet the whole time or you tend to get pissed off.'

'OK. So six is . . .?'

'Heaven, which we've talked about.'

'Uh-huh. And seven?'

'Seven is Guinness.' I was thrown for a second before I saw his empty glass. 'Just a half.' He smiled.

103

'OK if I have one too?'

'Like you said – you're over twenty-one.'

I picked up our glasses and went to the bar, where one of the alkies glanced blearily at me as I ordered. Christ, I thought, he did look vaguely animal, though I couldn't see any real animal getting itself into that state – too much self-respect. I obviously looked too long, because he suddenly scowled.

'What you staring at?' he slurred.

'Nothing,' I said.

'Then fuck off.' He took a step towards me, fists clenched.

I stepped back in alarm, but he kept coming. I took another step back, caught my heel in something, stumbled, felt myself falling, clutched at air, hit my head hard against the edge of the bar and . . .

Chapter Seven

Hospital. I woke up to find myself lying on a trolley in a cubicle in A&E. A nurse was asking someone how much I'd had to drink. 'Only a pint.' It was Geoff's voice. I flickered my eyes open in time to catch the heard-it-all-before expression on the nurse's face.

'I tripped,' I said weakly.

They looked over at me.

'Ah, back with us, are you?' said the nurse. 'How are you feeling?'

'Sore.'

'Well, you've had quite a nasty bash on the head. I'm going to stitch it up for you, but I'll have to give you a local anaesthetic first.' She produced a syringe the size of a knitting needle – and I fainted.

OK, I'm a wimp. I can't help it. Hospitals are my least favourite places in the world. Full of sickness and suffering and body fluids. Just visiting is enough to make me queasy: the reek of infirmity, the pukish colours, the sad unwell shuffling around in their dressing-gowns with tubes attached to God knows where and producing God knows what.

When I came round for the second time she'd already sewn me up and I was on my way to X-ray – standard,

105

apparently, for a head injury. Geoff was pushing the trolley. 'You OK?' he asked.

'Hope so,' I groaned, as the trolley banged through plastic swing doors. 'Did you see what happened?'

'You fainted.'

'In the pub.'

'You went over like a pine tree. Blimey, you gave your nut such a whack . . .'

'That alkie came for me.'

'What?'

'You know – threatened me.'

Geoff looked very surprised. 'The one nearest you?'

I grunted. 'That's why I tripped, trying to get away.'

'Well, he was the person who did most to make you comfortable. Made us put you in the recovery position, check your airways, see you hadn't swallowed your tongue.'

I was astonished. 'He was completely pissed.'

Geoff shrugged. 'Just goes to show.'

'What?'

'Can't judge a book by its cover.'

'He was going to thump me!'

'Why?'

'I don't know. Didn't like the way I looked at him, I imagine.'

'How did you look at him?'

'Fuck, Geoff, I don't know. Does it matter?' I could feel another bit of Buddhism coming on and I was not in the mood.

Geoff read the runes and clamped his mouth shut. The trolley squeaked along the corridor until we reached the X-ray department. Geoff handed over a pink card and the technician disappeared into a small office. Thankfully there were only a couple of other patients ahead of us. A thought struck me. 'Anyway, shouldn't a porter be doing this?'

'All otherwise engaged,' Geoff said. 'But if you don't want me here, I can go.'

'I didn't say that.' We lapsed into silence again. Then, from out of nowhere, a wave of anger surged through me. 'The thing is, Geoff,' I seethed, 'since meeting you things have been getting worse, not better. I've lost two jobs, I'm nearly broke, I've hit the bottle and now this. It's . . . it's . . .' I wanted to say 'not fair' but I knew that would only bring a Buddhist response. I just tailed off, spitting frustration.

Geoff was calm. 'You think there's a connection between meeting me and your bad fortune?'

'Well, you're the one who says there's no such thing as coincidence.' Ha – had him there.

He thought for a moment. 'You're stirring things up,' he said.

'What?'

'Your karma. You're trying to change your life so it's coming up. It's like—'

'Oh bugger off,' I said. He looked at me for a moment – and then he did.

***

I felt bad about it later. I sat in my flat, head banging despite the extra-strong painkillers the hospital had given me, feeling lonely, miserable, sorry for myself. I couldn't even have a drink; not because it might react with the pills, but because I kept hearing Geoff's voice explaining that 'the stairway to Heaven is also the stairway to Hell'. Or more precisely, because I knew it wouldn't stop with *a* drink. One would lead to two would lead to several; and I'd wake up tomorrow morning with a double headache. So he'd be right – curse him.

The fact was, he was just about the most interesting

bloke I think I'd met. Ever. He talked about stuff in a way I'd never thought of, that I didn't even agree with most of the time, but that made me look at things differently. And once you see something differently you can't unsee it, can you?

I'd been too hard on him, I decided. I'd been irritable because my head hurt and I felt foolish for falling over; and he'd come to the hospital to help me and – well, basically, I was a bad person. Selfish, self-centred, self-absorbed – all the things I'd listed as reasons why Angie had left. But, no good sitting here beating myself up. Use the tongue that told him to bugger off to make friends again. I called his mobile.

'What's seven?' I asked when he answered.

'Eh? Who is this?'

'Ed. You never told me what seven was. Or eight to ten.'

'Hang on,' he said. I could hear a strange hum in the background, which then disappeared. 'That's better,' said Geoff. 'I couldn't quite hear you in there.'

'What was that noise?' I asked.

'Chanting,' he said. 'I'm at a meeting.'

'You mean you do it all together?'

'Sometimes. So how are you feeling?'

'Embarrassed – for telling you to sod off.'

'Well, I probably deserved it. I should have been a bit more sensitive to your situation. Anyway, what's this about seven?'

'The Ten Worlds. You got as far as six.'

He laughed. 'I thought you'd had enough Buddhism.'

'So did I. But you can't leave me on tenterhooks.'

'Seven is the world of Learning, where you learn from other people. Eight is Realisation or Absorption, where you learn from your own experience and observation. Nine is Bodhisattva—'

108

'Altruism.'

'Caring for others.'

'Isn't that the same?'

'No, because it also creates benefit in *your* life – cause and effect. You helping others is a good cause for them *and* for you. So, strictly speaking, there's no such thing as altruism in Buddhism.'

'Ah. So coming to the hospital wasn't for me, then?'

'It was, because I wasn't thinking about my benefit. But I get it just the same, so you don't have to worry about that.'

I couldn't tell if he was taking the mick or not, but decided to let it go. 'Right, so that's another thing I've learned today – no such thing as altruism. Ten?'

'Buddhahood – wisdom, courage and compassion.'

'Right.' We'd been here before.

'And the key thing is each world contains all the others, so whatever life state you're in, you can be in a different one the next moment, depending on different internal and external causes.'

'I see.' I didn't quite, but I didn't want to keep him from his meeting much longer. 'So just let me check I've got them all. Hell, Anger, Animal . . . er . . .'

'Hell, Hunger, Animality, Anger, Heaven, Humanity, Learning, Realisation, Bodhisattva and Buddhahood. HH-AA-HH-LR-BB – OK?'

'Well, it's not the easiest mnemonic I've ever come across but I think I'll remember it. Thanks.'

'Oh – and I've got a possible job for you. Friend of mine. If you think you're up to it and don't mind getting your hands dirty.'

This was good news. 'What is it?'

'Landscape gardening. Look, I'll call you later. It's in my phone and I'm in the hall and the light's pretty bad – OK?'

'Sure. Thanks.'

'No problem. Speak later – and keep taking the tablets.'

'Will do. Cheers.' I hung up. I felt better already. Action – that was the key. Take action, make causes – and don't give up. I decided to call Geoff's friend as soon as I got the number. Whatever he was offering, I'd take it.

***

Early morning, two days later, and I was walking up to this FBH (fucking big house) in Hertfordshire. I'd got up at sparrow-fart and schlepped out there on the train, because Piers had been coming from Oxford and couldn't give me a lift. Sorry to say, I'd taken against him the moment I heard his voice on the phone: it was so far back he could have choked on it. I don't know what it is about the upper classes and the English language. I suppose being born with a silver spoon in the mouth makes pronunciation difficult. Anyway, my opinion wasn't helped by my first sight of him. His white mini-van was parked on the sweeping gravel drive of this FBH and he was unloading gear from the back, dressed in brown cords, green wellies, green quilted sleeveless jacket and flat cap. The complete Hooray Henry. Still, I crunched my way up to him and stuck out my hand.

'Hello,' I said. 'I'm Ed.'

'Ah! Thank God you've turned up!' He barked a laugh and shook my hand vigorously. He'd explained on the phone that his usual labourer – because that's what I was going to be – had put his back out and this job involved a lot of digging. 'Erm . . .' He looked at my feet. 'Those the only shoes you've got?'

Trainers. I nodded.

'Right. Well, tomorrow, assuming you come back' – he barked another laugh – 'boots or wellie boots, because you might have a bit of trouble with those. OK?'

110

'Air-Kiar,' I mimicked.

'Good. Um – I forgot to ask last night if you actually knew anything about gardening.'

'It involves plants.'

'Yes . . . Right, well – that's a start.' He gave me a quick smile, not sure quite what to make of me, and I started to help unload the rest of his stuff.

I knew I shouldn't be taking the piss but there's something about the Pierses and Johnnies and Olivers of this world that brings out the Bolshevik in me – you know, line them up against the wall, a quick burst from the Uzi . . . I mean, we took the tools and everything round the side of the house to the garden – 'park' would be a more accurate description – and this dowager-type in twin-set and pearls fell on Piers and kissed both his cheeks and asked after his mother and his sisters and 'Did they manage to get away at all this year?' and I thought, Well, there you go. Jobs for the boys, keep it in the family, don't on any account let in the hoi-polloi. Because I couldn't imagine too many horny-handed sons of the local area being invited to tender for this job. Still, I needed the money so the revolution would have to wait.

Our task was to take an oblong of parkland, sixty feet by fifteen, and turn it into a large mixed border. This meant digging out the turf, rotavating the soil and digging in a ton of compost and manure, all of which had to be barrowed across the park from where it had been dumped at the closest access point. Then we'd plant it up – shrubs, a couple of small trees, herbaceous plants – and finish off by burying five hundred daffodil bulbs in the long bank at the bottom of the garden. 'Should make a super display next spring,' Piers gushed.

'Lovely,' I said dryly. This looked like it was going to be bloody hard work.

'So – feeling fit?' He clapped his hands and rubbed them together.

'As a flea,' I lied.

'Excellent,' he said. 'Off we go then.'

It *was* bloody hard work. Just getting the turf up took most of the morning. But it was a lovely day and, to give him his due, Piers was a real grafter. First I cut and he lifted, then we swapped. We got a good rhythm going and talked, of course; and bit by bit my idea of him began to change. It wasn't really a surprise that he was a Buddhist – I'd half assumed it when Geoff gave me his number – but he seemed fascinated by how I'd met Geoff and what I'd gone through since.

'So you're trying to do it without the chanting, is that it?'

'I'm not sure I'm trying to do anything,' I grunted, lifting a sod of turf into the wheelbarrow, 'except get on. Some of the ideas make sense, and some just seem loopy, frankly. I'm curious, that's all.'

'But having a hard time?'

'I'll say.' I pointed to the large plaster on the back of my head. The pain had lessened but it was still sore.

'Hmm . . . Still, from sickness arises the mind that seeks the Way, eh?' He leaned into the cutting tool, slicing up another square of turf.

'How's that?' I said.

'Oh, sorry. Buddhist quote. It means sometimes you have to really go through it – you know, the mill – to wake you up, put you on track, Buddhist-wise.'

'Do you?'

'Well, I did, certainly.'

'How?'

'Oh, my dad,' he said, lifting the turf. 'Complete bastard. Drank, screwed around, rotten to my mother, gambled away the family fortune. Hated him – for years.'

'You mean, you haven't got any money?'

'Ha!' The laugh was rueful. 'You think I'd be digging flowerbeds if I had? No, I'm a fully paid-up member of the posh poor, I'm afraid. Cut-glass accent but no cut glass – or anything else, for that matter. Though we used to own a house bigger than this, believe it or not.' He waved a hand at the pile.

'What happened?' I asked, working away to loosen another sod.

'Daddy discovered the gee-gees. Blew the lot. Then he had a heart attack at Kempton one afternoon, during the 3.20, I believe, and that was that. We discovered a massive hole in the finances, and what with the inheritance tax – bye-bye family seat. Bye-bye everything, in fact. At which point I bumped into Buddhism.'

'And you started to practise?'

'Sort of.'

'I'm not with you.'

'Well, the chap who told me about it said you could chant for anything you wanted – material, spiritual, mental, emotional, whatever – and at the time I was a bit of a ladies' man, to be honest—'

'Like father, like son.'

'Exactly – although, of course, that was something I would absolutely flatly deny at the time. You know, you hate in others what you refuse to see in yourself.'

Do you? Interesting thought.

Piers ploughed on. 'Anyway, I decided, being the profound chap that I am, to chant to bed a Page Three Girl – something totally out of my league. It was a bit of a joke, really. But – and this is absolutely true – after ten days of chanting, twice a day, morning and evening, I met this girl at a party and blow me if she's not working for the *Sun*. We got on like a house on fire, one thing led to another and . . .

I couldn't believe it. It was like magic. Extraordinary. So was the sex . . .' He drifted away into a brief reverie, then snapped back. 'But,' he said with emphasis, 'it turned into the worst relationship of my life. God, I suffered. We both did. Excruciating. And it was only when it was over, mercifully, that I started to take the Buddhism seriously, because I realised what a shallow twat I was, and how disrespectful I was towards women. And, most of all' – he dropped his voice and leaned towards me, as if about to impart a secret – 'how much I resembled dear old daddy-o!'

'And you don't any more?'

'Well, of course I do. But I've managed to bring the more destructive elements under control. Plus I've stopped hating him, which is a big bonus. Frees up the energy for something more positive.'

I heaved a piece of turf into the wheelbarrow and stuck my spade in the ground. 'You or me?' I said, nodding to the barrow.

'I'll take this one,' said Piers. 'You have a breather.' He grabbed the handles and trundled off towards the compost heap hidden behind the shrubbery in a far corner of the garden.

As I watched him it struck me again how quick I was to jump to conclusions about people, to write them off on the basis of how they looked or sounded. Even that alkie. Perhaps I *had* looked at him in the wrong way. Perhaps I hadn't kept the contempt and disgust I'd felt out of my face, and he'd picked up on it, which is why he went for me. Hmm. I picked up the cutting tool to prepare more squares of turf, and as I cut I began to reflect on all the stuff that had happened to me over the past few weeks: Angie going, ItsTheBusiness crashing, getting and losing the job at Writers Inc., the Brummie Lino Man and The Carpet Tile Incident. And I started to wonder if there might not be something linking everything after all – something in me.

I was still musing and cutting when Piers returned with the empty barrow – except it wasn't quite empty. 'I found this by the compost heap,' he said, reaching in to take out a small plant. It was an acorn that had germinated. A thin shoot was growing upwards, topped by two small oak leaves, and a filigree of white roots downwards. 'It reminded me of that quote I told you earlier: "From sickness arises the mind that seeks the Way."'

'How?'

'Well, when I got into gardening I learned about how plants grow and reproduce and all that sort of stuff, and one of the things I learned was that some seeds, especially from trees, only germinate after they've been made very cold or very hot. Acorns, like this chap' – he gave it to me – 'need a hard frost to start the ball rolling, while some trees need a forest fire, would you believe? I was in Yellowstone National Park in the States a few years ago – have you ever been there?'

'No.'

'You should go. Amazing. Anyway, the place was completely covered in what looked like baby Christmas trees. Actually, they were young lodge-pole pine trees. They can't have planted all these, I thought. Up mountains, in valleys. Millions of them. So I asked a park ranger and he said there'd been terrible forest fires some years before and a decision had been made to let a lot of them burn out naturally, because it clears away all the mature trees and – this is the crucial bit – it germinates all the pine cones lying on the forest floor. So all this new growth springs up from the ashes and it's got the light and space to grow in.'

'Isn't nature wonderful?'

'Absolutely.' He either didn't hear the irony in my voice or chose to ignore it. 'But my point is – and that's why that little acorn reminded me – I think some people are like that. They've got a hard seedcoat around them – ego or illusion or whatever you want to call it – and it's not until they really suffer in some way that it's cracked and something fresh and new is able to emerge. That's what happened to me, anyway.'

***

I grew very fond of Piers over the next three days, and was really sorry when the job ended. He potted up the acorn for me in a bit of compost and it's sitting on my windowsill at this very moment; though I'll have to plant it out soon as it's getting quite big now. That's another thing he said: that practising Buddhism for him was like growing into an oak tree, bit by bit, day after day. He couldn't see it at the time, but when he looks back he realises how far he's come – from a weedy little seedling, through a sapling, to a sturdy tree. And it's the wind and rain and storms he's been through that have helped him grow and become strong. He was really quite poetic about it. And he saw Buddhism everywhere in the garden.

We were planting the daffodils, for example – three hundred Dutch Masters and two hundred Lothario – and I was finding it pretty bloody tedious. But not Piers. We were down on our knees, trowelling away, popping one or two bulbs in each hole, when he suddenly uttered, 'I think people are quite like plants, you know.'

'You don't say.'

He grinned. 'Have I mentioned it before?'

'Only once or twice.'

'Well, I do. I think everybody can grow, just like plants. But you have to give them the right conditions. I mean, some plants like shade, some like sun, some like clay soil, some will tolerate all sorts of conditions. But often you put

116

the wrong plant in the wrong place and it'll really struggle, even die. But in the right place every plant has the potential to grow completely, to its full extent.'

'It's a nice idea,' I agreed. 'But the problem is knowing the right conditions. I mean, I feel I have the potential to grow but I've no idea where the best place for that is.'

Piers looked up with a smile. 'Oh, I expect it's where you are right now, Ed.'

'How do you work that out?'

'Well, the thing about karma,' he said, 'and Geoff did explain karma, I hope?'

'Tried. I'm not sure I got it all.'

Piers grunted. 'Well, the thing about karma is it fits you like a glove. It's tailor-made for you. Which means you're always in exactly the right place at the right time to start to change things, to grow. You don't have to go anywhere. It all comes from inside you. The problem is, the vast bulk of people can't see that.'

I didn't understand, and said so.

'Take this bulb,' Piers said, holding up a particularly fat Dutch Master. 'Inside here is everything needed to become a daffodil. In Buddhism that's what we call the inherent cause. But it won't produce the flower unless it meets the external cause – good old Mother Earth.' He plunged his trowel into the ground and dug out a small hole, then dropped the bulb in and covered it up, firming down the soil with a light press of his hand. 'So it's the relationship of inherent and external cause that gives us the effect – a beautiful flower, OK?'

'OK . . .' I'd learned by now to treat Buddhist teachings of the blatantly obvious with patience – the twist often came at the end.

'Well,' Piers continued, 'it's the same with people. Our potential is all locked up inside us, and it's our messy old

117

daily lives that cause it to come out. That's the earth or soil in which we grow. It's like the Lotus Sutra – have you heard of that?'

'No.'

'A lot of people think it's the bees-knees in Buddhism – you know, *the* great teaching. Anyway, it uses the lotus flower as the symbol of our full potential – what we call Buddhahood – because the lotus grows in a muddy swamp. No swamp, no flower. So the swamp is our problems or our sufferings, and we need them to reveal our full potential.'

'That's lovely, Piers,' I said, 'except most people don't, do they?'

'Don't what?'

'Reveal their full potential. They live in a swamp and drown there. No flower.'

'Mmm. Absolutely right. Which is a terrible shame, don't you think?'

'I do.'

'Well then – so something has to happen to turn the swamp into a more growth-friendly environment, yes?'

'You tell me.'

'OK, take horse-shit. And don't pull that face – it's the gardener's friend.'

'Good for roses.'

'Marvellous. But not when it's fresh – far too corrosive. You have to leave it a while, let it mature. Then it becomes jolly good fertiliser. As shit it's useless, it's just shit. But the very same stuff becomes fantastic for growth.'

'So . . .'

'Well, it's the same with the swamp, our problems. As they are they can be shit.'

'You're telling me.'

'But they can also be transformed into the ideal medium for growth.'

118

'Yes – but how?' I was becoming irritated.

'By changing this.' He tapped his head.

'Yes, I know that,' I said, 'but *how* do you change it?' I stabbed hard at the ground with my trowel, frustrated.

'You have to meet the right teaching,' said Piers calmly.

We fell silent again. A light breeze rustled the leaves on the trees all around and above us as our trowels scraped and dug into the earth. Each time I dropped a bulb into the hole I made and covered it with soil, I couldn't help but see it as a cause – inherent cause, external cause, effect. There was something missing, though, something I still didn't get. But I couldn't put my finger on what it was. I just felt vaguely troubled. Piers must have felt something, too, because after a while he straightened up and looked across at me. 'Clear as mud, is it?' he asked.

'No, it is clear. It's just that – I don't know – there's something bothering me about it.'

'What?'

'I don't know.'

'Simultaneity?'

Eh? Bit of an odd segue.

'Only I should have explained that when I plant a bulb, according to Buddhism the effect's there at that very moment.'

'I don't understand.'

'In a latent form.'

I looked perplexed.

Piers picked up another bulb to demonstrate. 'The inherent cause and external cause' – he buried the bulb in the soil – 'won't produce what's called the manifest effect – the flower – straight away. There's a time lag. But that effect is . . . how can I describe it?' He searched for the right word. 'Implied – that's it. It's implied the moment the cause is made. So in Buddhism we talk about latent effect and manifest effect. You make a cause, the latent effect is instantly in your life but it'll only appear – become manifest – at some point in the future, when the conditions are right. Most people when they talk about cause and effect just concentrate on what they can see: external cause and manifest effect. But Buddhism is just as interested in what can't be seen: the inherent cause and latent effect.'

Ah! A penny suddenly dropped. 'That's it,' I said, waving my trowel at him. 'I understand it when you talk about daffodil bulbs, because there's a physical thing in the ground, and if I see a flower I know there must be a bulb down there, too. But what I don't get is this "the effect is instantly in your life" thing. Where?' I patted myself down, as if searching for it on my person.

'You know, that is such a bloody good question,' Piers said. 'I asked exactly the same thing when I first heard about this. And you know what the answer was?'

'What?'

'Coo.'

'Coo?'

'Short for coo-tie – K-U-T-A-I. The truth of non-substantiality.'

'And that's what?' I asked warily. I had the ominous feeling we were about to enter upside-down land again.

'Well, I imagine you probably think that either something exists or it doesn't – right?'

'Yes – like most people.'

'Actually, though, there's a third state – *ku* – where something exists but doesn't, all at the same time.'

I was right – through the looking-glass. I smiled faintly as I gathered my wits. 'So how do you work that one out?'

'Well, it's where something is real but there's nothing substantial to sort of back it up, as it were.'

'For example?'

'Your thoughts, or your memories. I mean, if I asked you to remember – I don't know . . . let's say losing your virginity, I imagine all sorts of things will instantly come rushing into your mind, yes?'

They did. Anne Rix – Trixie Rixie. I grinned.

'See?' said Piers, smiling. 'So, those images are totally real to you, but I can't see them. And where were they before I asked the question? In your life somewhere, but where?'

'Some part of my brain, I suppose.'

'Probably. But they're still not *things*, are they? They're non-substantial, without substance. But with the right cause or conditions they'll appear just as sure as the flowers will from these bulbs next spring. So they exist and they don't exist at the same time.'

This was just too weird. I'd signed on for four days as a garden labourer and here I was getting a lesson in the meaning of existence. But I couldn't argue with it, because the more I thought about it the more the stuff I just took for granted seemed to dissolve into . . . nothingness. Where was the past – my past? Gone. Some things remained: buildings and people and so on; but the experience, everything that was so real and important at the time, when I was living through it, where was it now? My experience was locked up inside me – somehow, somewhere – and so was my future. But the only thing I knew for sure was *now*, this present moment, digging in the earth of a rich woman's garden, planting daffodil bulbs. And moment by moment that experience passed, too, to join the stream of time, flowing back endlessly into the dark, distant sea of eternity . . . My head swam. I needed a lie down.

'Are you all right?'

I snapped to. Piers was looking at me, concerned.

'Fine,' I said. 'I think I've just had an epiphany.'

***

That was on our last day; the last afternoon, in fact. Piers gave me a lift to the station and pressed a wad of cash onto me and shook my hand, vigorously again; he said how much he'd enjoyed working with me and how he hoped we would again some time in the future but his partner would be back next week and so he didn't know when it might be and good luck with my writing and he'd look out for the book and would be first in line to buy it . . . And generally he seemed as sad to see me go as I was to say goodbye to him.

I sat on the train rattling back to London, trying to digest the experience – and keep the black cloud from descending. Because here I was again, unemployed, and with no idea of what to do next. But at least my head had stopped hurting – almost. And it occurred to me that while my life had become a lot less secure, it was also a lot more interesting. I was learning stuff, starting to see things from a different angle; waking up almost, it felt like. By the time we reached Euston I was feeling really quite cheerful. Perhaps life was going to turn out all right after all.

Then I bumped into Angie.

Chapter Eight

Old flames never die, they simply smoulder on; and with a bit more fuel, a little oxygen, a gentle raking of the embers – well, who knows what might happen?

Angie was crossing the station concourse as I was heading for the Tube. My stomach turned over the moment I saw her; she hadn't seen me and I hesitated to call out. But all the feelings I'd tried to kill in the weeks since we'd split up burst to the surface, and I heard myself shouting her name. She turned, searched, saw me with surprise and a confused smile.

'Hi. How are you? How are you doing?'

'Fine. You?'

Nothing. Inconsequential chat. Awkwardness. Until she saw the plaster on my head and sounded concerned. I made a joke of it, made her laugh – and we were away.

'Look,' I said, 'are you rushing off somewhere, or do you fancy a quick drink?'

Now it was her turn to hesitate, but with a nod she agreed. So off we went. One drink turned into two, three, then a 'quick bite', which became a long bite, and soon it was past ten – and approaching crunch time. The thing was, we had a really nice evening, despite her confessing to a brief fling with a guy she'd met through work – another

123

gut-churning moment for me. But I forgave her, because she was there, opposite me, and looking so slim and lovely and – hey – it was over, right?

For her part she was surprised by what I'd been up to since she'd left – she hadn't realised that ItsTheBusiness had gone bust, and I did my best to make light of my subsequent adventures. She found my tales funny and fascinating, and was intrigued about Buddhism. And then it was home time. Decision time.

'So,' I said, 'can I, er, walk you to the station?'

She didn't seem keen.

'Are you still living out in Walthamstow?' At the end of a long, lonely Tube journey.

She looked hard into my eyes, knowing exactly what I meant, and slowly nodded.

'Or,' I said, trying to make it sound as relaxed as possible, 'you could always come back to mine. Absolutely no pressure. I could sleep on the sofa and I think there's still some of your things there – you know, underwear and stuff.' I know how important it is to women to wear clean every day, but that's not why I'd kept it. I did because I hoped one day she might come back for it. Or just come back.

'Well,' she mused, 'it *is* a long way.'

'And late,' I added helpfully, knowing she felt unsafe on public transport at this time of night.

She looked up at me again. 'Are you sure you don't mind?' she asked.

Mind? Was she kidding? 'No problem at all,' I said straight-faced – while inside it was fireworks night. Bloody hell, she's coming back! Yippee! Hang out the bunting! Then – calm down. Don't get too excited, Ed. Nice and easy, that's the way. Let her make the running. Because doesn't the woman always decide?

Too right.

The trouble started in the taxi. I decided to splash out on one partly because I had a lot of cash on me, thanks to Piers; partly to spare Angie the public transport; partly to show off how generous and thoughtful I was; but mainly to get her back as quickly as possible, before she changed her mind. Alas, twenty minutes is a long time in an unstable relationship, and a lot can happen. Angie is Jewish, you see, and somehow the subject of karma came up during the ride back to my flat, and as I explained it her mood started to change.

'So it's the victim's fault, is it?'

I heard the danger signal in her voice, but it was too late. 'Not fault – responsibility. Fault's very judgemental, you see.'

'Right,' she said, 'But that still means the Jews were responsible for Auschwitz then?'

'Erm . . .'

'It must be, if you've got it right. You said Buddhism teaches everything is cause and effect – yes?'

I nodded, feeling a great black hole opening up.

Angie bulldozed on. 'Right, so if the effect is being herded into the gas chamber that means the Jews must have made the cause somewhere – doesn't it?'

'Well, I – er . . .' I didn't know what to say. The Middle East had been a running sore between us almost from the outset, when I'd innocently expressed some sympathy for the Palestinian cause.

Angie had reacted badly. 'Oh, so you think it's OK to bomb women and children at bus stops and pizza parlours, do you?'

'No, I don't think it's OK,' I'd protested. 'I'm just saying I can understand people being driven to do something like that, that's all.' Wrong – big-time. Since then the issue had weaved its way through our relationship like a malevolent subterranean river. It surfaced abruptly at times of tension, swept us along in its rapids for a while, then threw us gasping on the bank as it dived underground again – only to resurface at some inconvenient point in the future. Like now.

'Well?' Angie persisted. 'Did the Jews make the cause for the Holocaust or not?'

'I don't know,' I said, 'and I really don't want to talk about it now.' Our night of sweet passion was evaporating before my eyes.

'Why not? You wanted to talk about Buddhism all evening.' She sounded really hostile.

'Only because you kept asking questions about it.'

'I was trying to show an interest.'

'Oh, so it was for my sake?'

And so it went – downhill. By the time we got to my place we weren't even speaking. I saw that familiar 'This is such a bad idea' look on her face as I paid the taxi – and it was. I did sleep on the sofa, she slept in my bed; and I got such 'If you dare come anywhere near me' vibes from her before she closed the bedroom door that she didn't even have to lock it – although she did.

Next morning was polite, and strained – I'd slept terribly and felt totally knackered, and my head had started to throb again. Frankly, it was a relief to us both when she left for work. I crawled into my bed, still faintly warm and smelling of her, and instantly fell asleep.

***

Geoff listened without a word as I filled him in on the latest instalment of the soap that was my life. We were in a snug little pub he knew in Paddington. It was the end of a hard week and we hadn't met since I'd chucked him out of the hospital. I was starting to realise how much I'd

126

come to rely on him – not just for advice, but for a sympathetic ear, someone to really talk to. My friends had been Angie's friends, so when we'd split she'd got them in the divorce. The only other people I'd socialised with on any regular basis were Steve from ItsTheBusiness, who'd disappeared along with the company, and Derek, a mate from college who was a musician and always away on tour somewhere.

'Do you love her?' Geoff asked. He had a habit of going straight to the heart of things.

I was taken aback by his directness but answered as honestly as I could. 'Well, I love the idea of her,' I said. 'It's the reality that's hard. We just – I don't know – always seem to end up arguing.'

'Mmm,' Geoff murmured. 'My first marriage was like that. We fought like cat and dog, split up, got back together again, same thing happened. Took me a long time to see we'd created the karma to suffer with each other – and it wasn't going to change just through good intentions.'

I didn't like the sound of this. 'How do you mean?'

'Well, the thing about karma is it works below the level of the conscious mind, and drives it. It's in charge. I mean, you were planning a bit of nooky, right?'

I nodded sadly.

'But what happens? Give it the right trigger and up pops the bloody Middle East and all the arguments you've had in the past about it, and all the anger and resentment and God knows what.'

'Weariness, really. Very tiring.'

'Right. But you can't stop it. Or you can, but only after the damage has been done.'

I sighed deeply.

'You've created a pattern, see – a habit, karma, that's stronger than this.' He tapped his head. 'And trying to

127

change it with this' – tapping his head again – 'is like trying to lift a table while you're standing on it. Can't be done.'

'You're saying you can't change karma?'

'No, because you can. But not head-on. You have to come at it from a different angle. Like, when I chant I believe I'm going deeper than my karma, to pure life force; so that's like getting under the table and lifting it up because you can push against the ground.'

'And if you don't chant?'

'Good luck. But however you do it, basically you've got to change the part of you that's creating that pattern, that karma. Then the situation will change as a matter of course.'

I didn't quite buy this, but I remembered Piers and his daffodils. 'The trigger – that's like the external cause?'

'Right.'

'So what's the inherent cause of why we don't get on?'

'Sounds like the life state of Anger in both of you. Ego, conflict.'

Hmm. She was the one with the ego, but let it pass – for now. 'And the latent effect?'

'Well, the latent effect of your past arguments is this one, and the latent effect of this one will be the next one.'

'Great. Trapped.'

'Not necessarily.'

'But this thing always causes a row.'

Geoff shook his head. 'It's not the subject that causes the row, Ed; it's the way you are, your life condition, the inherent cause. That's the crucial thing about karma, and cause and effect. The causes you make in any of the Ten Worlds produce effects in that same world. This subject – the Middle East, Israel – has got mixed up with the inherent cause in your lives – Anger – to become an angry row. The latent effect is that it'll be another angry row at some point in the future, unless you do one of two things.'

'What?'

'Either avoid the external cause: never talk about the subject, switch off the telly when it comes on the news and so on.'

'Difficult.'

'Yes. Or change the inherent cause.'

'In me?'

Geoff nodded.

'But it's Angie who always picks the fight.'

'And you who always responds.'

'Not always.'

'Maybe not verbally, but I bet you're seething inside when you bite your lip.'

True. There was no escaping this bloke.

'It's like sediment at the bottom of a glass of water. If you stir it up with a stick the water goes cloudy. But if there's no sediment it can't go cloudy, no matter how hard you stir. The stick's the external cause, the sediment's the inherent cause, your life state.'

'And the water?'

'Could be anything – any subject, situation, relationship. In this case, it's Israel. So in this area, this "water", the trigger stirs up your Anger – and you row. But if the sediment was the world of Humanity, you'd be able to discuss it calmly. If it was the world of Learning, the trigger might set you off to research the subject more deeply. And if it was the world of Bodhisattva you might even be moved to go out there to try to help sort it out.'

'Ha!'

'Some people do.'

'And look at the result.'

'Doesn't affect the principle. You've got to deal with the inherent cause – life state.'

'Well, it does affect the principle, actually.' I wasn't

going to let him get away with this. 'Because Israel's the same problem as between me and Angie, only on a bigger scale. I try to see her point of view, to be calm, reasonable – which is Humanity, right?'

Geoff nodded.

'But she absolutely refuses to budge.'

'And what happens?'

'Well, either I just give up or . . .' I suddenly saw the trap.

'You get angry.'

'Irritated.'

'So the stronger life state wins,' Geoff said simply. 'Either the person in Anger brings out Anger in the person in Humanity, and they have a set-to; or vice versa: the person in Humanity will calm down Mr or Miss Angry. Life's a battle of life conditions, basically. Both in here' – he tapped at his chest – 'and out there.' He jerked a thumb at the room.

'God, it's all so bloody complicated,' I groaned, burying my face in my hands.

Geoff laughed. 'Not complicated, Ed – hard.'

I looked through my fingers at him. 'Pedantic – *moi*?'

'There's a big difference,' he insisted.

'Yeah, I know – we've been round this one before,' I said. 'Climbing Everest.'

'Cheer up, mate,' he said, slapping me on the shoulder. 'If you change, she will. She has to.'

'I doubt we'll ever see each other again.'

Geoff smiled. 'OK,' he said, 'here's a little game. You're a writer – yes?'

'Wannabe.'

'Right. While I get us a refill, I want you to imagine you're writing you and Angie as a story. How would you do it?'

'Why?'

'Just humour me.'

I thought – for about a second. 'I'd have her running back to me, tearful, apologetic—'

'Non-Jewish?'

'No.'

'So the problem would still be there? Israel, the Palestinians . . .'

'Maybe. But she wouldn't be so exercised about it.'

'Right. So in your story you'd give Angie a character makeover; basically make her more obedient?'

'Er . . .' It didn't sound very nice, put like that.

'That's OK – it's normal. Most people want to fix a relationship problem by changing the other person. But if you did that in a story it would seem totally unrealistic, wouldn't it? And ruin the story. Because what makes a good story – for most people, anyway – is where the hero has to go through all sorts of battles to win in the end. Boy meets girl, boy loses girl, boy really struggles to get girl back and does – classic love story. Boy meets girl, boy stays with girl, they live happily ever after – that's no story at all.'

'No, but a nice life.'

Geoff laughed. 'Or a fairy story. But anyway, that's not your situation, is it?'

He got up and took our glasses to the bar for a refill; and not for the first time I was left to think about the way I thought. Perhaps, deep down, I did want a fairy story – except even some of those were pretty bloody dark; full of child abuse, violence, treachery. And did I really want to win Angie back in the end? I didn't know. All I knew was that everything seemed to involve so much *effort*.

''Fraid so,' said Geoff as we started on our fresh pints. 'But that's what separates the six lower worlds from the four higher ones.'

I groaned. 'Not another principle – please.'

'Calm down, it's still the Ten Worlds. But the lower ones – the six from Hell to Humanity – come up in reaction to what's happening around us. Angie leaves – you're in Hell. You want another relationship – Hunger. You meet a woman, fancy her – Animality.'

'Who?'

'Just an example.'

'Oh.'

'Anyway, she laughs at you—'

'Cheers.'

'You're hacked off – Anger. She goes and you calm down – Humanity. And then Angie comes back – Heaven. Your life states are bouncing around, dictated by your environment. That's why they're called the lower worlds – because you're not in control.'

'Whereas . . .?'

'Whereas the other four all need effort.'

I tried to look enthusiastic.

'Take Learning. Seeing a book doesn't automatically make you read it. You have to make a conscious choice, and then put in the effort to read. Same with Realisation: you have to make the effort to look and listen, to observe, and then actually think, try to work something out. And with Bodhisattva it often takes tons of effort to help even one person—'

'As you're discovering.'

Geoff grinned. 'Let alone a community, or a country, or a continent, or the whole world.'

'And Buddhahood?'

'Chanting, studying, teaching others – never stops.'

'Sounds a bundle of fun.'

Another grin. 'It is, actually. And it generates a lot of life force.'

'I'll take your word for it.'

132

'You don't have to. But that's the point about the four higher worlds. You put in the work, you get the result. You become stronger, more capable. And you realise you don't just have to react to what's happening – you can make things happen, be in charge, make your life go in the direction you want it to.'

I looked round the pub. A couple of lads were playing pool. A fat bloke was feeding the fruit machine. A siren in skin-tight jeans was dithering over the juke-box. And all around people were chatting, drinking, smoking, canoodling. Enjoying themselves. I turned back to Geoff.

'I suppose the basic thing is – well, I like the lower worlds. I like fancying women, I like having a good time. I even like a good row every now and then. Whereas the higher worlds – a bit worthy, aren't they? Dull.'

Geoff slapped his hand on the table. 'You calling me dull?' He glared at me.

'No, not you personally,' I stammered, alarmed I'd offended him. 'It's just that, you know, the way you describe them . . .' I tailed off.

He suddenly grinned. 'Relax,' he said. 'The Ten Worlds are there the whole time – all of them – because they all contain all the others. Even the Buddha can suffer. So you can still drink, ogle women – whatever floats your boat. But in moderation. It doesn't dominate you, and because you aren't making causes based on those lower worlds the whole time, gradually you're creating karma based on the higher worlds, and so your life's gradually getting better, more solid, consistent. Happier.' He gave me a QED look and drank some more beer.

I studied him thoughtfully. 'It's got to be sales,' I said.

'What?' He looked puzzled.

'Your line of business.'

133

'Why?'

'Because you almost had me buying it there.'

Geoff laughed and took out his tobacco.

'OK,' I said. 'Now tell me the Buddhist view of the Holocaust.'

His face fell about a mile.

***

Angie sounded suspicious. 'A meeting? Why?'

It had taken quite a bit of courage for me to phone her, and the frosty response I got when she heard the sound of my voice told me this was going to be an uphill conversation. But faint heart etcetera . . . I had to plough on.

'I think you'd really like him. And I asked him your Holocaust question.'

'Uh-huh. What did he say?' She sounded a bit more interested.

'I think it would be better coming from him. That's one reason why I want you to meet.'

'Give me the gist.'

'I can't. But it sounded really, you know, balanced.'

'What do you mean, "balanced"? Between mass murder and what exactly?'

'Well, this is why you should hear it from him. Anything I say I'm just going to get wrong.'

There was a silence on the other end of the line, then a long sigh. 'You know, I don't think I'm really that interested, Ed. Sorry.'

This is what I'd dreaded. Frankly, I was using this 'meet Geoff and talk about the Holocaust' thing as a pretext for trying to re-establish contact; but Angie was too sharp not to guess my motive. There was only one thing for it.

'I don't have to be there, if that's the problem.'

'Look, I'm not going to meet some complete stranger, alone, to talk about the Holocaust. There's nothing he's going to say I want to hear.'

'That's open-minded of you.' The moment I said it I knew I shouldn't have.

Her voice could have cut steel. 'Bye, Ed.' The line went dead. So did my heart, my hope.

***

'You know your problem?' Dora said firmly. 'You've made this woman your *honzon*.'

I'd dropped in to Personal Personnel on the off-chance that a job for an aspiring bestseller writer might have come in since our last conversation, but Dora had asked me what was wrong – I must have looked even glummer than usual – and before I knew it I was talking about Angie. What was it about these Buddhists that made me want to confess all the time? 'My what?' I said.

'*Honzon*,' said Dora, 'It's Japanese for object of worship, or devotion.' Today was a cashmere sweater and figure-hugging ski pants day. She really was very curvy.

'I don't worship her,' I said. 'I hate her.'

Dora raised her finely plucked eyebrows.

'I do,' I insisted.

She was not to be diverted. '*Honzon* doesn't mean treating her like a goddess,' she said, 'or worship in a religious way. It's what's at the centre of your life, what you base it on.'

'Well, I didn't base it on her, so . . .'

'Then why are you so upset she's gone?'

Strange question. 'I shouldn't be? We lived together for two years. I thought we were going to – you know – get married and everything.'

'So she was the centre?'

'No.' I was starting to feel irritated by her persistence. 'But anyway, what does it matter? It's over.'

'The thing about a *honzon*, Ed,' she continued, ignoring my discomfort, 'is it's what gives your life meaning, purpose, focus.'

'Look, Dora,' I said, 'I didn't come here for more Buddhism. I came for a job.'

She looked me straight in the eye. 'If that's all, my darling, you could have phoned, saved yourself the journey. No, I think you wanted to talk about your woman – to a woman.'

Bloody hell – she was right. She knew me better than I knew myself.

'It's OK,' she said. 'I've got the time. Business is slack.' She flicked open her box of job cards, then glanced back at me. Her expression turned to one of alarm. 'Are you all right?'

I was blushing, turning bright red with embarrassment that she'd seen through me; and as she looked at me I felt it escalating into another of those hot flushes that would leave me looking as if I'd just stepped fully clothed out of a shower. 'Bit hot,' I said with a feeble smile. 'I'll – er – just get some air and . . .' I pushed back my chair, made straight for the door, and out.

It was a warm day, but I was so overheated the breeze down Baker Street hit me like a cool flannel. 'What is this?' I screamed silently. I thought back to the last time it happened, at ItsTheBusiness before my second meeting with Geoff, but I couldn't see any connection. I shook my head at the mystery of it all, waited for the flush to pass, then went back in to Dora.

'All right?' she asked as I took my place opposite her.

'Fine. I just have this problem with my thermostat. Goes a bit haywire sometimes.'

'Perhaps you should get it checked.'

'I would, only it's out of warranty.' I don't think she got the joke. 'Anyway, while I was out there I was thinking how you know me better than I know myself, Dora, because I realise I did come here to talk about Angie and, well, I'm just stunned that you saw that.'

Dora gave a little shrug.

'How do you do it?'

'I look after a lot of Buddhists – women mainly. You get to read people.'

'What do you mean – look after?'

'I encourage them in their practice, they come to me with their problems and I give them guidance. I've been at it a few years, you see.'

'Does that mean you're enlightened?'

She laughed louder than ever. 'Buddhism's a philosophy of the human heart. So I suppose my journey's been to understand that, a bit more each day if I can, and just share what I've learned with other people – like you and your girlfriend.'

'Ex-girlfriend.'

'Oh yes, you did mention it.' That twinkle again.

I smiled; we understood each other.

'You were telling me about *honzon*,' I said.

'Well, it can be anything,' said Dora. 'Your lover, wife, husband, family, kids, job, career, status, money; your philosophy of life, or religion or political beliefs. Your intellect. Your car, even.'

I looked surprised.

'You've never seen how some men treat theirs? Washing, and polishing and fiddling all the time. Then standing back to admire.'

I nodded; this was true.

'But the thing is,' Dora went on, 'a lot of people don't

137

know what their *honzon* is, because it's unconscious; until maybe it disappears for some reason. Then people know it, because they feel totally lost.'

'How?'

'You never come across the couple who've been married for forty, fifty years, then one of them dies and the other one goes straight after? Or the person who commits suicide because they lose all their money, or the star who falls out of the limelight and sinks into depression; or the priest who loses his faith and turns to the bottle? They lose their *honzon* and it's like their main prop's been kicked away from under them.'

This rang a painful bell. I'd never realised how many assumptions I'd built into my relationship with Angie – until she left. But as Dora was talking I suddenly saw that when we were together everything I imagined in my future had Angie in it somewhere. She *was* the base, the foundation. Even working at ItsTheBusiness had been bearable mainly because I could come home to her and complain about it; although now, from her point of view, I can see how being with me must have felt like living with one long whinge. But still I felt the need to argue with Dora.

'OK, but it's normal, isn't it? You've got to have something to drive you, to live for.'

'You're right – it is normal; which is why society's so messed up, in my opinion. Because most of these *honzons* aren't stable. They change, or just aren't reliable. Lovers come and go, kids grow up and leave, fame and fortune are a lottery. So trying to base your life, your happiness, on things like that is asking for trouble. It's like trying to build a house on a boat on the high seas.' She made a wave motion, up and down, with her hand.

'So what's your *honzon*, then?' I asked.

'Buddhism,' she said.

138

'Doesn't that change?'

'Yes and no. The core – the Law – stays the same; but how it operates changes to fit the times and the situation.'

'What do you mean by the law?'

'The basic Law of life, how things work. That's what I chant every day, twice a day. It's like my compass. So basing myself on that I can steer my way through life; it's constant but changeable.'

Here we go again. Religion, chanting, giving oneself over to mystical mumbo-jumbo – always the same sticking-point. And once again I felt the shutters going up.

Dora must have seen the glazed look coming over my face. 'I know you don't want to hear it, Ed, but that's why I can look at this business here and see it's struggling, and even know it could fail despite everything I might do, and not lose my sense of proportion. My happiness, my life, is not based on this. I know I'll survive, whatever happens, and build something even better in the future.'

'That's great, Dora,' I said, 'really great spirit. But how can you *know* that? You can hope it, and work for it, but you can't *know* it.'

'Well, you think like that, my darling, because you haven't done it. I have. I've been practising this Buddhism for fifteen years and every time I've had a problem or a so-called disaster, I've turned it round and built something better on it. Even this place. I was in Human Resources – it used to be called Personnel – for a large company. Six years ago it was taken over and our whole department was made redundant. Some of the people there thought it was the end of the world, but I chanted about what to do and – to cut a long story short – this is the result. So my faith, my belief, is based on my experience. No one can take that from me. And seeing you sitting there looking so handsome and so miserable, I just want to shake you.'

Handsome? It was a long time since anyone had called me that. I was quite taken aback. I quickly made a joke to cover my confusion. 'Please do.' I grinned.

She smiled. 'I thought you were stuck on this Angie girl. Isn't that the whole point?'

'Guess so,' I sighed.

'Well then,' she said briskly, 'I've said my piece, so let's see if I can help you in a practical way.' She riffled through her cards and pulled one out. 'OK, it's temporary and nothing to do with writing, but it's a job and you need some money, hmm? Gain.'

I nodded. 'What is it?'

'Sitting on the phone, trying to rent out an office space in the City.' She handed me the card.

I looked at it, then at her. 'I'll take it.'

***

I got home to find a message waiting for me on the answerphone: Angie.

'Hi, it's me. Look, I'm sorry for being so . . . short with you on the phone, and the other night. It's just that whenever Israel, you know . . . Anyway, I would like to meet your friend to hear what he's got to say about it, so give me a call and let's find a date, OK? Bye.'

I said people never fail to amaze me. Perhaps we were on again. Ish. I suddenly felt very happy. Then I checked myself. *Honzon* trap. She's nice to me – I'm up; she's not nice to me – I'm down. And I mustn't base my happiness on her moods – wasn't that the lecture Dora had just given me? Still, I couldn't help it. This was a good sign, and I mean *good*. I grinned, I whooped, I jumped up and down and punched the air, I sang 'Cecelia'. Perhaps, just perhaps, we'd turned a corner. Or were turning it. Or were slowing down, changing gear and preparing to make the turn. Perhaps. If Geoff talked to her like he talked to me, if he convinced her, charmed her, reassured her that this Buddhism thing I was getting interested in wasn't a load of old nonsense – well, perhaps we'd be all right after all. She wouldn't be a walk-on in the first act of my story; she'd be the girl the boy meets and loses and wins in the end. Perhaps.

Chapter Nine

Regence House was a low-rise block of glass and concrete in the heart of the City, close to the Bank of England. The space I was trying to flog was the entire fourth floor, which had been – irony of ironies – leased to a finance dot-com that had gone bust in the crash with massive debts. The whole space had been cleared out, apart from a desk and a fax/phone in a small side office, which didn't have a window. This was my base. A twenty-year-old in a pin-striped suit gave me a script and a long list of numbers – managing directors, company secretaries, property managers – and told me to work my way through them. It didn't matter that I knew nothing about commercial property, or letting, or that I'd be talking to people who did. As long as I stuck to the script everything would be OK.

'But what if they ask questions?'

'All the information you need's in the script,' said the pin-stripe. 'You've just got to whittle down the numbers, draw up a short list of who's interested and fax it through at the end of each day. We'll take it from there.' And with that he was off.

There's something very odd about being alone in a large and empty office when all around you throbs with activity.

142

The floor above was occupied by an insurance company, the one below by hotshot City lawyers, but nobody got out of the packed lift on my floor except me – to curious, questioning looks. 'Who's he? What's he doing there?' I was clearly an interloper, an outsider who didn't wear the City uniform and disappeared each day into the black hole formerly known as MoneyMoneyMoney.Com. I'd push through the swing doors, go past the bare and polished reception counter, and enter the still, parallel universe of the fourth floor. No one came to visit, the phone never rang, the world outside whizzed by. When I wasn't making a call the only thing I could hear was the sound of my own breathing. It was like being in a coma.

At regular intervals, to stop myself from going mad, I'd get up, walk out of my windowless cupboard, and cross to the thick panes of double-glazing that ran down the entire length of the office. The building opposite was another squat, ugly block, but it was full of people, and light – the only strip lit on my floor was in my little cubicle, leaving the rest of the space dim and gloomy. Down below in the narrow street black cabs and motorbike couriers and delivery vans accelerated and braked, and honked horns and yelled abuse at each other; but the sound was distant, muffled by the glass. Craning my head right I could just see the corner of the Bank; while craning left, at the end of the street a tower of steel and glass rose into the sky, out of my eyeline. I felt like a kid pressing his nose up against the window of the shop called life.

It was during one of these sanity visits that events took an unexpected twist. I'd just had a long series of rejections – office space wasn't exactly at a premium, since so many dot-coms had bitten the dust in the past few months – and I needed a break. My ear hurt from having the phone pressed against it for so long, my back ached and I was hungry. I walked to my usual window, straight across from my cubby-hole, and looked down. Traffic, bicycle courier, pretty girl with fat friend. I looked right. Bank of England, power, traffic snarl-up at road junction. I looked left. Steel and glass tower. A cradle holding a man in blue overalls – a window-cleaner – was being lowered to the first floor, and I started wondering idly how often the windows were washed; or if it were a constant process, like painting the Forth Bridge.

Then I stopped. There was something about the figure in the cradle that seemed familiar. He was about sixty yards away and had his back to me, and I was looking from a tight angle, but even so. I looked harder, squinted, then rushed out of the office, past the empty reception and dashed down the stairs to the street. I don't know why I was running, as the bloke couldn't really go anywhere. But I hurried along, dodging pedestrians and traffic as I hopped off and on the pavement, all the while keeping the cradle and its occupant in my sights. I got to the T-junction, right opposite where he was cleaning, and looked up. His back was still turned to me. I called out his name but the traffic was too loud and he was too far away. I crossed the road and climbed the steps to the entrance. The cradle was still a good twenty feet above me, but I called his name again. The man in the cradle stopped, then looked down over the side, searching for the source of the voice. He saw me with surprise. It was Geoff.

***

A few minutes later the cradle bumped gently to earth and Geoff climbed out. 'Hello,' he said simply.

'So this is what you do?' I asked.

He nodded.

'Helping people see more clearly at all levels?'

144

'That's right.'

'As a window-cleaner.'

He nodded again. We stared at each other. He was looking to see how I'd react, and I was trying to work out how I would. I was stunned; then, hurt, offended. Not just because he'd kept this from me but because he knew where I was working; I'd told him when I'd got the job. So why hadn't he been frank?

'Were you hoping I wouldn't find out?' I asked.

Geoff gave a slight shrug.

'I'm working just down there!' I pointed towards Regence House.

He looked uncomfortable. 'I didn't tell you because . . . well, I didn't know how you'd react.'

'What do you mean?'

'I didn't think you could take knowing what I did.'

'Why?' I was trying hard to keep the hostility out of my voice, but couldn't.

'You really want to know?'

'Yes.'

'Well, it's because you struck me from the outset as very dismissive. Closed. I might have got you wrong, but I thought that once you could label me, put me in a box, you'd dismiss or label everything I said, too, if you didn't like it.'

Talk about a punch in the guts. I stood there staring at him, lost for words. I felt a bit dizzy, as if my world had wobbled.

Geoff must have seen my pain. 'Sorry,' he said.

I shook my head, as much to clear it as to show my bewilderment. 'I thought we were friends.'

'We are – I hope.'

'Then why didn't you trust me? Why let me believe you were some sort of life-coach or something?'

'You believed what you wanted to believe, Ed.'

' "Helping people see more clearly at all levels?" What was I supposed to think?'

Geoff sighed. 'Look, I'm sorry if I've offended you. I just did what I thought was best – all right?'

I looked at him, stupefied. My immediate reaction was to walk away and have no more to do with him, but then I remembered I needed him for this meeting with Angie. Except that was even more high risk now, wasn't it? What if she didn't like what he had to say *and* she found out he was window-cleaner? Well, that was easy – I just wouldn't tell her.

Then it hit me. The fact that I automatically decided to hide his job from Angie wasn't just because of her status snobbery – it was because of mine, too. Geoff was right: I wouldn't have reacted to him in the same way if I'd known what he did. But this was too much to admit at this precise moment, standing on a busy street in the City of London, even to myself.

'So, any other secrets I should know?' I asked bitterly.

'No,' he said coolly. 'Though it's nice of you to ask.'

'What do you mean?'

'Well, in all the time I've known you, Ed,' he said, 'that's only the second question you've asked me about myself, apart from my job.'

Whack. Another one into the solar plexus. I felt the need to fight back. 'I know lots about you.'

'Bits and pieces – but only because I've told you. You've never asked, you've never shown any interest in me. It's all been about you.'

A right hook. I was reeling. 'Well, that's because you seem so sorted.'

'Look, mate, don't get me wrong. I'm just saying that maybe one reason why you're in the situation you are is

146

because your focus is all on yourself. You start to widen your vision more, think about the world more, other people, society, what you can do to change things for the better – well, you might find a lot more satisfaction, fulfilment and, dare I said it, happiness, than you're getting at the moment. Self *and* others, that's the way. Now, if you'll excuse me.' He pointed to the tower looming above us, then climbed back into the cradle, hit a button on a small console and was lifted slowly into the air. He hit another button and started to crab sideways – he was obviously going to work his way up the next column of windows to the top of the building, then down again; up down, up down, till they all sparkled. And everyone could see clearly, at all levels.

***

Trying to sell overpriced office space to uninterested senior managers didn't come easy the rest of that day. I felt like shit. Geoff was the one who was out of order, who hadn't been straight, yet I was the one feeling guilty. But yet again he'd put his finger on it. I hadn't shown any interest in him whatsoever. It was just like that night when I'd realised how the only things I cared about were me and Angie, then narrowed it down to just me. But isn't everyone like this? I thought. At heart, underneath it all, don't we all care about ourselves above everything? We set up a direct debit to some charity or other to salve our consciences, convince ourselves we're helping the poor or the sick or the planet, but actually isn't it just a down-payment on more personal consumption, more hedonism, more Me-Me-Me?

I thought about my mum, who was always doing good, especially when she retired. Sitting on committees, raising money for the local hospice and Oxfam, visiting the old and the lonely. But she'd been a Christian, part of the

Church, which I couldn't stand for its sanctimony and piety and disapproval of virtually everything I rated, e.g. sex and drinking. I suppose I associated one with the other – religion and do-goodery – and somewhere, deep down, rejected both. Was I any the better for it, though? Looking at her life, I remember thinking how boring it seemed: endless meetings and minutes, and phone calls to soothe the ruffled feathers of some irate member of this or that committee. It all seemed so petty. But was my life any more exciting, or fulfilling, or valuable? Shuttling between my flat, the pub and the limbo known as the fourth floor, Regence House, I couldn't honestly say it was.

The face of a bloke from college swam into my mind. Red Pete, we'd called him, because he was always up in arms about something: Third World poverty, US 'imperialism', Palestine. Whenever you bumped into him – and you didn't want to, believe me – he'd always have an armful of leaflets about some rally or meeting or injustice somewhere in the world. And it was always the fault of the rich, bloated, capitalist West, with the US President and his henchmen in the Pentagon and/or Big Business cast as Evil Incarnate. I felt sympathy for some of the issues – it was a quick read of one of his pamphlets that shaped my basic view of the Israel–Palestine problem (shaky ground, I later realised, for 'debating' it with Angie). But Pete was always so bloody angry and saw the world in such black-and-white terms – or should that be red-and-white? – that in his own way he was just as boring as my mum. He was all about changing the world and she was all about helping your neighbours, and neither appealed. I just wanted to get laid, drink – oh, and become a famous novelist. And how boring is that? Except to me.

So, it was true. My life was narrow, self-absorbed and pretty bloody shallow. And I began to get the uneasy inkling that maybe it was no coincidence I was all alone in this bleak, windowless office, in a dim and empty space. What had Geoff called it? The oneness of life and its environment. What's outside is simply a reflection of what's inside; the inner and the outer self are a perfect match. If that was true – yikes. But how to change, how to change . . .?

***

Angie was looking gorgeous – as ever. She'd come straight from work and had on a narrow pencil skirt and a little jacket that showed off her curves a treat; all topped off by the prettiest face and a mass of brown curls. I looked at Geoff to see his reaction, but he was giving nothing away. He just got up, smiled and held out his hand.

We were in a tapas bar I knew Angie liked – a smoky, noisy pub didn't seem the best place to discuss the Holocaust, and certainly not with her. She was class. I'd called Geoff to confirm the arrangement a couple of days after our confrontation in the street, and had brushed off his apology for not being frank about his job. It didn't matter, I said – though it did. Everything he'd told me might be true, and his evaluation of me might be spot on, but part of me still felt deceived, manipulated almost. Perhaps I was over-reacting, but you can't help how you feel, can you? Well, Geoff said you could, but I had a big question mark against that, too. Still, here we were, the three of us, going through the preliminary chit-chat and about to dive into very deep waters. Danger-opportunity . . .

'So,' said Angie after a while, 'Ed says you've got a Buddhist explanation for the Holocaust.'

Geoff smiled. 'It's my explanation,' he said. 'It's not an official line or anything. It's how I've made sense of it, through Buddhism.'

'Can you make sense of it?'

'I've tried.'

'OK. Fire away.' Angie sipped her wine and smiled sweetly, but I knew that look. Inside she was coiled, ready to pounce on any statement that in any way suggested the victim was culpable.

Geoff took a deep breath and launched in. 'Right. Well, first off, I want to make it clear that nothing I say should be taken in any way to justify what the Nazis did. That was disgusting, an atrocity, and the people who did it and supported it are totally responsible for their actions. OK?'

Angie nodded and sipped her wine, watching him closely.

'And from a Buddhist perspective they've created terrible karma for themselves in doing what they did.'

'Karma – that's the punishment they're going to suffer in the future?'

'Not punishment, exactly. It's the effects you experience as a result of causes you make, good or bad. So if you cause suffering at some point you'll suffer in return.'

'Which means all the Jews who were murdered in the Holocaust must have made the cause at some point to die like that – which I absolutely refuse to accept.'

Attagirl – get in there, straight to the jugular. She was staring fixedly at Geoff. So was I. How was he going to deal with this?

'That sounds outrageous to you?'

'Totally.'

Geoff grunted. 'Ed said members of your family were killed.' He glanced at me.

'On my mother's side, yes. Her mother's parents, two brothers, cousins, uncles and aunts. My grandmother was the only one who got out, on the kindertransport. If she hadn't I wouldn't be here.'

150

Geoff shook his head. 'Terrible. So anything that even hints the victim is somehow responsible feels like a real insult.'

'Yes.'

He sighed. 'I know. It's very hard, even if you believe in the eternity of life, like I do. But for me the question isn't so much what causes did these people make to suffer like this, because I think that's impossible to answer—'

'That's convenient,' said Angie tartly.

'For me,' said Geoff, ignoring her tone, 'the important question isn't what causes people made in their past lives but what people do in *this* life. What makes people behave like the Nazis did to the Jews? Why did other people let it happen – or not? In Denmark, for example, the vast majority of Jews were hidden by the non-Jewish population, or helped to escape, whereas in Poland they weren't. And for me, above all, the crucial question is what can we all do to make sure it doesn't happen again?'

'Only it has, hasn't it?' I said. 'Rwanda.'

'Exactly,' said Geoff.

'Exactly what?' said Angie, still seething. But at least she hadn't walked out, which I suspect she would have done by now if it had been just the two of us.

'Well, I reckon,' said Geoff, 'everything boils down to what Buddhism calls the world of Anger. Which isn't just losing your temper. It's ego, identity, how you define yourself as separate from other people; the rest of the universe, in fact.'

Angie crossed her arms and legs and gazed at him, aggression shining from every pore.

Geoff ignored it. 'One way we do it is in opposition to other people, or groups of people, often putting "them" down to make "us" – our group – feel better or superior.

151

You see it in football supporters, nations, religions, political groups – everywhere.'

'And?' Angie's tone was harsh, impatient.

'And taken to extremes,' said Geoff, 'that attitude can be used to justify anything "our group" decides is good for us, and to ignore anything "that group" says or wants. They don't count; our needs come first. So time and again through history you see groups of people who've wiped out other groups they've classed as enemies or a threat or inferior in some way. The Mongols did it right across Asia. We Europeans did it to millions of "darkies" during the whole period of colonialism. White people wiped out or ethnically cleansed millions of indigenous people when they settled the Americas. And we're still doing it.'

'How?' Angie sounded incredulous, and even I was taken aback.

Geoff ploughed on. 'Every year,' he said, 'millions of people in developing countries die from poverty, disease, hunger, malnutrition; more people every year than died in the six years of the Second World War, including the Holocaust. In fact, some people call this the Silent Holocaust. We know about it but we let it happen – because it suits us, our lifestyles.'

Angie looked floored for a moment. 'How do we let it happen?'

'Because a lot of this death is the result of international debt and unfair trade policies skewed towards the West. We benefit, so we do little or nothing to change it.'

Angie's eyes narrowed. 'If you're saying that me buying a cup of coffee from Starbucks or wherever is the same as the Nazis shovelling men, women and children into the gas chambers . . . well, that is such complete crap. And trying to make the link, to make them equivalent – I find that disgusting.'

Geoff didn't turn a hair. 'I'm not saying it's equivalent. I'm saying what the Nazis did isn't unique or even unusual. It's an extreme case of what human beings have done since for ever: denigrate, devalue, disregard other human beings when it suits them.'

Angie stared at him with naked hostility, and inside I groaned. If I'd known he was going to start sounding like Red Pete I'd never have put him anywhere near her, because she was basically a *Daily Mail* editorial on legs. But he hadn't said any of this to me. He'd talked about history, about how Christians had felt insulted by Judaism because it denied that Jesus was the son of God; and how the Jews were often feared as alien because they were a tight-knit and self-reliant community, forced into separate development by persecution. And a lot of the time people were simply jealous of them because they were so successful in trade and business. 'Look at how Jewish businesses were destroyed by the Nazis, or stolen,' he'd said. 'That shows where a lot of anti-Semitism was coming from: greed and envy.'

But – and this was the bit that brought me up short – he'd also wondered how the Jews calling themselves the Chosen People might have affected non-Jews. 'Anyone who sets themselves up as special in some way – even if they are special – is always going to be targeted by other people,' he'd said. 'It's not nice, but it's a fact. Like, we had this rich kid at school who really thought he was a cut above us, and we all hated him, wanted to bring him down to size. So we bullied him – including me, I'm ashamed to say. And with the Nazis – well, they were the Chosen People too, weren't they? Aryans, the Master Race. And you can't have two Chosen People, so they tried to wipe out the Jews. Horrible.'

I'd had to think hard about all this. It went beyond labels

like 'good' and 'evil' to basic human attitudes like resentment, fear and jealousy. It sort of made sense to me, but then I wasn't Jewish. I didn't know how it would sound to someone more closely involved – like Angie. I hoped she might *just* be able to consider it without getting all worked up. But somehow the conversation had taken the wrong track and come off the rails. Time to rescue the situation. I opened my mouth – but too late.

'There is no way,' Angie hit back, 'that you can equate people starving in the Third World to the Holocaust. That was genocide – one group deliberately targeting another people and trying to exterminate them. And even talking of them in the same breath is an insult to the six million Jews who were deliberately, wilfully, systematically murdered.'

'Fair point,' I said, desperate to appease her. Geoff wouldn't budge.

'If governments follow economic and trade policies that they know result in massive numbers of deaths,' he said, 'does it matter what it's called? And how different are we from people living in Germany during the Holocaust if we know our governments are doing this but turn our backs on it?'

I winced again and waited for the explosion.

Angie looked at Geoff as if he were from another planet. 'So now I'm as bad as the people who supported Hitler?'

'Look, I don't want to upset you, Angie,' Geoff said.

She snorted with derision.

'All I'm saying is the Nazis blamed their problems on the Jews and consciously decided to get rid of them. We sacrifice other people indirectly, by building our wealth on structures and systems that cause incredible suffering in poorer parts of the world. And basically we think that's OK, or not enough of us care enough to stop it.'

Angie sighed and stared at her empty wine glass.

I leapt in. 'Another one?'

'No, thank you.' Her answer was clipped, terse. She composed herself and looked up at Geoff. 'Is this Buddhism – or communism? Because it sounds identical to the sort of crap you hear from those people who riot about the "evils of globalisation" and capitalism. Despite the fact that every society, when it gets freedom, freely chooses the free market.'

'Actually, I did used to be very left-wing,' Geoff admitted cheerfully, 'till I realised neither communism nor capitalism's got the whole story. And if you base your society on ideas that are incomplete, sooner or later you're going to hit the buffers.'

'What do you mean by "incomplete"?' Angie asked, her critical antennae still quivering furiously.

'Ideas that don't understand cause and effect properly, or don't reflect life accurately. Or exclude whole groups of people – like women, or savages, or Jews, or non-Aryans, or non-Christians, non-believers, the rich, the poor, the working class, the bourgeoisie. You name it.'

'Meaning, I suppose, every idea except Buddhism.' The contempt in her voice was so heavy I sensed the conversation might be drawing to a close.

But again, Geoff sailed over it. 'Well, even most Buddhist teachings are incomplete,' he said. 'Some of them say women can't become enlightened, for example.' He flashed her a warm smile, but it was far too late for that.

'How very enlightened,' Angie replied – her one joke of the evening.

'Exactly. Not the sort I practise, though.' He smiled again.

'So there is hope for me,' she said dryly. 'As long as I follow your example, hmm?'

'As far as I'm concerned,' said Geoff, 'the important thing isn't what people practise, or even what they believe – it's how they actually behave towards each other.'

Angie looked at him a moment. 'Right,' she said. She held his gaze a while longer, then gave a short sigh, grabbed her bag and slung it over her shoulder. 'Well,' she said, getting to her feet, 'it's been very informative. Thank you for the drink.' She headed for the door.

I jumped to my feet and ran after her. 'Angie!'

She turned and looked at me.

'Come on, stay for another one.'

'No thanks,' she said, glancing daggers over my shoulder at Geoff. 'I've had a long day and I want to get home.'

'Angie . . .' I pleaded.

'OK?'

The two letters were laden with a warning that froze me dead. Helpless, I watched her push open the door and turn out of sight along the street. Out of sight and out of my life – for ever?

156

Chapter Ten

Every once in a while a person has to choose; has to make a conscious decision about something really quite important. Where to live, who to marry, which way to go in life. And who their true friends are. That was the decision I had to make about Geoff, because I was starting to have serious doubts about whether associating with him was doing me any good at all.

After Angie walked out I dragged myself back to my seat, desolate, but Geoff didn't seem too bothered that she'd stormed out. 'Spiky, isn't she?' was all he said. And he shrugged off the fact that he'd not repeated anything he'd said to me about the Chosen People and how the jealous tear down those who are special, etcetera, etcetera. She hadn't given him a chance, he explained. She was 'closed' and hadn't wanted to listen. 'Sorry if this is stamping all over your heart, Ed, but I can see why you split up.' Of course, I hadn't told him what I'd had riding on the meeting. After our encounter in the City I hadn't wanted to confide in him, because if someone's not open with you it's only natural you won't be open with them – right? So I decided to spend the rest of that evening making up for the lack of interest I'd shown in his private life – by interrogating him. If he passed

157

the test – well, maybe I might keep in touch. If not – sayonara.

I knew he'd been divorced, and had been a builder. That evening I discovered he'd been married for fourteen years and had two daughters, now both in their twenties. One he saw, the other he didn't. 'It's difficult,' he said, 'but I'm working on it. She still blames me for what happened with her mum.'

'What did happen?'

'Another woman,' he said ruefully.

'Ah. You still with her?'

'No, that didn't work out either.'

I pressed him for more details and he told me he'd started an affair about ten years into his marriage.

'We just rowed the whole time,' he said. 'Couldn't see eye to eye on anything. It got to be like going home to a war zone every night. Either hot war – a row; or cold war – the big freeze, no communication, nothing. How we managed to share a bed for so long is beyond me. Anyway, I met this other woman who I got on with, could talk to, have a laugh with . . .' He shrugged.

'Was this before or after you became a Buddhist?'

'After.'

I raised an eyebrow. 'I thought you were supposed to get wiser when you practised.'

'I'd only been at it a couple of years,' he said, but he could see I wasn't impressed. 'Gaining wisdom's a process. You do what you think is right at the time. And if it turns out wrong – well, the question is do you learn from your mistake and grow? Or do you keep on making it again and again?'

'You tell me.'

'Well, the pain I caused for everyone involved – my wife, kids, the other woman, me . . .' He blew out his cheeks at the memory. 'I wouldn't want a repeat of that. Talk about cause and effect. So that lesson isn't just up here.' He tapped his head. 'It's here, too.' And he tapped his chest.

'No pain, no gain.'

'You said it. Growing pains. Human revolution. Did I tell you about that?'

'A bit.'

'It's when you transform some crappy part of your character and gradually a better you emerges. But some of the thicker specimens among us, like me, have to really suffer the consequences of our stupidity before we get the message and change.'

I had a flash of the acorn Piers had given me, growing on the window-sill back home. 'So what about your building work? What happened to that?'

Geoff smiled. 'All part of the same mess. I had my own firm but it was based at home and when my wife kicked me out it was impossible to keep on top of things – you know, the admin, cash-flow, paying the guys. Bit by bit it went down the toilet, and me with it.'

'And the other woman?'

'She took me in for a bit but that went pear-shaped pretty fast. So then there was a period of kipping on friends' sofas, till I started running out of friends. 'Cos I was knocking back this stuff' – he lifted his bottle – 'like there was no tomorrow. I was headed for the streets, basically.'

'What – and you were still being a Buddhist?'

'Well, that's the funny thing. Chanting twice a day was the only stable thing I had. I'd do it religiously, if you'll pardon the pun. And if I woke up with a stinking hangover and couldn't do my morning practice I'd get really pissed off with myself, because I knew what a difference it made to my day. And in the end I thought, Either you get

159

yourself together, son, and turn this situation around, or you'll end up as a pathetic old wino living out of bins.'

'So?'

'So I persuaded a mate to lend me some cash, bought a bucket and a ladder, and started washing windows. Bit by bit I got out of the toilet, got my life back together – and QED.' He stared into the middle distance, reliving for a moment the memory of that time.

'How long ago was this?' I asked.

'Thirteen years.'

'And you've been washing windows ever since?'

'I really enjoy it,' he said, laughing. 'I like being outside, I meet a lot of people, go to lots of different places. Like, where you saw me – that's my biggest gig. Takes a week, once a month. The rest of the time I'm all over the City and the West End, doing everything from hotels to shops to restaurants to private houses – you name it.'

'It's still just cleaning windows though, isn't it?' I said. 'I mean, after having your own company . . .'

'God, the hassle in that,' he countered. 'Fussy clients, architects, the spec always changing, or guys never showing up for work, or skiving off, or always trying to cut corners. No. What I do is simple, straightforward, gives me enough to live on, and when I finish a job it's finished. I go home, no worries, no paperwork in the evenings, and I sleep bloody well.' He smiled and toasted me with his beer. A contented man.

And yet.

As I sat listening to Geoff's life story, and how practising Buddhism had saved him from destitution, I kept thinking, Yes, but you're still only a window-cleaner, aren't you? I couldn't help it. And Piers was only a gardener. And Dora ran a small employment agency . . . Was that it? This 'human revolution', 'enlightenment', 'Buddhahood' – was

160

it just an elaborate way of coming to terms with the ordinary, humdrum stuff of daily life? Of going all round the houses in search of meaning, only to arrive back where you started and know it for the first time? (To quote the only bit of A-level T.S. Eliot I could remember.) But I didn't want to 'come to terms' with my life: I wanted to bloody change it!

'So,' I said, 'before you became a Buddhist you had a wife, a family, a successful business. And now you're a window-cleaner, single and estranged from one of your daughters – is that it?'

Geoff laughed. 'Sounds great, doesn't it? But I had all those things and I wasn't happy. Looked good on the surface but underneath . . .' He shook his head.

'Perhaps you should have been a bit more grateful,' I suggested, gently twisting the knife. 'A lot of people would give their eye teeth for what you had.'

'Without a doubt,' Geoff agreed. 'And now I am grateful. I get on well with my ex, and my elder daughter. And I think my younger is coming round, slowly. And OK, I don't have as much money and I'm still looking for Miss Right. But you can only start from where you are, can't you? I met Buddhism at a particular point, I had these experiences, and now I'm older, wiser and, deep down, happy.'

Sigh. The H word again: happy. I really didn't know what it meant. Not in the way Geoff or Dora used it. The only happy I knew was what they labelled Heaven or Rapture – what you feel when you get something you want; or pleasure, like being in bed with Angie. Happy. Happy, happy, happy. Say it often enough and the word sounds almost childish. Happy the Clown. Happy chappie. Happy clappy, lose your mind in religion. Was that what I wanted? Is that what Geoff was offering? If so, it just didn't appeal.

Needless to say, by the time we parted I still hadn't made up my mind about him.

***

I got home to see the light blinking on the answerphone. My stomach lurched. Angie? I hit the button.

'Hi, Ed. Martin here.' I groaned. 'Just calling to see if you fancied meeting up some time.' No bloody way. 'Only I really enjoyed our discussion that time and I'd like to know more about this Buddhism you're getting into.' Eh? I'm not. 'Except it's nothing like anything I've read about since our talk. It's Buddhism, Jim, but not as we know it.' In a poor imitation of Mr Spock. 'Anyway, give me a call when you get a moment.' In your dreams, mate. 'Oh – and when are you going to get a mobile? Byeeee.'

I dialled 1471. His was the last call, at 6.37. Nothing from Angie. So that was that, then. I was tarred with the same brush that had dismissed Geoff. Only one thing for it. I went into the kitchen, took the Scotch from the cupboard, the Coke from the fridge, and mixed myself a half-and-half – which is one stiff drink, I can tell you. I went back into the sitting-room, turned on the television and sat flicking moronically from channel to channel. But I wasn't watching it. I was churning over the evening with Angie.

She was my *honzon*, all right, my anchor; and with her gone I was adrift. I could see it all now, even through the alcoholic fug that was fast descending. From the moment she'd walked out my attitude to everything had changed. Basically, nothing really mattered any more except the agony I was going through. That's why I'd had the row with Martin that week. His problems, ItsTheBusiness, the Lino Man: it was all so petty, so meaningless, set against my suffering. At the time wiser counsel would have said I was

162

getting things out of perspective, but from what I understood that's the whole point of your *honzon*, isn't it? It gives you perspective, and when it goes . . .

Suddenly, an uncomfortable thought unfurled in my brain: that ever since Angie had left I'd been fighting a deep, unconscious urge towards self-destruction. Calling Martin a tight-fisted git had been a challenge to sack me. The booze – this ridiculous amount of whisky in my hand right now – what was it if not a drive for oblivion? And what did my characters want to do when I tried to write? Commit suicide. That was their way out, their natural, inevitable choice.

But there was another urge here, too. Survival. That's why I'd latched onto Geoff. He offered hope, life, growth through Buddhism. That's what I was attracted to *and* fought against. Or rather, My Evil Friend did. Because he was always lurking somewhere – around the corner, under the beer mat, in the bottle – to jeer and mock, criticise and taunt. He didn't want me to be happy, because then what would he do? Who would he play with? He'd be alone, and he couldn't bear the thought of that.

I smiled at the image of his discomfort. But there was something discomfiting me; something beneath these drunken musings, like the pea under all those mattresses the princess tried to sleep on . . . Abruptly I stood up and swayed over to the answerphone. I hit the button and replayed Martin's message, the part that said: 'I'd like to know more about this Buddhism you're getting into. Except it's nothing like anything I've read about since our talk. It's Buddhism, Jim, but not as we know it.'

That was it. Even though I was drunk – or perhaps because I was – I realised in a flash what was wrong. I was making Geoff my new *honzon*. I had started relying on him to give new meaning to my life, almost to become his apprentice. That's why I'd been so shaken to discover he'd not been straight with me. And now this: 'It's Buddhism, Jim, but not as we know it.' What did it mean? That what Geoff had been telling me wasn't really Buddhism at all? I mean, I'd taken it all on trust, hadn't I? I hadn't done any independent research, or checked it out with other Buddhists. Sure, what Dora and Piers had told me basically tallied, but they were all part of the same thing, weren't they? Perhaps it was all made up, like so many of these Eastern 'religions'; a mish-mash of teachings taken from all over the place, then whizzed together in the spiritual blender of some guru's imagination and peddled to gullible Westerners as the antidote to their middle-class neuroses.

All my doubts about him came rushing back to the surface. Oh God, I thought. Oh God . . .

***

Another morning, another thick head – and another excuse for not going in to work. I just couldn't face it. I phoned the twenty-year-old pin-stripe to say I thought I had food poisoning. His 'Right . . .' was so knowing he could have been looking at the empty whisky bottle in the kitchen bin. But I didn't care. At least I could spend the rest of the morning in bed. By lunchtime I'd recovered enough to consume four rounds of toast and a couple of cups of tea. And then I went straight down to the public library. I had to look up the address in the phone book, as it's not one of my local haunts. But it wasn't too far and the walk cleared my head.

For a while. Wading through the encyclopaedia entry on Buddhism totally did it in again. Talk about difficult. Obscure, abstruse, full of strange words in italics with lots of unpronounceable consonants and dots over odd letters.

164

Even the bits I could read I couldn't understand, like this:

The twelve-linked chain of causation teaches the causal relationship of ignorance and suffering. (1) ignorance gives rises to (2) action, which causes (3) consciousness, which causes (4) name and form, which cause (5) the six sense organs, which cause (6) contact, which causes (7) sensation, which causes (8) desire, which causes (9) attachment, which causes (10) existence, which causes (11) birth, which causes (12) ageing and death.

Which means what, precisely? Some parts I could get, just about; but how the hell does action cause consciousness, or attachment cause existence? Clear as mud. I put the encyclopaedia aside and turned to something lighter, a sort of beginner's guide to Buddhism, where I came across this:

The four noble truths is a fundamental doctrine of Buddhism clarifying the cause of suffering and the way of emancipation. They are (1) the truth of suffering – all existence is suffering; (2) the truth of the origin of suffering – suffering is caused by selfish craving; (3) the truth of the cessation of suffering – the eradication of selfish craving brings about the cessation of suffering and enables one to attain nirvana; and (4) the truth of the path to the cessation of suffering – the eradication of selfish craving can be achieved through the eightfold path. This consists of right views, right thinking, right speech, right action, right way of life, right endeavour, right mindfulness and right meditation.

165

A fundamental doctrine, eh? And yet Geoff hadn't even mentioned it. Plus there was nothing in what I read about the Ten Worlds, or *ichinen*, or *kyo chi gyo i* or *ku* or human revolution or the oneness of life and its environment or *anything* he had told me. It might have been interesting, it might even have made sense, but it wasn't Buddhism – at least, not according to these books. I would have to talk to him about it – tomorrow, before my faith in him was blown away completely. By my reckoning he would still be cleaning his corporate tower, so I planned to hook up with him at lunchtime and have it out there and then.

***

Things didn't go quite according to plan.

I get to Regence House at my normal time, just before nine, ride up in the packed lift and squeeze my way out at the fourth floor. Through the swing doors, past the polished reception desk, into the twilight zone – and stop. The strip-light is on in my cubby-hole. I hear a voice – female. I go closer. She's talking on the phone, smiling, animated. She hangs up, sees me, is surprised – we both are – and it turns out she's working here. 'But I work here,' I protest. She's confused, I'm confused, I call the pin-stripe – and I'm told I've been replaced. She was going to sit in just for the day, but she generated so many leads – almost twice as many as my average – that they've decided to keep her. So goodbye, Ed. I object, get cross, bluster, but it's no use. I'm only a temp and I should take it up with the agency. Which I try to, but Dora's not answering her phone for some reason. Defeated, I yield the floor to Miss Twice-As-Good-As-Me with as much grace as I can muster – which is none – and five minutes after arriving find myself back on the pavement outside Regence House. Now what?

Obvious. I turned left and headed for the tower. At the end of the street I looked up. The window-cleaning cradle was high above me, way out of hailing range. I counted – it was three floors from the top – then ran up the steps and pushed through the plate-glass doors into a large atrium. A couple of sullen guards sat at a desk in front of me. A pair of escalators rose behind them to the first floor, with banks of lifts to the left and right.

'Yes, sir?' One of the guards had spotted that I wasn't at home.

'Er, Yellowhammer,' I said, glancing quickly at the long list of company names on the wall.

'Nineteenth floor,' he said. So much for security.

I got into one of the lifts and looked at the buttons. There were thirty floors, so I pressed for twenty-seven. A few moments later I stepped out into a carpeted area high above London. To my left and right were large, plate-glass windows onto a panoramic view of the city. Outside the one to the left ran two vertical steel cables. I went over and looked down. Geoff was in the cradle, wiping off the window of the floor below. I thumped on the glass but he didn't react. I looked around, saw the sign for the emergency stairs, dived through the door and down a couple of flights. Geoff was just hitting the down button on his console when I confronted him through the glass. He looked shocked and jabbed at the console. The cradle juddered to a halt.

'What's up?' he shouted. I couldn't hear him, but read his lips.

'I need to talk!' I shouted back.

He frowned, not understanding.

'Talk!' I shouted again, opening and closing my hand like a glove puppet.

His expression brightened – he'd got it. He stabbed his

finger towards the ground, pressed a button on the console, and sank slowly out of sight. I turned from the window to see half a dozen office workers, freshly disgorged from one of the lifts, staring at me with blank curiosity.

***

'What's the matter?' Geoff asked. The cradle had got down to where I was waiting at the foot of the tower, by now feeling pretty foolish.

What could I say? 'Why didn't you tell me about the four noble truths?' It was hardly so urgent I needed his immediate attention, was it?

'I, er . . . I lost my job again,' I said lamely.

'Ah.'

'And Dora's not answering her phone and um . . . I need to talk to someone.' God, what must he think of me? I'm starting to sound like one of those crazy people who lose all sense of proportion. But then, I had – hadn't I? No *honzon*, no anchor. Perhaps this was what a nervous breakdown felt like.

Geoff didn't turn a hair; he just looked at me. 'I need to work, Ed,' he said, jerking a thumb at the tower.

'Yes, of course you do,' I said, embarrassed. 'I don't know what I was thinking of. Sorry.' I started to turn away.

'But if you don't mind heights . . .'

I realised he was offering me a place in the cradle with him.

'It's quite safe,' he said, 'as long as you're clipped on.'

I saw there were a couple of spare harnesses hanging from one of the handrails. I looked up at the tower. It was bloody high.

'Up to you,' he said. 'But if it's an emergency . . .'

'Is it allowed?' I asked.

168

'Well, you'll have to work,' he said. 'Then you'll be covered by my insurance – as my trainee, if you like.'

I hesitated, then decided. 'OK.' I climbed in beside him, he fitted the harness around my waist and clipped me on; and then, with a judder, the cradle started to rise gently up the side of the building. My nervousness rose with it; not because of the height, but because I realised I was going to tell Geoff . . . well, that I didn't trust him, basically.

I stuttered and stumbled through how Dora had explained what a *honzon* was and how I felt I'd lost mine – Angie – which was why I'd been so all over the place and found Buddhism so interesting but I didn't want to make another mistake and put all my eggs in the wrong basket, so to speak, which was why I kept giving him such a hard time about it, but yesterday I'd read all this stuff that didn't sound anything like what he'd told me and it said the four noble truths were a fundamental principle which was news to me and—

'So this isn't about losing your job at all?'

'Well, sort of. It just – you know – brought everything up.'

'"Everything" meaning if what I've been telling you is true.' Straight to the point – again.

'No. Yes. I mean – well, I just don't know.' I grimaced an embarrassed smile and waited for his reaction.

Geoff sniffed. We were now hundreds of feet up, looking down over the rooftops of one of the world's major finance centres, and rocking gently in the wind. Geoff peered in towards the building, then squeezed the console. We stopped. 'Twenty-fifth floor,' he said, and grabbed a short-handled mop from the corner. 'Wash or dry?'

For some reason I didn't answer but looked over the edge of the cradle. I wished I hadn't. Far below me the street started to sway and swim out of focus.

'Don't look down,' Geoff barked.

I snapped my eyes back to his face. He was still holding up the mop.

'Wash or dry?'

I dithered, regaining my equilibrium.

'Washing's easier,' he suggested.

'I'll wash then.'

He handed me the mop and pointed to a small round trough where it had been standing. It was full of soapy water.

'The whole cradle's plumbed in,' he explained. 'Clean water's fed down here, and the dirty stuff's sucked up the other side.'

I saw for the first time that a long hose ran down the length of each steel cable, attached at intervals by metal rings.

'So I don't have to keep going up and down to refill the bucket. And the detergent I mix like so.' He twiddled a little tap above the trough and a thick, whitish liquid dribbled out.

'Cunning.'

'Very.' He rubbed his hands together. 'Right then – a short history of Buddhism, in twenty-five floors.'

***

We worked our way back down the side of the building as Geoff talked. At each level I dipped the mop in the trough, then wet the glass from top left to bottom right. Geoff was right behind me with the squeegee, wiping off the windows with deft, graceful flourishes as he galloped through two-and-half-thousand years of Buddhist development.

'The historical Buddha was this Indian bloke called Siddartha Gautama. He was prince of a tribe called the Shakyas, so when he became famous people started to call him Shakyamuni, which means "sage of the Shakyas". Anyway, as a royal he lived high on the hog till he realised life for people outside his palace was full of suffering. So one day he gives up being prince and sets out on a journey to find out how to overcome what he now thinks are the four unavoidable sufferings of life: birth, sickness, old age and death.' He hit the console button and we sank to the next floor.

'Birth?'

'Into a world full of pain.'

'OK.' We jerked to a stop, I wet the mop and we started on the next window.

'So he travels about,' Geoff continued, 'and tries all sorts of teachings and practices, but eventually he realises he has to look for the solution inside himself. So he sits under this tree and meditates for a long while, until – eureka – he gets the answer.'

'Which is?'

'Well, that's the problem. What he's understood is so deep and mind-blowing that when he tries to explain it to other people no one knows what he's on about. So he has to work out a way of teaching people that'll gradually bring their understanding up to a point where he can share his insight with them. It's been described as like Einstein trying to explain relativity to nursery school kids.'

I grunted. 'Never understood that, either.'

'Ditto,' Geoff said, and hit the console button again. We were making good time, working to a good rhythm, which always seems to help the talk flow. 'Anyway,' he said as we reached the next floor, 'the four noble truths was one of the early steps he taught to sort of lay the basic ground rules of understanding. But he didn't stop there. He developed his teachings over the years until eventually, in the last years of his life, he just taught the Lotus Sutra, which he said was the only sutra that was full and complete. In other words, it contained everything he'd understood.'

171

'Piers said it was the "bees-knees" of Buddhism.'

Geoff laughed, giving his squeegee a wipe with his chamois. 'The bees-knees? Very Piers, that is. But I think he's right.'

'So – problem solved then. Read the Lotus Sutra.'

''Fraid not,' said Geoff. 'Because it's very obscure – full of flowery language, weird creatures, fantastic events. Very difficult. Plus it's not consistent. What's taught in the second half contradicts what's in the first half; and the whole thing contradicts virtually everything else Shakyamuni taught during the rest of his lifetime. In fact, it's so different from most of the other stuff he said that some people wonder if he taught it at all.'

'I don't understand.'

'Some people say it was made up by other Buddhists hundreds of years after his death.'

'Can't you check?'

'How? Shakyamuni taught a long time ago, before writing was invented, even. Everything was memorised and passed on orally.'

'That's a bit dodgy, isn't it? I mean, how do you know if he said any of it?'

'We don't. But some people say it doesn't matter who taught it. What matters is what it actually says.'

'But if it's all full of contradictions . . .'

'Exactly. Which is why there've been so many arguments for such a long time about what Shakyamuni really meant; since the moment he died, virtually.'

'Hmm.' I thought about this as I mopped over another window. 'So why have you gone for the Lotus Sutra, then? Because that's what your practice is based on, isn't it?'

'It is,' said Geoff, rocking from side to side as he drew the squeegee right, then left, then right across the plate glass. 'It's because it deals with this world, the one I'm living in.

For example, most of the other sutras talk about desire as being the root of all suffering, right? You suffer because you want things you can't have, or you get attached to them and then you lose them.'

'Like Angie.'

'Exactly. So those sutras basically teach that the answer lies in training yourself to not want anything. *Nirvana* means to blow out, like blowing out a candle flame, and is supposed to be the state you reach when you've got rid of all your desires. But how realistic is that? Even wanting to reach that state is a desire, so to me it doesn't make sense.'

'What does the Lotus Sutra say?'

'That desires are part of life, they're inescapable. And instead of trying to get rid of them you can transform them, from negative to positive, destructive to constructive.'

I thought about this. Seemed reasonable.

Geoff pressed on. 'Plus the Lotus Sutra is totally democratic. It's the only sutra I know that says everyone can become enlightened – men, women, children, evil people, *everyone* – in this lifetime, here and now. Whereas all the others put riders on it, like saying women have to be reborn as men first, or you have to practise all kinds of austerities for millions of years – which I don't really have time for. Or you have to be reborn in some faraway heaven, which doesn't appeal, frankly. I don't want to escape from daily life. I want something that helps me deal with it – the whole messy, wonderful, business of it.'

I looked at him. 'Wonderful?'

'Yes,' he said, smiling. 'Life's wonderful, death's wonderful. It's all fucking wonderful!' He threw out his arms and yelled into the City sky.

I didn't get it. Death – *wonderful*? Geoff tried to explain about how life and death were just two phases of an unending cycle, and death was like a night's sleep in the eternity of one's life, so it needn't be feared; in fact, coming to terms with it was the basis of true happiness. And I had to admit that he did seem to be living proof of that. But the more he talked the more I realised what a distance there was between us. For me the Big Chill was curtains, finito, The End. And frankly, discussing it while suspended on the outside of a building a couple of hundred feet up in the air gave me the willies.

'Is that why you can do this sort of a job?' I asked with a strained smile.

'How do you mean?'

'Well, it doesn't bother you if, you know . . .' I mimed him falling over the side and splattering on the pavement below.

He looked surprised. 'You think I got a death wish? No way.'

'Well, I just thought that if you don't mind dying . . .'

'I like *life*, Ed. And I like it all the more because I'm not hung up about death, that's all. Besides, not looking after your life is a form of slander.'

'Slander?'

'Anything that denigrates, disrespects, disregards life – yours or someone else's – in Buddhism is called slander and it's a cause for suffering. That includes putting yourself down, or other people, not caring about yourself or other people. Buddhism's about the opposite – caring about yourself and others. Treasuring life, including your own. So in here I wear this at all times.' He rattled his safety harness.

We worked on in silence for a bit as I took this on board. Slander. According to Geoff's definition I was a master at it. Denigrating myself and others came as easily to me as the air I breathed. I let out a long, depressed sigh.

'You all right?' Geoff sounded concerned.

'Fine.'

He studied me for a moment longer, then made a decision. He hit the console and the cradle sank towards the ground.

'What are you doing?'

'Having a break,' he said.

'I'm OK,' I protested.

'Well, I'm not,' he said. 'I need the bog.'

I didn't argue. A minute or so later we reached the street and got out. I was relieved to be back on the ground, to tell the truth, and when Geoff said he might be a little while I took the opportunity he was giving me to push off. I had to see Dora about the Regence House fiasco. Geoff tried to press some cash on me before I went: 'You've earned it,' he said. But I didn't want his money. His time and his knowledge were what I valued, and for now I'd had plenty of both during our ride down the side of the building. So I waved him goodbye and headed for the nearest Tube station – and Dora. Did she know I was going to be chopped? Had she helped arrange it? And, most important of all, could she get me another job?

Another surprise was waiting for me, though, when I got to Baker Street: Personal Personnel was closed. I looked through the glass door but the office was dark. No wonder the phone hadn't been answered. I knocked on the window, just in case she was in the back, but no one came. Maybe she'd taken the day off. But as I was about to turn away I thought I saw a movement. I looked harder. Someone had peeped around the doorway of the small kitchen at the back, I was sure of it. I knocked again, and this time a figure appeared – Dora. She hesitated, then came to the door and unlocked it. I saw at once why she'd been hiding. Her eyes were puffy and her face was streaked with mascara. She'd been crying.

Chapter Eleven

No man I know carries a handkerchief these days; not unless he's over seventy and wears a hat. My dad used to: a neatly folded and ironed square of material that smelled faintly of aftershave. I never saw him blow his nose on it, and I never saw him offer it to a female in distress, either. Even so, when Dora opened the door in tears I immediately started to search my pockets for a handkerchief I knew I didn't have. Perhaps it's some deep male instinct that can't bear the sight of a woman with smudged make-up and a runny nose.

'God, Dora – what's wrong?' I asked. She ushered me in and locked the door behind me.

'The bank,' she sniffled. 'They've called in my loan.'

'What – on this place?' I was shocked.

She nodded and wiped away a tear with a long, polished fingernail, careful not to get any mascara in her eye.

'Excuse me,' she said. 'I was going to wash my face when you knocked.' She disappeared into the back again.

Blimey, and here was me thinking all that talk about possibly going under was just joshing to make me feel better about my situation.

After a short while Dora reappeared, face rinsed and trying to be brave. 'Would you like a cup of tea?'

'In time of crisis what else is there?' I followed her into the 'kitchen', which was no more than a narrow passage containing a sink, a kettle and a stationery cupboard, with the loo behind the door at the end. 'So what happened?' I asked, as she busied herself with the tea.

'The dot-com bust,' she said simply. 'Hiring's been drying up over the summer, and the bank's decided I'm not a good bet any more.' She sighed, tired, and threw a couple of teabags into mugs.

'Bit harsh, isn't it?'

'Not really.' She shrugged. 'I never made any real money, even when times were good. Overheads are too high, competition too fierce.' The kettle clicked off and she poured the boiling water into the mugs. 'Been a long time coming, really.'

'So what are you going to do?'

'Don't know,' she said. 'Milk?'

'Please.'

She fished out the teabags and poured a little milk into each mug.

'Thanks,' I said, as she handed me one.

'Well, that's not strictly true,' she said. 'First I'm going to wind things up here, because I do have a few clients in jobs.' A thought struck her. 'Speaking of which – what are you doing here?'

That answered that question, then: she hadn't known anything about me being replaced. I explained what had happened, my previous day's 'illness', but Dora wasn't buying it.

'Hangover?'

'No,' I lied, trying to sound offended.

Dora grunted. 'Hmm. Well, they didn't call here for a replacement – not surprising if the staff I supply aren't reliable.'

177

'I was ill,' I protested.

Dora sighed again. 'Never mind,' she said. 'Your commission wouldn't have made any difference. Anyway, once I've let everyone know what's happening, I shall go home and chant my little socks off about what to do next and how to pay off my debt.' She sipped her tea.

'How much is it?' I asked.

'More than you've got, Ed.' She smiled. 'Unless you've had a nice fat advance for your bestseller?'

I laughed ruefully.

Then came the question I'd been dreading. 'How's it going, anyway?'

'Erm . . .'

'Or isn't it?'

I looked into my mug sheepishly. 'I got halfway through chapter two and just . . . I don't know. It wasn't any good.'

'Nothing comes of nothing, Ed.'

I sighed deeply. 'I know. I'm useless.'

'No you're not!' she said with sudden fierceness. 'No one's useless. And if you chanted you'd be able to see that and bring out all the fantastic stuff that's locked up inside you. But you won't, will you?'

'No, I won't,' I said, surprising myself with the force of my words, 'because frankly I can't see what difference it makes. I mean you and Geoff and Piers are all very nice people and I admire your attitude to things; but your business has just gone bust, Geoff had a business and now he's a window-cleaner, and Piers is poor, by his own admission—'

'Posh poor,' Dora corrected me. 'Which isn't what you and I understand by poor.'

'OK, but even so, you say how great this thing is you all do and I'm sure it makes you feel better; but as far as I can see it's just another way of rationalising failure.'

178

Dora looked stung.

At once I regretted being so blunt. 'I'm sorry,' I said. 'I didn't mean—'

'No,' she said stiffly. 'You're right. Actual proof's important. For some people, how you cope with difficulty is enough. But other people want to see hard results – and that's important, too.'

'I didn't mean I think you're a failure, Dora,' I said, squirming. 'Of course you're not. Just getting this place going is proof of that. And it's not your fault it's folded, is it?'

'I'm not sure about that,' Dora said. 'I don't think I'm a very good businesswoman.'

'Well, it's more than I've ever done, for God's sake, so who am I to talk?'

'Don't worry.' Dora smiled. 'I'm not offended. I think what you're saying is you want to meet a rich, successful Buddhist – right?'

'No.'

She looked surprised. 'Why not?'

Because it makes me seem shallow and materialistic, I thought. I said, 'Because religion isn't about that, is it? It's about higher things – you know, the spiritual side of life.'

Dora smiled enigmatically and went through to the office. I followed. She was writing a name and telephone number on a Personal Personnel compliments slip. 'Liz Wylie,' she said. 'Makes TV films – and lots of money.' She handed me the slip. 'I'll tell her to expect your call, shall I?'

'Erm . . .' This sounded interesting, but what was I supposed to say: I'm broke, confused and talentless and Dora thought you might be able to help?

Dora saw my hesitation and laughed. 'In for a penny, Ed!'

I looked up from the slip and saw her beaming at me. 'Er . . . OK. Thanks.'

'No – thank you,' she said, and kissed me on the cheek.

'For what?' I said, surprised.

'For coming by, cheering me up.'

'How?' I didn't understand.

'Sometimes, just seeing a friendly face is enough,' she said. 'Like a flower in the desert.'

True. I smiled at her. She smiled at me. I waved the compliments slip. 'I'll call her.'

***

But not at once. First I had to go through my usual agonising. What would she think of me? What did I want? Should I pitch her some TV ideas? Did I *have* any TV ideas? If not, why not? Where could I get some? But what if I gave her a good idea and she nicked it, ripped me off, etcetera? All the usual nonsense, building the whole thing up in my mind, looking at it every which way, imagining all sorts of scenarios, until I was practically rigid with indecision. The paralysis of analysis. Or so I told myself; until finally, sitting in my flat looking at the phone number on the compliments slip, I admitted the truth. I was scared. Being with successful people made me feel totally inadequate, especially if their success was in a field anywhere close to my ambitions – writing, film, television. They had 'It' and I didn't. They'd made it and I hadn't. I was a wannabe, they were the real thing. And they'd sniff out my desperate, servile longing the moment I was ushered into their presence.

Low self-esteem – *moi*?

Then I remembered Dora. 'In for a penny, Ed!' I couldn't let her down, could I? Feel the fear and do it anyway. Faint heart never won fair lady. Nothing ventured, nothing gained. Courage – that's what I needed.

And then I had one of those moments when a whole string of disparate thoughts just come together. 'Courage' and 'encourage' – they had to be related. Dora and Geoff and Piers had all been encouraging me in one way or another, trying to give me courage. Or rather, urging me to summon up my courage, because it was definitely in there somewhere, only sleeping. And then I thought about wisdom and compassion, the other two parts of the trio they said made up this thing they called Buddhahood; and for some reason *The Wizard of Oz* came into my mind because I suddenly realised it was talking about exactly the same thing. The tin-man and the scarecrow and the lion were all aspects of Buddhahood. The tin-man needed a heart – compassion. The scarecrow needed a brain – wisdom. And the cowardly lion needed courage. They went off to see the Wizard to get what they needed, but he taught them that they all had those qualities inside themselves already.

I was so knocked out by this revelation that I couldn't move for a while. It might not sound much, but it was as if what Dora and Geoff and Piers were telling me had suddenly been validated by an external, independent authority – the bloody Wizard of Oz! And was it just a coincidence that this independent verification came through a film, *and here I was about to make contact with a Buddhist film/TV producer*? That really was bollocks, of course, because in no way am I superstitious. Although there is no such thing as coincidence, right?

Anyway, all this eventually convinced me that I had to make the call. And the moment I did . . .

'Oh yes. Dora said you'd be calling. You've got some questions about Buddhism.'

'Erm, well, yes, if er—'

'No problem. I could do with a break; if you're free a bit later, say three o'clock?'

Simple as that – which made all my agonising seem pretty foolish. But then, if I hadn't tormented myself like that I wouldn't have had my realisation, would I? No pain, no gain. I allowed myself a little smile: I was starting to sound like a Buddhist.

***

Liz Wylie lived in an FBH in Notting Hill, just up the road from Holland Park. It dripped money. Just keeping the outside white and gleaming must cost thousands, I reckoned, climbing the front steps. An attractive but harassed-looking woman in her early forties opened the door to me. She was barefoot, in jeans and baggy jumper, and had a cordless phone clamped to her ear.

'Liz?' I asked tentatively.

She nodded.

'I'm Ed.'

She smiled and pointed to a front room off the hallway. I made for it as she continued her conversation. 'Yes,' she said, 'I understand all that. But the bottom line, Frank, is that Discovery want the changes and if you're not prepared to do them I'll have to find someone who is – OK?'

The front room was an office, drowning in scripts. They bowed the shelves that lined the walls on three sides. They covered the old, leather-topped desk by the window, and the battered Chesterfield sofa by the fireplace. They stood in piles all over the floor, like termite hills. It was hard to know where to put my feet. A framed quotation on the desk caught my eye: 'A great revolution of character in just a single individual will help achieve a change in the destiny of a nation and, further, a change in the destiny of all

182

humankind.' Hmm. Liz entered before I could pursue the thought, still on the phone.

'Fine, Frank – then think about it. But not too long, because I need to know by first thing tomorrow . . . Right.' She ended the call and looked at me brightly. 'Writers, eh?'

I laughed – yeah, what a bunch. 'It's very good of you to see me,' I said.

'No, it's my benefit,' she said, moving a pile of scripts from the Chesterfield to the floor and gesturing me to sit down. 'This business is madness and dropping a bit of Buddhism into the middle of the day helps restore a speck of sanity, you know?'

I didn't but smiled anyway.

'So, how can I help?'

'Erm . . .' I decided to plunge in. 'Well, I suppose the problem is I'm interested in applying the theory, the philosophy, to my situation. But I'm really not into all the praying stuff – you know, the chanting.'

'Yes, Dora said to keep off the religious side.'

'Really?' I sent her my silent thanks.

'Well, if it's any help,' Liz continued, 'what hooked me was that you could use Buddhism practically, and let the religious bit come later, as you started to see the benefit.'

'Sounds interesting.'

It was. She'd met the practice via a TV director while working as a continuity girl on 'some crummy series', and was really impressed by how he handled the pressure and always seemed to be able to turn things round. She wanted to get on in the TV business but felt stuck, so at his suggestion she gave chanting a go. 'Miraculously' – her word – soon afterwards she was offered a job 'out of the blue' as a script reader for a long-running series, and thought that with chanting as her ace in the hole it was only a matter of time before she worked her way up to producer, executive producer and, eventually, 'God'. Then she hit the buffers.

'I started to feel more and more uncomfortable about chanting for success, about using a religion – and Buddhism, at that, because it had always seemed so other-worldly to me – about using religion to gain material benefit. It just didn't feel right. I was OK about using it to feel better about myself, or to get stronger, or chanting for other people or world peace or whatever; but actually to get more money? A better job, a bigger house?' She shook her head. 'And then I realised I had this basically Christian view about religion and the material world – you know, they don't mix.'

'Render unto Caesar that which is Caesar's?'

She nodded. 'Exactly. And unto God that which is God's. They're totally separate realms, dealing with totally different things and values; and basically, the religious, spiritual realm is "higher". You know, it's all about love and self-sacrifice and saving your soul; while the material world is grubby and selfish and animal.'

'Sounds like we went to the same school.' I laughed.

'Well, that's the funny thing,' she said. 'I didn't have a religious upbringing at all. I'd just sort of absorbed these attitudes from my surroundings. Anyway, it took me quite a time to understand that Buddhism doesn't teach this separation.'

'No?'

'No. It teaches *shikishin funi*, the oneness of mind and body, or the material and non-material aspects of life.'

This was starting to sound familiar. 'Is this the Three Truths?' I asked.

Liz looked surprised. 'It's based on it, yes.'

'Geoff told me about it.'

'Geoff who?'

My stomach suddenly lurched. I realised that I didn't even know his second name. How self-absorbed is that? 'Geoff the window-cleaner,' I said. 'He's the one who put me onto Dora.'

'Oh, I know,' said Liz. 'I was on a course with him a couple of years ago. A study course.' Then she frowned. 'Are you all right?'

I was starting to overheat again. A deep flush was creeping up my head from my collar, and it was only a matter of time before the sweat popped out all over.

'Don't worry,' I said, forcing a smile. 'Wonky thermostat.' Same joke, but she hadn't heard it.

'I don't think the heating's on,' she said, straight-faced.

'I mean, my thermostat. It's OK – it'll pass in a moment. Go on.'

'Well,' said Liz, trying not to be distracted by my imminent spontaneous combustion, 'the Three Truths applied to living beings is expressed as the oneness of mind and body. What happens in your body is also expressed in your mind, and what happens in your mind is expressed in your body – they're just different aspects of the same life. So physical illness tends to make people suffer mentally, for example, while unhappiness also produces physical effects.'

'I see,' I said – and I did. Because wasn't my Niagara of embarrassment a prime example of what she was saying? This spectacular blushing was due to something completely intangible and abstract, a profound mental disturbance that only I was aware of, and which other people would probably find extremely silly – knowing which only made it worse. I sensed it was somehow linked to how I saw myself; because when that mental image was shaken, for some reason I exploded into this welter of sweat and confusion. It was a psychosomatic short-circuit;

185

a sudden, unexpected and overwhelming system breakdown that I could do nothing to avert or control. I simply had to suffer and wait for my self-righting mechanism to bring everything slowly back to balance. But why the reaction was so extreme – well, that was a complete mystery.

All this I teased out afterwards, as I tried to make sense of the experience. For now, I blinked through the sweat and tried to concentrate on Liz's words.

'But Buddhism applies the Three Truths to everything. There's a Buddhist quotation – "No affairs of life or work are in any way separate from the ultimate reality" – which basically means that the spiritual side of life isn't "up there" in Heaven, or hidden behind or beyond everyday life, but is actually an intrinsic part of it and revealed in ordinary, everyday stuff.'

'Right . . .' I sort of understood what she was talking about, but mainly I was aware – thank God – that I was cooling down again.

Liz looked at me intently, not sure if I had fully grasped her point. She stood up, thrust a hand into a pocket in her jeans and pulled out a pound coin. 'Take this pound coin,' she said. 'It's the physical aspect of an entity called a pound sterling. Its value – what it can buy – is the non-physical aspect. Both have changed massively over the years. For example . . .' She pulled open a drawer in the desk and rummaged through it. 'Here we are.' She produced a white envelope, and from it an old pound note. 'Remember these?' She handed it to me. 'That was the last version of the pound note before they abolished it. I don't know what it bought then but I know it wouldn't be the same as today, even if you could use it. So its value isn't the same and physically it isn't the same, but it's still a pound sterling. It's got a unique identity that doesn't change; in fact, which stretches back to some point in the eighth century. I know because I did research on it for a programme once.' She smiled.

'Right,' I said. 'So . . .?'

'So in Buddhism there's no rendering unto Caesar that which is Caesar's and unto God that which is God's, because they're just different aspects – physical and spiritual – of the same thing.'

'Right,' I said again. 'And so . . . ?'

'And so with Buddhism you have a religion that concerns itself both with the material *and* the spiritual aspects of life. One's not "higher" or more worthy than the other. Both are important, and part of the challenge of being happy is finding a balance – the Middle Way – between the two.'

'Ah. I understand now,' I said – and again, I did. The flush had passed, normal service was resumed and I could think – and see, now the cascade of sweat had dried up – clearly.

Liz continued. 'For example, lack of money – the physical – produces suffering, which is mental-stroke-spiritual. But too much money can also produce suffering, if you don't know how to use it.'

'Really? I thought you couldn't be too rich or too thin.'

Liz smiled. 'If you met some of the people in my business you'd know that neither of those is true. Basically,' she said, 'what I've learned is money's neutral. It functions according to our life state.'

'The Ten Worlds?'

'Dora's explained those, has she?'

'Geoff.'

'Right. How about *esho funi* – the oneness of life and its environment?'

I nodded.

187

'Well, money's just a part of our environment, so it reflects our life state.'

'How?'

'OK,' she said, 'take Hell. Money can make us suffer. And I don't mean being broke but actually having it. Like this friend of mine, Yorkshire lass, very pretty, non-Buddhist. She married an Arab who wasn't just rich but obscenely rich. His family had a huge estate in Saudi, somewhere up in the hills, where the wedding took place – which is where she really started to suffer. She was brought up Protestant, you see, and not to be ostentatious, and she found it incredibly hard to accept the huge gap in wealth between her husband's family and the peasants who lived on their estate. The worst moment, she said, was when she was literally showered with money by people who had virtually nothing; who'd scraped together what little they had for this wedding to show support for their local lord. She said she was almost physically sick.'

'That would have been one for the album: bride chucks up on wedding day.'

'Well, the marriage didn't last long – which wasn't a complete surprise. But the odd thing is she's struggled for money ever since.'

'Why?'

'My guess is deep down she's afraid that having money will corrupt her in some way – which is probably a hangover from her upbringing. You know, "the love of money is the root of all evil." Which I think she might interpret at some level as "the hatred of money is the root of all good." Who knows?'

'Deep.'

'Deeply hidden, yes. But I think a lot of attitudes about money are.'

'Right, so that's Hell.'

She nodded.

What's next? HHAAHH . . . 'Hunger?'

'The world of desires. Well, that's more obvious: we want money, desire it, crave it. Although – strange paradox – fundamentally, people dominated by Hunger don't really want the thing they think they're craving.'

'No?'

'No. They want to fill a vacuum at the centre of their lives, and fix on money – or drink or drugs or sex or serial relationships or whatever – as the means to fill that vacuum.'

I had a flashback to the alkies in my local where I'd bashed my head.

'There's a not very good script up there somewhere,' said Liz, waving at the shelves, 'about an addictive gambler – obviously written by one. But the message that comes across is he's not really interested in money.'

I looked surprised.

'He's addicted to uncertainty, to the excitement of possibly winning money, but also possibly losing it. It's the buzz he's after, not the result. Or look at Robert Maxwell. As soon as he closed one deal he'd be off hunting the next. But when he got it he seemed to lose interest and would have to go after more. Until everything exploded – like that huge guy in Monty Python's *Meaning of Life*.'

'Mr Creosote.'

'That's the one. A final after-dinner mint he doesn't even want and – boom.'

'So you're saying that no matter how much or how little you've got, if you're in Hunger you stay in Hunger.'

'Exactly. You can't change any basic life condition just by changing your environment. Princess Diana lived in a palace and was still unhappy.'

You can't change any basic life condition just by

changing your environment: was this true? I filed it for later mulling and looked round the room. 'So what does this environment say about *your* life condition?' I asked, nodding to the piles of scripts.

Liz laughed. 'It's actually very organised, believe it or not. We try to read them all but it's a constant struggle. Once people know you're in films and telly you get scripts from everywhere. The ones on the shelf are read, rejected and eventually recycled. The ones here' – on the desk – 'are current projects. These' – on the sofa – 'are possibles. These' – on the bookcase behind her – 'are projects we've actually made. And the rest' – waving a hand at the termite hills– 'are in the waiting-room.'

I plucked up some courage. 'Need any help?'

'Reading?'

I nodded. 'I love films.' Which wasn't completely true, as I hadn't been to the cinema for months. But as long as she didn't ask me about any recent releases . . .

She didn't. She hesitated slightly, then pointed to an especially tall pile. 'OK. That one's got copies of everything. Take a couple and let me know what you think.'

'Thanks,' I said, taking two at random.

'I can't pay you, I'm afraid.'

'That's OK. It's as much for my benefit – to see how it's done.'

'Or not, more likely.'

I smiled, happy: I was back in the film business. 'So where were we? Money and the Ten Worlds. HHA . . . Animality.'

'Is foolishness. So it relates to people who basically do dumb things with their money. Like lottery winners who spend, spend, spend until all the money's gone and they've got nothing to show for it. People in Animality live for the present – eat, drink and be merry for tomorrow we die.

Except usually we don't. We just wake up broke, with a hangover.'

I gave a little laugh, but squirmed inside. This sounded like me. So was I dominated by Animality? But then, Hell and Hunger rang pretty loud bells, too. Three out of three of the lowest life states – a nap hand. 'Anger?' I asked, moving swiftly on.

'Very interesting. For people in Anger, in the Buddhist sense – ego, competitiveness, that sort of thing – money's essentially a means of keeping score. You see it a lot in this business; well, in business generally. Money's a weapon, a means of fighting and winning, and to show others who's top dog.'

'Well, that's one I definitely don't have any experience of,' I said, relieved.

'Me neither,' she said. 'But my husband did. He was a producer out in LA when he started to chant – basically, to be more successful, because he'd co-produced a minor Hollywood film and wanted to move into the big-time. But competition out there's intense, and even though he had this decent credit on his résumé he found it hard to get good work. He turned down a lot of rubbish because it was all beneath him, and since he had money in the bank he could afford to. But after a year it started to run out – and so did the job offers, even the rubbish ones. Anyway, to cut a long story short, eventually he had to take an office job and move to a small apartment out of town.'

'Was he still chanting?'

'Like fury.'

'What – even though it was having the opposite effect to what he wanted?'

'Well, the thing was, he kept having all these realisations about himself.'

'Like?'

'Like he realised that, fundamentally, he didn't really like himself. Deep down he didn't think he was worth anything as a person and had chased success to prove to everyone – including himself – that his life meant something. The money and the big house and the glamorous jobs he'd had were just the score, what he presented to the outside world. But inside, basically, he felt there was nothing.'

'And that kept him going?' To my ears he sounded a bit of a masochist.

'Well, that and meeting me.' She flashed a smile. 'Benefit comes in all forms.'

'You were already chanting?'

'Yes. I met him through the practice.'

'And you were attracted even though he was having such a hard time?'

'No – *because* he was having a hard time and was so incredibly cheerful and positive about it. And funny. He was a comedy producer, you see. It's hard to get out of the system.'

'Right.' I knew nothing; nothing about women, anyway. She was attracted to a failure – because of his attitude. I remembered something my dad had once told me: that no woman will stay with a man for whom she's lost respect. So perhaps the real failure wasn't the loss of external success but something inside. I thought of Angie. She hadn't been attracted by my success – I'd never had any – but by something she saw in me. Promise, perhaps; some sort of light, maybe; but something intangible. And when that went, she did too. Hmm. Maybe there was something after all to this 'inside-outside self' thing, this oneness of life and its environment.

'Sounds an interesting bloke,' I said, after this moment's reflection.

192

'He is.' Liz smiled. 'It's a shame you can't meet him but he's out in LA at the moment. We're producing a major drama-doc with Discovery about the Japanese War Crimes Tribunal.'

'Sounds a bundle of laughs – for a comedy producer.'

She smiled again. 'He's had to branch out. That's one of the things he learned from his experience. Anyway.' She glanced at her watch. 'You want to hear the rest of the Ten Worlds and money, or . . .'

'If you've got time.'

'Quickly, yes. Only Tim will be calling from LA soon.'

'As quick as you like.'

'OK. The world of Humanity and money is where we do the sensible thing: we make a budget, live within our means, more or less, and would probably like a bit more money but aren't really fussed enough to do a lot about it. It's where we're level-headed, realistic and basically prudent – but with a little flutter now and then, perhaps.'

'OK.'

'Heaven – or Rapture – is when money makes us feel good. When it comes unexpectedly, or at just the right moment, or as the reward for our efforts or talents. Or when we realise that thanks to this money we can get something we want, for ourselves or someone else. But the feeling doesn't last. So shopaholics, for example, have to keep buying new things to try to hold onto that rapture.'

'So it's like Hunger, then?'

'It's closely related, yes. Hunger's the world of desires. Heaven or Rapture comes when a desire's satisfied.'

'Right.' I was beginning to join the dots, I felt.

Liz glanced at her watch again and pressed on. 'If you think about money in a detached, intellectual sort of way, that's Learning and Realisation. A student reading economic theory in a textbook is in the world of Learning, while someone like Keynes, who developed the theory from observing how economies actually work – or how he thought they did – is an example of the world of Realisation.'

'OK,' I said, doing a quick mental count. 'That's eight. Hell, Hunger, Animality, Anger, Humanity, Heaven, Learning and Realisation. Bodhisattva?'

'A Bodhisattva uses money to lessen suffering. You've heard of Andrew Carnegie?'

'As in Carnegie Hall?'

'That's right. He was the Bill Gates of the nineteenth century. Made a fortune from iron and steel. Anyway, he once said that, "The man who dies rich dies disgraced." So he gave away most of his money before he died to things he considered deserving causes. He probably made his money in the worlds of Hunger and Anger – because apparently he was a ruthless shit in business – but when he gave it away he was in the world of Bodhisattva.'

'Interesting. So what's the Buddha's attitude to money?'

'Basically, that money isn't the root of all evil – we are. But we're the root of all good, too. So it's all up to us. Money's just another fact of life. Treat it with respect but don't worship it or base your life on it. Use it to create the maximum value in any situation.'

'And if you haven't got any?' Like me.

'Well,' said Liz, 'someone once said that money's like the air we breathe. It's all around us. The problem is, some of us are asthmatic.'

I started a fake cough.

Liz laughed. 'So the solution is to develop healthy lungs.'

'Which means what, exactly?'

'Personally,' she said, 'since it was a Buddhist who said it, I think it means to develop the life condition of Buddhahood. You create good fortune through developing your

194

wisdom, your courage and compassion.'

'And if you're not going to practise Buddhism?' Like me.

'Then I suppose you could interpret it to mean changing how you look at money, think about it, use it – all that. I used to be very easy-come-easy-go about it, so there were times I was flush and others when I wasn't. Animality, basically. Now I'm a lot more methodical – boring, but very effective; which means I've been able to accumulate some.'

I looked round the room. 'So I see.'

'And Tim turning things round hasn't hurt.'

'And how did he do that, exactly, apart from chanting?'

'Gratitude. And sincerity.'

'Sincerity?'

She nodded.

'As in, once you can fake that you can fake anything?'

'Well, that's just the point,' she said. 'He learned not to fake it.' She gave me another smile – my cue to leave.

As she showed me to the door one more question came to me. 'What about Dora? You know about the bank pulling the plug on her?'

'She told me, yes.'

'Well, she's been practising a long time. Where's her good fortune?'

Liz tapped her chest-bone. 'Inconspicuous benefit,' she said. 'It's in here: her life state, her attitude.'

'OK, but she's still broke.'

'When someone in Buddhahood has money,' said Liz, 'he – or she – uses it to create the maximum possible value. When they don't they're naturally supported and protected by their environment, including the people around them who recognise their true worth. And from a deeper perspective, they use their misfortune to teach others.'

'Teach others what?'

'That they can overcome any suffering and become stronger, more courageous, compassionate and wiser.'

'Through Buddhism?'

'Yes, or maybe just through encouraging them not to give up. So perhaps somewhere deep in Dora's life she actually wanted this to happen.'

I laughed – absurd.

'To teach you.'

The sceptical smile disappeared from my face; she was being serious. But before I could ask her more the phone rang.

'That'll be Tim,' said Liz.

'Thanks for your time. And I'll let you know about these.' I waved the scripts.

'No hurry,' she said with a smile. 'And good luck.' She closed the door.

196

Chapter Twelve

Going home on the 27 bus, crawling along Westbourne Grove, I kept thinking about the phrase Liz had tossed out to sum up her past attitude to money: 'Animality, basically.' Because that same easy-going attitude was mine; and her description of other aspects of the life state rang all sorts of uncomfortable bells. So did that mean I was dominated by Animality, always living for the present, not really thinking about the consequences of my actions, driven by animal instinct?

I tried to join some more of the dots. Fancying Angie – that was certainly very animal, but it didn't really count because you were allowed to fancy women in this Buddhism, right? So, swearing at Martin – definitely. Almost got me fired. In fact, falling into that job in the first place was totally unplanned. I'd met him in a wine bar, we'd got chatting, he offered me the job and I'd said yes on the spot. Then there was running out to check if the window-cleaner was Geoff – very impulsive. Then getting in the cradle with him – ditto; I had no idea what might happen. Plus there was getting plastered that night, knowing I should be going in to work the next day, so losing the gig – stupid. So was telling Geoff to piss off at the hospital, when he was trying to help me. And confiding in Dora about Angie without thinking it

197

through. And setting up that Holocaust meeting between Geoff and Angie just because I wanted to see her again . . . It was all stupid, foolish. There was no thought in any of it. I just did what I felt like at the time, and if it didn't work out, I simply moved on. And where would that get me in the long run? Nowhere.

Hang on, though. What about writing my book? That wasn't Animality. If I'd understood properly, that was Realisation – trying to make sense of the world through my own efforts and observation. Except I hadn't kept it up, had I? As soon as I got stuck it was 'put-this-bloody-thing-away-it's-too-hard-and-have-a-drink-to-cheer-up'. So, Animality again. An image flashed into my mind: a cartoon of a bloke lying in bed in some poky flat. All you could see were his feet sticking out from under the duvet and a thought bubble rising from the other end of the bed: 'Of course, what I'd really like to do is direct.' Angie had stuck it on my fridge as a joke, but even at the time I'd felt a sting, like she was trying to tell me something. Perhaps if I'd listened harder back then she'd still be around.

That cartoon was next to one I'd stuck on the fridge myself. A group of Japanese monks with bald heads are kneeling at the feet of the chief monk, all very serious, and he's saying to them, 'The road to enlightenment is long and difficult – which is why I asked you all to bring sandwiches and a change of clothing.' At the time I just thought it was funny but perhaps there was a deeper reason for keeping it. No coincidence, again? And what about this whole Buddhism thing, anyway? That couldn't be Animality, surely. Talking to Geoff and Dora, even making this trip to see Liz – that was Learning, wasn't it? Trying to better myself through knowledge gained from other people. So maybe I wasn't just an animal after all.

Until it occurred to me that most of what they'd been

telling me had gone in one ear and out the other, and the thing they all stressed – this chanting business – I absolutely refused to have anything to do with. But was that Animality – or reason? If something doesn't make sense, that doesn't automatically make you stupid, does it? It might just be a bunch of bollocks, like that Indian bloke who persuaded a whole load of middle-class Westerners to give him all their money because he was supposed to know the meaning of life – and then shagged all the women and drove around in a fleet of white Rolls-Royces. And still they worshipped him! How stupid was that? So maybe not wanting to chant was wisdom, not Animality. And wisdom's part of Buddhahood, isn't it? Except chanting's supposed to give you that, so . . . I stopped. This was doing my head in.

Then I remembered the scripts. Liz had said that becoming a script-reader had been how she'd moved into a new career, so why not for me? I looked at my pick. Neither title inspired much confidence – *Diamonds Are For Eva* and *The Basement* – but *Diamonds* was a good half-inch thinner, so I opened it up, turned three pages of dramatis personae and character notes, and started on the film proper.

FADE IN.

EXT. LUAWAMBA MINE. DAY
WIDE SHOT of a vast, open-cast diamond mine somewhere in Africa. Black WORKERS, carrying baskets of the rich, red earth on their heads, swarm over it like ants, their taut, muscular bodies glistening with sweat in the equatorial sun. PULL BACK to reveal a blond SS man watching them – FISCHER. He's also sweating, in full uniform, and carries a riding-crop that he taps impatiently against his shiny, black boots. Nazi GUARDS are stationed all around the top of the mine, some in machine-gun nests.

Suddenly, a shout goes up. FISCHER looks across to the top of a long ladder down into the mine. A GUARD is struggling with a worker – or should that be SLAVE? Other GUARDS rush to help and the SLAVE is quickly over-powered. Calmly, unhurried, FISCHER walks over. The GUARD forces open the SLAVE's hand. CU – HAND: it is holding a single, small diamond. FISCHER takes it from the SLAVE. Their eyes meet: FISCHER's – cold, merciless; the SLAVE's – terrified, pleading. Calmly, unhurried, FISCHER takes the Luger from his belt and puts the barrel end to the SLAVE's head. The SLAVE screams. CU – TRIGGER: the finger squeezes. Bang.

CUT TO:

INT. REICHSCHANCELLERIE. DAY
CU – RING ON FINGER: it is encrusted with diamonds.

EVA (OOS)
Oh, Adolf – it's beautiful!

Reveal EVA (Braun) admiring the ring on her finger. In the background HITLER is studying a large map of Russia that shows the Red Army pushing back the Germans – in all sectors.

HITLER
It ought to be. It cost me enough.
EVA
(surprised)
You paid for it?
HITLER
(grunts)
With a division of my finest men.

Which was as good as it got. The plot, boiled down, has Eva Braun giving Hitler a hard time unless she's kept in a constant supply of diamonds – *or so Hitler wants British Intelligence to believe*, because while she gets the big, flashy stuff, his real interest is in the industrial diamonds he needs (eh?) for his pioneering nuclear weapons programme. The SOE rumbles the operation and have to blow up something crucial just before it . . . well, that's literally where I lost the plot – and the will to live. *Raiders of the Lost Ark* meets *Heroes of Telemark* meets *A Pile of Crap*.

I glanced out of the window. We were inching along the Marylebone Road, snarled in rush-hour traffic. Nothing for it but to investigate *The Basement*. Again, it started promisingly.

FADE IN.

EXT.   SUBURBAN STREET.   DAY
Pleasant music over a sunny Sunday morning in a bog-standard suburban street in a bog-standard suburb of a bog-standard town. CHARLIE JONES is walking back with the Sunday papers and a carton of milk. He waves cheerily to a NEIGHBOUR mowing his front lawn. Another NEIGHBOUR is trimming his front hedge. CHARLIE nods to him with a smile, then turns up the path to his house. He takes out a large bunch of keys, opens his front door and turns to survey the street with a look of satisfaction. He enters, the door closes.

CUT TO:

INT.   KITCHEN.   DAY
A brief montage of CHARLIE cooking and eating a full English breakfast: bacon sizzling in the pan; tomatoes under the grill; bread going into the toaster;

eggs being fried; tea being made; toast popping up; CHARLIE eating while reading the paper; his empty plate being pushed back – all to the sound of *Desert Island Discs* on the radio in the background.

Finally, CHARLIE finishes the paper and glances at the kitchen clock: nearly midday. He sniffs, picks his teeth, then takes his big bunch of keys and gets up from the table.

CUT TO:

INT. HALLWAY. DAY
CHARLIE comes out of the kitchen. In front of him is a door under the stairs. CHARLIE selects a key from his bunch and unlocks the door.

CUT TO:

INT. BASEMENT. DAY
As the door opens, light floods into the darkness; we are at the bottom of a flight of stairs, looking up. CHARLIE enters, flicks on a light, and comes down the stairs. Unsettling music in the background.

CHARLIE reaches the foot of the stairs and turns on another light. We see the basement has been fitted out like an S&M dungeon. OK, we think, so he's into kinky sex. Big deal. He goes round the room, checking out the equipment, pulling on restraining straps, swishing a cat-o'-nine-tails, opening and closing handcuffs with a key from his bunch, feeling the point of a long, sharp spike. He smiles – all seems in order. His smile fades. Slowly, he turns around. Facing him is a large wardrobe. He chooses a key from his bunch, licks his lips in anticipation, then unlocks the door. He opens it.

Inside is a YOUNG WOMAN. She is naked, gagged, her hands tied to a hook above her head and her feet bound tightly by cord. She screws up her eyes against the light and tries to scream, terrified, but the gag won't allow her. CHARLIE waits. Gradually, the YOUNG WOMAN calms down and opens her eyes. She sees CHARLIE and whimpers with terror. He smiles and reaches out to her. She flinches, but all he does is remove her gag. 'See?' his expression seems to say. 'Nothing to worry about.' But she watches him closely, her breathing shallow, fearful. She's about to speak when CHARLIE puts his finger to his lips – ssh. Then suddenly, from behind his back, he produces the spike. He holds it up, between their faces. His is gleeful, hers horrified.

CUT TO:

INT.   HALLWAY.   DAY
The YOUNG WOMAN's piercing scream.

CUT TO:

EXT.   CHARLIE'S HOUSE.   DAY
The YOUNG WOMAN's piercing scream ...

CUT TO:

EXT.   SUBURBAN STREET.   DAY
The YOUNG WOMAN's piercing scream . . . is not heard by the NEIGHBOUR mowing his lawn. Or the NEIGHBOUR trimming his hedge. Or anybody.

Bloody hell, I thought; this is powerful stuff. Gruesome, but compelling. I was hooked, which is the whole point of an opening (I'd read somewhere). I turned the pages, expecting a tale about the dark, subterranean murk that runs under the banal normality of our so-called 'civilised' society.

What I got was torture. Then more torture. Then even more torture. Each scene was more elaborate and more painful than the last, and with each one I felt more and more nauseated. And then, probably as a defence mechanism, the scenarios became so ludicrous that I started to laugh in disbelief; until even that wore off and I became bored, then irritated and finally, as the bus ground its way at last to my stop outside Camden Town Tube, deeply troubled. I glanced again at the name on the title page: Greg Emerson, 14 Whittingdale Drive, Grimsby, Lincs. Perhaps I ought to call the local constabulary, I thought, and suggest they check out Greg's basement – just to be on the safe side.

I felt vaguely depressed as I trudged the couple of hundred yards to my flat. These two writers had both had good ideas – or so they thought – and had slaved God knows how long over their computers to turn them into scripts. Both had tried hard, had done their best, had troubled to print out their efforts, bind them, post them off – probably to several companies. And yet both had come up with total garbage. But at least they'd finished. I hadn't got beyond chapter two, which was just as well, maybe. For who's to say if my offering wouldn't be dismissed with the same mixture of contempt and annoyance I was showing towards *Diamonds Are For Eva* and *The Basement*?

By the time I got home I'd made a decision. They might not be great scripts, but I owed the writers some respect – there but for the grace of God, etc. I would sit down and write a proper report on each: a brief summary of the plot, observations on strengths and weaknesses, and suggestions for improvement. They might not help the writers but they might impress Liz, which was much more important. Perhaps I could become a script editor or, better still, a script doctor, one of those anonymous guys who rewrites other people's screenplays and gets paid vast sums for his trouble.

I set about the task with gusto. Taking apart someone else's work is always a lot easier than struggling to produce something original yourself. It was like being back at uni, doing Eng. Lit. As I worked I started to notice how both stories relied on an incident of extreme violence up front to grab the audience's attention; and then more violence – with a sprinkling of sex – whenever the narrative started to flag, which was often, especially in *The Basement*. The overall effect was of unpleasant characters being unpleasant to other unpleasant characters; the strong dominating the weak and people basically treating each other like animals . . .

I froze. Animals . . . Animality . . . Surely not. But there was no way round it. Out of all the scripts I could have chosen, I'd picked two that were riven with – gulp – Animality.

'Life and its environment are one . . .'

Nah, I told myself, this is just superstition. Most scripts are full of sex and violence, so the chances of picking a couple like this are actually quite high. True, the other half of me said, but that just means you're drawn to a business dominated by the stuff, by Animality. Which brings you back to this life and environment thing. *Funi*: two but not two, not two but two.

I flicked back through the scripts. Perhaps I was reading something into them that wasn't there? But no – there was barely a page on which anyone did anything halfway decent for anyone else. No Humanity, let alone Bodhisattva or Buddhahood, but certainly lots of Hell and Anger, and the Learning and Realisation were all geared towards hurting and/or killing others. Even the Heaven/Rapture was cruel – characters really enjoying the suffering they were causing. And the good guys, the commandoes who blow up the mountain to divert the river and flood the Luawamba mine, even they kill with cold, ruthless satisfaction and barely turn a hair at drowning so many of the black workers in the process. 'Collateral damage,' their leader reassures his team as they fret briefly about what they've done. 'Unavoidable.'

So what did this mean: that I was trapped by this life state? That Animality was to be my destiny? That no matter how hard I tried, I would run up against it wherever I turned, just like My Evil Friend?

I froze again, then juddered as a sudden shiver ran through me and the hair stood up on my arms. My Evil Friend, that grinning toad forever lurking in the shadows, waiting to do me down – was he part of this? Was he the inner voice of my Animality: fearful, mistrustful, seeing threats and danger everywhere, and so getting his retaliation in first? Fight or flight – that's what animals do, isn't it? And that's what My Evil Friend did, too. Anything he didn't know or recognise or sense as safe, he'd attack. Or run away from, reject. In a way, he was trying to protect me, but all he was doing was keeping me locked up, like some over-anxious parent. I could see it all with such clarity I was stunned.

Moments like this are very hard to explain to other people. Inside, you feel that something enormous has happened, that a tectonic plate has shifted; but from the outside there's nothing to see at all. But I was so excited, so overwhelmed almost, I had to share it with someone. Geoff. Because this all hooked up with his slander thing, too. From the way he'd described it, it was obvious that My Evil Friend slandered me, slandered other people; in fact, it seemed to me that MEF *was* slander.

I called Geoff's home, then his mobile, but no reply. I left a message on both, then paced around the flat for a while, trying to get rid of my nervous energy. In the end, there was nothing for it but to sit at the desk and write it down, just to get absolutely clear in my mind what it was I'd understood. Because, somehow, it felt like a turning-point.

***

206

'And you worked all this out by yourself?' Geoff sounded impressed. It was after work the following day and we'd hooked up in The Three Crowns, the pub where we'd first met over the stinking inspection pit. He'd suggested the venue because he was going on to a local Buddhist meeting a bit later and this would be his only chance to get together for several days. It was odd being back where it had all started. Shirley was still behind the bar, but had assured us that the drains were finally fixed – properly. 'That's why I'm back,' Geoff had joked. 'I heard it was safe.'

So here we were in the corner by the fire – the evenings had started to get chilly – me with my beer, him with a lemonade and lime. 'Because I don't like to drink before a meeting. Afterwards – fine; before – no.' I'd just shown him the two sides of A4 I'd written the previous evening. 'Yes,' I said, taking it back, 'all my own work.'

'No chanting?'

I shook my head. 'Nope. Besides, I don't know how to do it.'

'Well, you just want to know the theory, don't you?'

I pulled a face; was that still true?

'And from that,' Geoff continued, pointing to the paper, 'it looks like you've got it really well.'

'Really?' I perked up.

Geoff nodded. 'Fear's a key part of Animality, and it can be either positive or negative. It can protect you from danger, but also restrict you. So linking that to your Evil Friend, and slander – fantastic insight.' And he raised his glass to me.

'Thank you,' I said, chuffed. A moment's silence as we both drank.

'So now what?' he asked, wiping his mouth.

'Sorry?'

'Well,' he said, 'you've realised how powerful Animality

207

is in your life, and how it manifests itself in all sorts of ways, including your Evil Friend. So what are you going to do about it?'

'Er . . .' Another moment's silence, this time for thinking. 'Well,' I said after a while, 'I'm not entirely sure yet. But knowing your enemy's half the battle, isn't it?'

'Certainly is,' said Geoff, and looked at me. Another few seconds went by.

'Look, I know you want me to chant,' I said finally. 'And I might do – one day, maybe, who knows? But not—'

Geoff beamed.

'And don't smile like that.'

'Like what?'

'Like you've got me.'

Geoff raised his hands in surrender. 'Ed, it's entirely up to you. I'm here because you wanted to meet, not the other way round.'

'Well, I just wanted to check out I was on the right lines, that's all.' For some reason I was starting to feel all defensive again.

'And you are – I said.' He smiled again, like a teacher pleased at the progress of a particularly difficult pupil.

'Plus,' I said, pointing an accusing finger at him, 'I remember sitting in here with you weeks – months – ago, and you refusing to answer a very important question. Not about your job, but exactly why it is that changing yourself changes your environment.' I sat back and folded my arms like I'd won an argument or something. I knew I was trying to cover up my concession that I might possibly one day chant –the first crack in the dyke – and I knew Geoff knew it, too. But I did also want to know the answer. Was picking up those scripts just coincidence, or was there really some mystical, invisible thread between the churning, inner reality of my life and the great outdoors of the rest of the world? It seemed important to know.

Geoff sucked his teeth, stared into his glass – and then uttered. '*Ichinen sanzen*,' he said.

'Come again?'

'Three thousand realms in a moment of life.'

I shook my head – still did not compute.

Geoff tried again. '*Ichinen* – life moment, remember?'

I nodded.

'*Sanzen* – means three thousand, but actually stands for everything. Basically, *ichinen sanzen* means that moment by moment your life both embraces and permeates the entire universe.'

He looked at me. I looked at him.

'Oh, of course,' I said. '*Ichinen sanzen*. I see. Thanks.'

'It's not easy,' he said.

'Pah!' I retorted. 'Little me, the universe, embrace, permeate – what's the problem?'

He grinned. 'It took me quite a while to get my head around it. But once you grasp it, it's hard to see things any other way.'

'Go on then,' I challenged. 'Do your best.'

'Well,' he said, taking a deep breath, 'it's about how everything connects up: the physical side of life, the spiritual side, the past, the present, life, death. Everything.'

'A modest little principle, then?'

'It's the Buddha's enlightenment, Ed, so you can't expect it to be a piece of piss, can you?'

'Fair enough. Go on.'

'Right. Well, you actually know a lot of the bits already.'

'Do I?'

'Mmm. *Ichinen sanzen* just sticks them together into something consistent.'

'Oh.'

'So you start with the Ten Worlds – Hell, Hunger and so on.'

'HHAAHHLRBB.'

'That's it. And all of them contain all the others, so one moment you can be in Hell, say, and the next in Anger, or Bodhisattva or still in Hell. That's called the mutual possession of the Ten Worlds and is very important.'

'Why?'

'Because it means whatever your life condition, whatever your reality, theoretically it can change at the very next instant. You're not doomed by fate to suffer, for example, or you don't have to die and go to Heaven to be happy, or be reborn again and again to pay off your karma. You can become fulfilled and happy in this lifetime – right now.'

'Theoretically.'

'Well, we're talking theory, aren't we?' He sounded a bit irritated.

'OK, keep your shirt on. What's next?'

Geoff took a sip of his drink to compose himself and continued. 'The Three Truths, the physical, mental and essential aspects of life, are also part of *ichinen sanzen*. So your life condition, your Ten Worlds – which change moment by moment in the depths of your life, its essential aspect – is revealed moment by moment in your physical and mental aspect. So if you're in Hell, how you think and feel and look is different from if you're in Heaven, say, or Anger.'

'OK.'

'And these different life states all have different power. In Hell sometimes you can't even get out of bed, as you know.'

'Yep.'

'But when you thought you might be back on with Angie you were walking on air.'

I nodded ruefully.

'Hunger – there can be great energy there; restless, eager, driving. And Anger can be very powerful, both positively and negatively. So the inbuilt power of these life states is also part of *ichinen sanzen*, along with their influence – the way they affect the environment.'

'How do you mean?'

'Power is potential. Influence is when that potential is activated. An angry thought has a certain amount of influence; it might show in your face, for example. An angry word has more influence on your environment, an angry act even more.'

'I see. So power and influence are directly related.'

'That's right – but not always in proportion.'

'I don't understand.'

'Well, a baby, for example, has very little power. It's only a baby. But once it starts screaming – Christ, everyone comes running. It has a lot of influence. And the opposite's also true. Everyone – and I mean *everyone* – has enormous power as a potential. The problem is they can't release it or access it, and so they tend to have very little influence. That's why they're unhappy. They're frustrated, unfulfilled. Which is where Buddhism comes in.' He grinned.

'OK, you can spare me the sales pitch,' I said (in a nice way). 'I'm half-sold already.'

'Good.'

'*Half*-sold. Because you still haven't explained how the external world is supposed to be this sort of magic mirror to what's going on inside here.' I tapped my chest.

'I'm coming to it – all right? Blimey, it took Shakyamuni years of searching and self-examination and fasting and austerities and God knows what to understand all this, and you want to get it all in the time it takes to sink a pint.'

'Be fair, Geoff.' I laughed. 'I have been mulling it over for a few months.'

Geoff raised a hand. 'My apologies. And I hereby acknowledge your rigorous mulling.'

I raised my glass. 'Apology accepted. So . . . ?'

'So we've got the Mutual Possession of the Ten Worlds, expressed through the Three Truths, power and influence. But in a sense that's all static. What makes it active is cause and effect. This causes that, makes things happen. You make a Hellish cause, you get a Hellish effect. You make an Angry cause, you get an Angry effect, and so on. Not straight away necessarily, but eventually – unless you do something in between to negate or soften that effect. So part of *ichinen sanzen* is something called "consistency from beginning to end".'

'Which means?' I was struggling to keep up.

'Let's say the essence of your life at this moment is – what do you want it to be?'

I didn't hesitate. 'Animality. Stick with what we know, eh?'

'All right. The essence of your life right now is Animality. So basically you're thinking like an animal – the mental aspect – and physically obviously you are an animal, but at this moment your animal senses and instincts are totally alive and honed. You could be on the lookout for food or sex – or a fight, maybe.'

'Sex.'

He laughed. 'All right. So you have a certain potential in that life state – power – and if you activate it that power will have an influence in the environment. You could see a woman, for instance, and attract her with your animal magnetism.'

'Which is considerable, when I choose to turn it on.'

'I've no doubt. Anyway, power and influence are made active by cause and effect. Seeing the woman is cause, and chatting her up is effect. And the cause is a combination of what's outside and what's inside. Outside – the woman; inside – your Animality; specifically, your desire to pull. And all these things – beginning with the essence of your life in Animality and ending with you chatting her up – are consistent from beginning to end. If you were in a different life state you would think and behave differently, make different causes and so on, but everything you thought and did would be still consistent from beginning to end with that life state. If you were in Anger, for example, seeing the woman might lead to a row rather than nooky. See?'

'Erm . . .'

'Good. Now—'

'Hang about. I just need a second to process all this.' I closed my eyes, trying to concentrate, to bring together everything I'd just heard. 'Basically,' I said carefully, 'what you're saying is that your life state totally affects the way you think and behave and relate to your environment, from moment to moment, in a consistent way. Is that it?'

'Almost. Your life state *is* the way you think and behave moment to moment. At that moment, your total reality *is* Animality or Hell or Hunger or whatever life state you're in. You perceive and experience the whole of your reality according to that state. And that's your inner reality and the external world. They're not separate. They're two but not two, not two but two. *Funi.*'

I screwed up my face in an effort to understand, but it was no good. 'I can't see the distinction,' I said. 'Sorry.'

'Don't apologise, mate!' said Geoff. 'This isn't easy stuff.' He scratched his head a moment, searching for a way to explain. 'I know. When my ex-wife was pregnant with our first child, there was a period when I saw pregnant women everywhere – on the bus, on the street, in shops. I wasn't looking out for them, I just saw them everywhere. But after she gave birth these pregnant women suddenly disappeared. I never saw one. But guess what I did see.'

'Babies?'

'Absolutely. The world was full of them: in buggies, in prams, being carried around, screaming, puking. I couldn't move for babies. And now my kids are grown up – no babies. Someone's hidden them, too.'

I smiled. 'You're talking about a preoccupation, though, not a life state.'

'A preoccupation is an expression of your life state.'

'Ah.'

'An animal's preoccupied with survival, a Buddha with transforming suffering. Anyway, the point is: the world hadn't changed, I had. Without even knowing it.'

'OK,' I said, and now I felt we were coming to the heart of it, 'but what you're talking about is how you experience things, how you perceive things. The objective reality stays the same – right?'

'In this instance, yes.'

'OK. But I'm not interested in just *experiencing* things differently. I want to *change* the objective reality.'

'I totally agree. That's crucial.'

'So?'

'The final part of *ichinen sanzen* is called the Three Realms, because your life operates in three areas: the self, living beings, i.e. society, and the physical environment. Separate but all part of a whole.'

'*Funi.*'

'Yeah – basically. Anyway, the point of the Three Realms is that if you want to be happy you need to create good, positive relationships in all three. You need to be at one with yourself. And you need to have good relations with the living beings around you – other people. And you've got to respect and protect your physical environment, because in the end that's what supports your life.'

'Well, that doesn't seem so radical.'

'It's not. It's common sense. But it puts everything together, and fundamentally it says everything comes down to *connection*. Are you connected to your true self, what you really want and need to make you happy? Are you connected to other people in a creative way? Or at all? A lot of the unhappiness I see around me is because people are isolated from each other, which historically is not a natural way for human beings to live – especially if physically they're very close to each other.'

'You're never so lonely as when you're in a crowd, eh?' I tried to sound ironic, but actually this was something I was feeling more and more – simple loneliness. Especially since Angie had gone. In fact, I'd been aware for some time that half the reason why I wanted to talk to Geoff was just because I craved some decent human company.

'Exactly,' he said, ignoring my tone. 'And a lot of environmentalists, for example, say one reason our society's so screwed up – mentally, spiritually, physically – is because we've lost our connection with nature.'

'OK,' I said. 'I can accept all that. But how does it relate to your life condition "permeating the universe"? And, coming back to my question, to me actually changing things?'

'Consistency from beginning to end again,' he said. 'Your life condition – whatever it is – permeates the realm of your self, your social environment and the physical world, which extends ultimately to include the whole universe.'

'But how?'

'Because everything joins up, that's how.'

I frowned, frustrated. I didn't understand.

Geoff glanced at his watch. 'Look, I'd love to talk some more, Ed, but I've got to go to this meeting.'

'Oh. OK.' I couldn't keep the disappointment out of my voice.

'But . . .' He looked at me. 'No.'

'What?'

'Well,' he said, 'where I'm going right now is to chant in preparation for a discussion meeting tomorrow night. Now, you won't want to come to this one, I suppose?' He looked at me cautiously.

'A meeting to chant about a meeting?'

'That's it – to put our life state in the right place for tomorrow.'

I shook my head.

'No, I didn't think so. So why not come and ask your question at the discussion meeting tomorrow?'

'Discussion meeting?'

'There's a little bit of chanting – just a few minutes – then an open discussion on a topic we can all join in with.'

My eyes narrowed with suspicion. 'What topic?'

'Well, tomorrow it's "What's the meaning of life?"'

I threw back my head and roared with laughter.

Geoff looked puzzled. 'What's so funny?'

'You Buddhists. Bloody hell – intense or what?'

Geoff grinned. 'Actually, it's a good laugh. And interesting. And you'll get an answer to your question – several, probably. But look, have a think about it and if you want to come, give me a call on the mobile and I'll give you the address – OK?'

'OK, but don't hold your breath.'

'I'm not. Like I said, it's up to you.' He drained his glass and got to his feet. 'Either way, see you soon, yeah?'

He stuck out his hand with a warm smile, and as I took it for a brief second I felt such an overwhelming sense of fondness for him, for his ordinariness – and his extraordinariness at the same time – that my throat tightened and I could feel the tears about to come. Fuck, I thought – what *is* going on? It was like I was in love. Not in a sexual way, but in the way you love your parents. Or should do, in an ideal world. But then we're often disconnected from them, too, aren't we? I certainly had been. I coughed hard to clear my throat and regain control. Feeling love towards someone I hardly really knew, a window-cleaner – and a bloke! – well, that was completely out of the question. 'Yuh,' I said huskily. 'I'll call you.'

***

I walked home. It took about an hour, but whenever I talked to Geoff there was so much to think about that I needed time and space to digest it all.

I was actually feeling sorry for myself when I filled up, I reasoned. Geoff leaving just reminded me of my loneliness, the pain of disconnection. And yes, I did want to be whole. I didn't want to be stuck alone in my flat night after night, getting slowly pissed in front of vapid TV. I did want to be connected – with a woman, a family, friends, society. I looked up. Even with the stars, I thought. It was a clear night and the major constellations were quite visible. I remembered reading somewhere that the stars you see are so far away and the light's taken such a long time to reach you, that when you look at the night sky you're actually looking thousands, maybe millions of years back into the past. So if that was true, and we are all stardust, all part of the Big Bang, and some minute residue of that event was in me at this very moment, was it totally ludicrous to believe that my life could somehow permeate to the distant fringes of the universe?

'Watch it!'

I looked down from the starry heavens to see an irate

man in his fifties glaring at me. He'd been forced off the pavement to avoid a collision.

'Sorry,' I said. He scowled, then walked off muttering to himself.

'Well, there you go,' said a voice. 'That's what happens when you get all poetic and metaphysical – you literally can't see where you're going.' I stopped. It was a voice I knew. My Evil Friend. 'And it's all a bunch of bollocks anyway. It's—'

'Fuck off!' I said it out loud – and instantly he disappeared. I looked round quickly to check that the Irate Man hadn't heard me, then hurried homewards. But I was sick of My Evil Friend. More and more I could see it was him, his voice, that stopped me doing things, blocked the very connections that deep down I wanted. By the time I got home I'd decided I would go to that meeting tomorrow night, because what's to lose? If I hated it I'd just chalk it up to experience, and if I loved it, well, who knows?

I let myself in to my flat and immediately looked over to the answerphone. No blinking light, which meant no messages, no connection . . . no Angie. This is why we like phones, I thought: to feel connected. Getting letters: same reason. I hit the replay button on the machine. 'Hi, Ed. Martin here. Just calling to see if you fancied meeting up sometime. Only I really enjoyed our discussion the other week and I'd like to know more about this Buddhism you're getting into. Except it's nothing like anything I've read about since our talk. It's Buddhism, Jim, but not as we know it. Anyway, give me a call when you get a moment. Oh – and when are you going to get a mobile? Byeeee.'

I made two more decisions there and then. First, to buy a mobile phone. And second, believe it or not, I called Martin to fix up a lunchtime drink the very next day. Connection.

218

Chapter Thirteen

Empty wallet. That's what I'd forgotten to factor into the day's proceedings. I didn't realise it till later, because I decided to forsake public transport and walk the couple of miles into the West End. I felt good, fit, focused, and I wanted to connect to everything around me. This is what being alive is all about, I told myself as I strode down Camden High Street – *ichinen sanzen*. How everything's a part of me and I'm a part of everything. I didn't really understand it, of course, except in a vague sort of way, but I was determined to be positive, to keep My Evil Friend deep in his hole, and face each moment bright-eyed, fresh and cheerful.

And it was great – until I got to the phone shop. Or more precisely, until my credit card was rejected. I'd spent half an hour poring over the different models, agonising about the different styles and payment packages and how many ring tones they offered; and when I finally made up my mind the bloody computer wouldn't accept my card. I was mortified, but the Asian shop assistant didn't bat an eyelid. All he said was, 'Have you got another one?'

'No,' I said, and then – oh God – the unmistakable prickle that signalled the start of another mega-blush. 'I'll get some cash. There's a machine just down the road.' And

I practically bolted from the shop. The blush subsided, thank heavens, but there was no joy at the ATM. It just informed me – a bit sarcastically, I thought – that I 'appeared' to be out of funds, and asked me to contact my branch. Well, obviously my branch – or the vast computer it was hooked up to – knew full well if I was out of funds. I'd wheedled another couple of hundred on my overdraft limit soon after losing the Writers Inc. job, but hadn't had the bottle to keep an eye on the balance since then. I knew, of course, that 'money out' at regular intervals but 'in' only sporadically – and recently, not at all – was not the best way to manage my finances, especially when allied to the classic head-in-the-sand philosophy that had served me so well in days gone by. And all through that long conversation with Liz the producer I'd felt this vague unease, like mild indigestion, that my time – or rather my money – was running out. But I'd done nothing about it – Animality again. And so – *ipso facto*, *cogito ergo sum* – here I was completely, stony broke.

Bloody hell. Now what? I was supposed to be meeting Martin in twenty minutes. Well, Christ, I told myself, he can at least buy you lunch, seeing how much he owed you when he went bust.

'But that means admitting you're penniless,' said a familiar voice. MEF was back.

'Why shouldn't I be penniless?' I countered. 'It's him who's put me in this position.'

'Sure,' said MEF. 'But what about all that brave Buddhist talk you gave him about "danger-opportunity" and problems helping you grow and *kyo chi gyo i* and all the rest of it? What's he going to think?'

'Look,' I said, 'do you want to eat or not? Because if he doesn't cough up for lunch it's walking home on an empty stomach, beans on toast and then God knows what till I can find some money from somewhere.'

'Fine,' said MEF mildly. 'I'm sure you'll handle it wonderfully. Let's just hope he's not broke too.'

That's the thing about MEF. Like him or loathe him – and increasingly it was the latter – he had a habit of making me face things I didn't want to see. I thought for a moment, then decided. If Martin was as broke as me he could hardly look down his nose at me, and nothing I'd told him about Buddhism implied it was a quick fix to all of life's problems. And if he wasn't broke – well, whatever he thought, at least I'd eat. A no-brainer, really.

***

He wasn't broke – far from it. He was flush, and ridiculously pleased to see me. 'It worked!' he said, pumping my hand hard.

'Eh?'

'I did *kyo chi gyo i* and it bloody worked! What are you having?'

He explained as he bought me a pint. 'I thought about it a lot and it seemed to make sense, so in the end I decided to give it a hundred per cent; you know, full throttle, no holding back. So I totally took on board what you said about fixing your *kyo*, your goal.'

'Really?'

'Absolutely. So I thought, what do I really want? Well, obviously it was to keep my property and avoid bankruptcy. But I couldn't see how it could be done. What I'd put into the company was secured against the flat and the bank was at the door, you know? And then I remembered what you'd said about *kyo* involving creating value for other people—'

'Did I?'

'You bloody did and that was the trump card, I tell you,

221

because I thought, Hang on. Here I am trying my hardest to avoid paying my debts, and everyone's on my back. So what if I do a one-eighty, turn the problem around and try my hardest to do the exact opposite?'

'Meaning?'

'Pay everyone back!'

'Blimey.'

'You said it. I decided to go to every creditor and absolutely promise to honour my debt, with an agreed rate of interest, even if it took me the rest of my life to pay them off. A few were sceptical, but in the end, everyone's agreed.'

'What about the staff?'

'I'm coming to them. Because I only had this idea last week, when I called you. Anyway, once I decided this was what I was going to do, the only thing to work out was the how – *chi*. Which actually was quite simple.'

'Was it?' I was growing more and more incredulous.

'Yes.' Martin laughed. 'I went to one of my mates who'd put a bit of dosh into the company, and explained my thinking, and he was quite impressed. And basically, I asked him to take over the whole debt – which is pretty much small change in his terms – and mortgaged my flat to him as collateral.'

'And that covered it?'

'Not all of it, no. But I also convinced him to let me work off the rest.'

'How?'

'Well, that's the beauty of it. He puts another slice of cash into a property development portfolio that I manage for him. I get a small salary and ten per cent of any profit and he gets the rest.'

'So you're paying him off with his own money?'

'Not exactly. His money and my skills are making more money – for both of us. And in the meantime, everyone gets paid. *Kyo chi gyo i.*' He beamed, totally pleased with himself.

'But why would he trust you with more money when his last investment that you managed went bust?'

'Because he knows that wasn't my fault. The market collapsed. Whereas bricks and mortar – you can't go wrong, can you? I'm doing up five houses right now, OK? When they're sold we make two hundred grand profit, easy. He gets one-eighty, I get twenty, and so we go on. Bob's your uncle.'

I didn't know what to say. The thought did occur that he was an arch blagger with a gullible mate, and had simply transferred his debt from the dot-com bubble to the housing bubble; but hey, what did I know? The net result was that he had money and I didn't. The obvious question sprang to my lips.

'So does that mean you can pay me the two grand you owe me?'

'Ed, you are first in line,' he said with a laugh. 'You showed me the way.' He took out his cheque book. 'Only I can't do it all in one hit, if that's OK?'

'Fine.' I gulped. He was throwing a rope to a drowning man.

'Five hundred now and the rest over the next three weeks?'

'Great.'

He started to write.

'Only – could I ask a favour?'

He stopped and looked at me.

'Could that be cash?'

***

He was very understanding. He bought lunch, then marched down to the bank with me and took out £500 in

223

crisp, new twenties. He handed them over with a smile and waved away my thanks. 'No, Ed,' he said, putting a hand on his heart, 'it's me who should be thanking you. And for such an interesting lunch.' Because I'd spent most of it regurgitating everything I could remember that Geoff and Co had told me about Buddhism. 'You know,' he said, just before we parted, 'I might actually become a Buddhist. It's bloody magic!'

Maybe for you, mate, with your rich friends, I thought, as I watched him go – but for me? To say I was bewildered wouldn't come close. A totally unexpected piece of good fortune had come to me from a bloke whose guts I'd hated only a few months ago, who'd turned things around based on advice I'd given him, but which I couldn't make work myself! I stood there shaking my head. I needed to talk to someone. But that's the problem when you're single: no partner to share all your triumphs and disasters with. Unless you've got a friend who's prepared to put up with your wittering . . .

I thought. There were only two candidates, and Geoff would be up a ladder somewhere. Which left Dora, but was her office still open? Give her a call, I reasoned; and then I remembered what I'd been doing when I'd discovered I was skint.

The Asian guy in the phone shop looked surprised to see me. He'd obviously written me off as a time-waster, so it was very satisfying to peel off a series of notes and walk out with a brand-new mobile. I felt like I'd rejoined society somehow. Connection. OK, maybe it was an extravagant purchase for someone living hand to mouth, but I had cash in my pocket, and the fifteen hundred quid Martin said he was going to send would at least put me under my overdraft limit for a few more weeks. I had time to sort myself out.

So – Dora. I called her office on the new mobile but her number was permanently engaged, which meant either she was there but busy, or there was a fault, or . . . what? There was nothing for it but to make a visit. It wasn't far, so I decided to walk again. It was a day for Shanks's Pony.

***

My good mood faded as I approached Personal Personnel. Two men were loading Dora's desk into a white box van. The rest of her office was already aboard – a couple of filing cabinets, four chairs and a crate of odds and ends. Not much to show for six years' hard graft. I went inside. The office looked bare and grubby, like every room does when it's been emptied of life. The phone was on the floor, with the handset not properly on its cradle. I put it straight and went through to the kitchen. Dora was making a final cup of tea. 'Hello, handsome,' she said with a smile. 'Just in time to toast the end.' She passed me the mug and took another from the cardboard box she'd packed with her tea things. She was in a tracksuit and trainers, no wig, no make-up – stripped bare, like the office.

'I'm really sorry, Dora,' I said as she made a second cup. It was lame, but I didn't have anything else to offer.

'Pah,' she said. 'What doesn't kill you makes you stronger.'

'Does it?' I'd never thought so.

'In my case it has to,' she said grimly.

A voice came from the other room. 'All loaded, love!'

'Thank you!' Dora shouted. We heard the door close. Dora sighed, then squeezed her teabag hard against the side of the mug and dropped it into a plastic bag of rubbish. She raised her mug in mock salute. 'The future.'

'The future.' We clunked, then sipped in silence.

225

'So,' she asked, trying to be bright, 'what blows you in here?'

'Doesn't seem important now,' I said, because it didn't.

'Come on. You didn't come all this way for nothing.'

She gazed at me with her big brown eyes and I found myself thinking, Why does this woman wear make-up when she doesn't have to? Underneath it she's really very pretty.

'Well?' she said, mistaking my silence for reluctance.

'Well,' I said – and told her all about my morning, and my encounter with Martin. 'I just can't make sense of it,' I finished.

Dora laughed. 'Protection,' she said.

'Sorry?'

'When the Buddha nature manifests from within it receives protection from without. This is one of Buddhism's fundamental principles.'

'Is that a quote?'

'Mmm. And a fact.'

Now I was even more confused. 'You're saying I manifested Buddha nature?'

She smiled and nodded.

'When?'

'When you first taught him about Buddhism, about *kyo chi gyo i* and so on. And again this lunchtime, by the sound of it.'

I was nonplussed. 'I don't understand.'

'Teaching others about Buddhism is an aspect of Buddhahood. It's one way it manifests itself.'

'What – even if you don't mean to?'

'Well, look at the effect,' she said. 'He's thinking of becoming a Buddhist.'

'He was only saying that.'

'How do you know?' She sounded indignant. 'He's

completely surprised you already. Who's to say he's not going to do it again?'

She was right. And what she said tied in completely with what I always say about people: that they never fail to surprise you. In fact, I was about to surprise myself, wasn't I? Time for a sheepish confession. 'Speaking of which,' I said, clearing my throat, 'I'm sure you'll be pleased to hear that Geoff has finally persuaded me to . . . er . . . go to a meeting.'

Dora raised her eyebrows – high.

'Tonight. Just to listen.'

Her eyebrows returned to normal. 'Sure. Great.'

'Anyway, so . . .' I shrugged, at a loss.

'What's the topic?'

I gave a little chuckle. 'The meaning of life.'

Dora smiled faintly. 'One of Geoff's favourites. In fact . . .' She went through to the office. On the floor in a corner was a box I hadn't seen. In it were various books and magazines. Dora crouched down and rummaged through it, then brought out a small, battered paperback. She gave it to me.

I read the title. '*Man's Search for Meaning* – Victor Frankl.'

'Geoff gave it to me, right at the beginning of my practice,' she said.

I opened the cover and saw there was an inscription. 'To Dora. And may all your days be meaningful. Geoff kiss kiss.'

Dora smiled. 'He introduced me, you see.'

'Really? Geoff did?' For some reason I was surprised.

Dora nodded. 'It's not about Buddhism but it's very Buddhist,' she said. 'Anyway, if you get time before tonight read it. There's a whole page on the meaning of life.'

'A whole page?'

She smiled and nodded again.

'OK,' I said. 'But if I borrow it I'll have to know how to get it back to you.'

'You want my address?'

'Tell you what,' I said, producing my new mobile with a flourish. 'How about you do me the honour of being the very first person in my new phone book?'

She clasped a hand to her chest, wide-eyed. 'Ed,' she said, 'I'm speechless.'

***

I started reading on the bus home. What a book. What a bloke! A man who could find meaning even in a concentration camp! I literally could not put it down. I almost chose to stay on the bus past my stop just so I could go on reading. But reluctantly I marked the page and jumped off, then hurried, ran almost, back to my flat so I could start reading again. Dora was right: Frankl deals with the meaning of life in a single page. And what a page!

The Meaning of Life

I doubt whether a doctor [*he was a psychiatrist*] can answer this question in general terms. For the meaning of life differs from man to man, from day to day and from hour to hour. What matters, therefore, is not the meaning of life in general but rather the specific meaning of a person's life at a given moment. To put the question in general terms would be comparable to the question posed to a chess champion: 'Tell me, Master, what is the best move in the world?' There is simply no such thing as the best or even a good move apart from a particular situation in a game and the particular personality of one's opponent. The same holds for human existence. One should not search for an abstract meaning to life. Everyone has his own specific vocation or mission in life to carry out a concrete assignment which demands fulfilment. Therein he cannot be replaced, nor can his life be repeated. Thus, everyone's task is as unique as is his specific opportunity to implement it.

As each situation in life represents a challenge to man and presents a problem for him to solve, the question of the meaning of life may actually be reversed. Ultimately, man should not ask what the meaning of his life is, but rather he must recognise that it is *he* who is asked. In a word, each man is questioned by life; and he can only answer to life by *answering for* his own life . . .

My jaw dropped at the utter simplicity, the profound wisdom of this. Of course! There is no Meaning 'out there' waiting to be discovered, like a distant land on the other side of the world. It's here, in us and our circumstances, waiting to be realised – or created, perhaps. And Dora was right: this was all very Buddhist; or at least it sounded a lot like the stuff she and Geoff had been telling me.

Geoff! I looked at my watch with a start. Six o'clock, and I hadn't called him yet to say I was going to the meeting; because after this I most definitely was.

He was delighted to hear it and gave me the address, which was just up the road in Kentish Town. 'Want me to pick you up?' he asked.

'That's OK,' I said. 'It's not far.'

'OK. It starts at 7.30.'

'See you there,' I said and put down the phone. Then I started to pace. I felt such a buzz, so alive, that I couldn't keep still. I could hardly wait to connect with other people; talk with them, share, discuss. It was like Frankl had been speaking to me directly. And I don't know why – perhaps I was in some heightened state, I don't know – but it struck me as sort of amazing that words on a page, marks of black ink, could have this effect on me. I know the written word is just speech set down on paper, but all of a sudden the whole thing seemed wonderful – that we can transmit what we know and feel through this abstraction of symbols. Just like music. A composer hears a melody, or feels it maybe; then he writes it down, using another weird set of symbols, and when others play it the music is reproduced and stirs the same feelings in the listener. Very odd – and very ordinary at the same time. So there had to be something in me, too, just waiting for the right stimulus to be triggered; some inner sense of . . . truth? Some part of me just waiting – for Frankl's words, as it turns out – to punch the air and shout, 'Yes!'

I looked at my watch again. No time for a meal before I went out, so I just made myself a couple of rounds of toast and ate them leaning against the cooker. To my right was the fridge and my favourite cartoons: 'What I'd really like to do is direct' and 'The road to enlightenment is long'. I smiled. To my left was the window-sill and Piers's acorn. It had sprouted a couple of new leaves. I smiled again. Very symbolic. I was in an extraordinarily good mood.

I finished my toast, put on my jacket, got my keys, wallet and – oops, nearly forgot – new mobile phone, and was almost out of the door when the phone rang. I stopped and waited for the answerphone to kick in. When it did there was a heavy sigh on the line. In the background I heard noise, laughter, faint music. Another sigh.

'Never mind,' said Angie. 'Maybe give me a call some—'

I dived for the handset before she could finish. 'Angie?'

'Oh – you're there.'

'I was just on the way out. What's the matter?'

'Oh nothing. I just . . .

'What?'

Another sigh, sad this time. 'You've forgotten, haven't you?'

'Forgotten what?' I desperately racked my brain. Not her birthday, or –

'It's our anniversary. Was.'

'Ah. I, er, didn't think we were celebrating that any more.'

She laughed bitterly. 'Look, do you want to know the truth, Ed?'

'Er, OK . . .' I steeled myself for something terrible – or wonderful, like she'd finally realised she couldn't live without me.

'I asked this bloke at work out for a drink because . . . well, I didn't want to be alone this evening, and now we're here I've just told him to piss off. I'm a cow, aren't I?'

'No, no . . .' My synapses were exploding. What did this mean? This woman flip-flopped faster than Olga Korbut.

'Anyway, you were going out. I'm sorry, forget it.'

'Did you want to get together or something?'

She laughed again. 'I don't know what I want. But look, go to your whatever. I'm making you late.'

'It doesn't matter,' I said. 'It was only a drink with a mate. I can blow him out.'

'Really? Won't he mind?'

'Really – don't worry.' I was sure Geoff would understand. I mean, a stroke of luck – sorry, good fortune – like this, the second in a day. Bloody hell, maybe I'd turned a corner. And there were bound to be other meetings I could go to, so the meaning of life would have to wait. Besides, hadn't I sussed it now I'd read the book? I told Angie to stay where she was – a pub in Soho – and I'd see her in

231

thirty minutes. Then I slipped Frankl into my jacket pocket to finishing reading on the Tube and practically sprinted to the station.

***

Angie was nursing a spritzer, looking sad and nervous and gorgeous all at the same time. She jumped up awkwardly when she saw me to give me a quick peck on the cheek. It felt like a first date, almost. Not a bad sign, maybe, if we were going to give it another go.

'Who was it?' she asked.

'Who was who?'

'Your mate? Or was it a date?'

'No.' I laughed. 'It was . . . just someone I did a job with a few weeks ago. Nothing serious.' I felt a bit of a heel, but I wanted to steer well clear of anything that might be a red rag to her, like Geoff and Buddhism. Which was fine, except she immediately spotted the book sticking out of my pocket.

'What are you reading?' she asked.

'Oh, it's something I thought you might be interested in,' I lied, wrestling it out and passing it to her. 'Viktor Frankl. He was a Jewish psychiatrist who survived Auschwitz.'

She opened the front cover and read the inscription. 'Geoff? The Fascist Buddhist?'

'Eh? How do you make him a Fascist?'

'Apologist for the Holocaust.'

I bit my tongue. I hadn't heard any apology for the Holocaust at that meeting, but the last thing I wanted now was another argument. 'Actually,' I said, 'I picked it up at a second-hand bookshop, so I don't know who the people are.'

Angie nodded, seemingly content with this explanation,

232

and started reading the back cover. I did feel disloyal, but I remember Geoff himself explaining the difference between truth and value, and that sometimes only a barefaced lie will do. Except this wasn't the Nazis coming for Anne Frank; this was me trying hard to stay on good terms with . . . it suddenly struck me – with my *honzon*, my object of worship. And we'll sacrifice anything to protect that, won't we? Like morality. Or perhaps it's your *honzon* that shapes your morality.

'Mmm, it does look interesting,' said Angie. 'Can I borrow it?'

'Sure,' I said. 'That's why I brought it.' Inside I apologised to Dora and promised I'd get it back to her – eventually. And if the worst came to the worst I could always say I lost it and buy her another copy. I'd even get Geoff to inscribe it again.

'Thank you,' said Angie brightly, and planted another kiss on my cheek – warmer this time, and a bit longer. A good sign. And things got steadily better. Another drink and we both relaxed. We teased each other about our shortcomings, made a solemn pact that we wouldn't discuss the Middle East, laughed about the first, disastrous Christmas we'd spent with her parents – and then abruptly she went all serious. 'Do you know what I miss?' she said.

I shook my head.

'The intimacy. Being close to someone – it takes time, you know?'

I nodded.

'And going through all that again with somebody else . . .' She glanced at me, nervous, searching for a response.

I didn't know what to say. Connection again. We all want it, need it. I cleared my throat. 'Are you saying you want to . . . try again?'

She smiled bravely. 'I told you, I don't know what I

want. Except another one of these, while I go to the loo.' She drained her glass and handed it to me, then stood up and swayed unsteadily to the ladies'.

Christ, I thought, she's pissed.

'How many have you had?' I asked when she came back. Another spritzer was waiting for her.

'I don't know,' she said. 'A couple before you came?' Meaning four or five. 'Why – do you think I'm drunk?'

'Merry, maybe.'

'Well, that's good, isn't it? You always said I didn't know how to let my hair down.'

True. I'd only seen her drunk once in all the time we'd been together – that same first Christmas with her folks. She'd been so nervous about how they'd take me that she'd completely overdone it on Christmas Eve and spent most of the next day in bed, sick as a dog. 'Have you eaten anything?' I asked.

'Not since breakfast.' Which for her usually consisted of an apple and a banana.

'How about some food, then?' I suggested.

'Well, I am hungry,' she agreed, then leaned close. 'But not for food.'

Oh my God, I thought, she's up for it. A sexy smile and a hand on my knee confirmed it. I swallowed hard. 'Your place or mine?' I said, trying to keep it light, fun.

'Mine, I think,' she said with mock seriousness. 'There's something about your place that—' She stopped.

'What?'

'I find it hard to relax there.'

'OK,' I said. 'Cab?'

***

Forty minutes later we were outside the door to her flat in Walthamstow. She lived in a small block that overlooked the reservoir, which had a kind of bleak beauty at this time of year. Not that you could see much at night, other than the yellow reflections of the streetlights on the far side, fractured by the breeze that constantly rippled the surface of the water. She'd snuggled close in the taxi, closed her eyes – and promptly fallen asleep. Which had added to the growing uneasiness I was feeling about this whole thing. One half of me was rejoicing, but another part – guess who – was not so sure.

'It'll only end in tears,' said MEF.

'Bog off.'

'Look,' he said, 'what does it tell you that she has to get pissed before she takes you to bed? Do you seriously want to rebuild your relationship on the basis of a drunken shag?'

But before I could answer, the cab went over a speed bump and she jerked awake, then looked up at me with a sleepy smile and pulled my head down to hers. The kiss was deep and intense, but somehow I didn't feel part of it at all. It was like I wasn't really there, just watching. Like I was watching now, as she fumbled her key drunkenly into the front door.

Inside, Angie led me straight through to the bedroom, where she clicked on a small bedside light that cast a soft glow around the room. 'Make yourself comfortable,' she said, nodding to the bed. 'Just got to pay a visit.' She stroked my face and went out.

I heard the bathroom door open and close, and realised this was my cue to get undressed. I stripped quickly and slipped under the duvet, shivering at the chill of the sheets. Or was it nervousness? This was a fantasy come true, but it felt all wrong. Why?

'Because she doesn't really want you,' said MEF. 'She's lonely and confused and . . . actually, come to think of it, maybe that's why you got together in the first place. Two lonely, confused people searching—'

'Shut it!' I hissed, just as the bedroom door opened and Angie came back into the room.

'Sorry? Did you say something?'

'Er, I just prefer the door closed.' I smiled.

'There's no one here,' Angie said, but obliged anyway. She was wearing the silk dressing-gown I'd given her two birthdays ago – and nothing else, as I saw when she dropped it from her shoulders and slid into bed next to me.

'Mmm – warm,' she murmured, gliding her hand up and down my torso and kissing my chest.

Half-heartedly I stroked her back and neck, as I knew she liked, and waited for the inevitable question. It wasn't long coming.

She slid her hand lower, then stopped. 'What's wrong?' She sounded genuinely puzzled.

'Erm, I think it's just nerves,' I said. But it wasn't.

'Nerves?'

'Well, yes, you know, it's been a while and . . . you know – out of practice.' I gave a nervous, pathetic little laugh.

Angie looked at me seriously, then brightened. 'I know what you want,' she leered, and dived under the duvet. She resurfaced a minute later, red-faced and just a bit cross. 'What's the matter?' she said. 'Don't you fancy me any more?'

'Of course I fancy you,' I said. 'It's just a bit . . . overwhelming, that's all.'

Angie threw herself onto her back with an angry sigh and stared at the ceiling. 'God, I knew this was a bad idea,' she said.

Cheers, I thought. And when I didn't immediately contradict her she turned her back to me with another harumph, pulled a pillow over her head and – well, that was that, basically. Chalk up another conquest to the Don Juan of Camden Town. Before long her deep and regular breathing told me she'd fallen asleep. I lay next to her wondering what to do. Stay and try to rescue the situation by manufacturing a bit of passion – or go, and in going know that I'd be driving the final nail into the coffin of our relationship? The trouble was, my heart – or rather, a more crucial part of my anatomy – just wasn't in it. The oneness of mind and body. What a way to learn that lesson. But why wasn't it? I'd rushed to meet her with such enthusiasm – and now? Perhaps I'd summed it up more accurately than I knew that time with Geoff: I loved the idea of her, but there was something about the reality that just didn't work. And possibly never would.

I got out of bed.

***

I walked home, all the way from Walthamstow – eight miles. End the day as you'd begun it, I thought. I'd left a note saying sorry and I hoped she'd understand, and that it wasn't her fault, it wasn't mine – it was simply something that happened between us. Whatever intention we started with, things just went wrong. Karma. (Though I left out that last word – didn't want to antagonise her any more than she was already.) And I walked through the night not because I couldn't find a cab or because I'd missed the last train. I just wanted to think; me and MEF. Except he didn't seem so evil at the moment, more a warning voice; and it was becoming increasingly hard to tell when he was being which.

I thought about me and Angie; about what had brought us together and kept us together: physical attraction, sense of humour, a way of seeing the world. But it wasn't enough. If you don't share a vision of the future, what you want to do together as a couple – anything from bringing up a family to running a business to saving the world – I guess it's pretty hard to sustain a bond when you both change, or the very things that had attracted you start to get on your nerves. She was good-looking but vain; I made her laugh but then never wanted to be serious. Ho hum.

And I thought about sex. Not in a lustful, lascivious way, but trying to understand what had happened with Angie. My performance – or, rather, lack of it – had truly astonished me. I'd never failed to rise to the occasion before, so I knew this was significant. But I'd always thought that sex was sex; almost an automatic thing, at least for men. Clearly not, though. But why? As I pondered, trudging through the halogen-lit streets of north-east London, it occurred to me that perhaps you could apply the Ten Worlds to sex, in the same way that Liz had applied them to money. I had time on my hands, so I decided to give it a go.

Hell and sex. Well, that was easy: it's when you simply don't enjoy it. Although, as some comedian once said, even bad sex is pretty good. Except, I told myself, when it's forced on you, like rape or child abuse or some other crime. OK. Hunger: the world of restless, insatiable desire. Easy again. Nymphomaniacs and whatever the male equivalent is called. Animality. Should be easy for me . . . I guessed it had to be when people couple and use each other just like animals, taking no interest in each other except to satisfy a bodily urge. Anger. Hmm – tricky. Anger wasn't being angry, I reminded myself. So what was it exactly? Ego. And then I remembered Liz saying that in the state of Anger money was just a way of keeping the score, so I supposed with sex it was piling up a string of conquests, or going for particular partners not because you like them especially but because being with them or sleeping with them made you look good.

Tranquillity. Normal, boring, run-of-the-mill sex? Take-it-or-leave-it sex? Can't-really-be-bothered-about-it sex? All of these might be possible, I suppose. And Heavenly or Rapturous sex? Orgasms, obviously, but also romantic sex, when you're deeply in love.

So that was six, and the next three I could rattle off easily. Learning: reading sex books, learning new techniques. Realisation: studying sex, researching it, like Masters and Johnson did. And Bodhisattva: sex therapists, or just using sex to cheer someone up. But Buddhahood? That stumped me. Wisdom, courage and compassion didn't seem to have much to do with sex; at least, not in my experience. It did occur to me, though, as I reached Finsbury Park, that Angie and I had experienced all of the other nine worlds during the time we'd been together.

Pulling her in the first place had been a definite conquest. And for a time we were deeply into each other and quite romantic – and were at it like rabbits. Hunger and Animality and Heaven all rolled into one. And then we slowed down and started to experiment and learn from each other, and discovered all sorts of things about ourselves we hadn't known before. And when I was feeling depressed Angie knew exactly what to do to raise my spirits. Then, towards the end it tailed off into middle-aged, married-couple mode: once a week if I was lucky, and that without much passion or excitement. And what was that little scenario just now if not Hell?

By the time I got back to Camden Town I was feeling a lot clearer, and quite positive. I'd ended it. My body had shown me something that I already knew deep down, and finally I'd taken charge and made a decision. As I climbed the stairs to my flat I felt sort of empty but not unhappy. I was ready to be filled with a new reality, where Angie was a lesson in the past and who knew what lay ahead?

There were two phone messages waiting for me when I opened my front door. The first was Geoff.

'Hi, Ed. Just ringing to make sure you're OK. It's 9.20 and some of us have gone on to The Chequers on Kentish Town Road, by the station. We'll probably be there till closing-time so come along if you get this in time. Great meeting, by the way. Anyway, maybe see you later. Cheers, bye.'

For a moment I felt a pang of guilt at standing him up, but then I thought that I'd never have worked things out about Angie if I hadn't gone to meet her. I played the second message – Geoff again. He sounded more anxious this time.

'Hi, Ed. Geoff here. Look, I know I'm probably being a bit of an old woman but you were so definite about coming tonight and then you weren't at the pub either . . . It's probably totally innocent but – well, just give us a call when you can, OK? Cheers.'

He was worried about me! I checked my watch: it was gone 1 a.m. I'd explain it all in the morning. Correction – later this morning. But right now I needed my bed. I crawled into it and fell instantly asleep.

***

I woke up feeling incredibly refreshed, like something had shifted. I got out of bed hungry and demolished two bowls of Bran Flakes and several slices of toast and marmalade. And then I worked. I had this surge of energy – life force – and decided to put it to good use. So I finished both script reports, printed them off and trundled down to the post office to send them back to Liz – all before lunchtime. Causes, I told myself. Effects come from causes, and it was time to multiply them. I got back, looked round the flat for more to do, and realised that I couldn't put it off any

240

longer: I had to call Geoff. I decided to do it mobile to mobile; that way I'd surprise him with my new number. I'd apologise and then tell him all the news I'd been planning to relate at the meeting. I was sure he'd understand – be proud of me, even. OK, I hadn't gone to the meeting but I felt I'd done some 'human revolution', all by myself. I'd learned something, grown, and was ready to move on. I listened to his messages again before calling his number. He sounded genuinely concerned. I was touched.

His phone rang for some time, then an unfamiliar voice answered – a woman . . .

'Hello.'

'Er, hello. Is Geoff there?'

'Who is this, please?'

'Who's that? Is that Geoff's phone?'

'Yes, but you've come through to St Mary's, Paddington.'

'What? I don't—'

'I'm afraid Mr Aston's had an accident.'

A sudden chill gripped me. 'What sort of accident?'

'Are you family?'

'No, a friend.'

'Well, I'm sorry, but we can't give out any information until we've contacted his family.'

'Is he all right?' My alarm was growing.

'I'm sorry,' she said again, 'we can't give out any information until we've contacted his family.' There was something in her voice, a tone of hidden regret, that set my mind racing to a terrible conclusion.

'Fuck,' I said. 'He's not dead – is he?' Her hesitation told me everything.

Chapter Fourteen

Karma. Destiny. And death. Geoff dead – just like that. Dead. So suddenly, without warning. Dead and gone. Where? Why? One day here, alive, breathing. The next . . . None of it made any sense. And so young: *fifty*. That was nothing these days. It was all so . . . unfair, so meaningless. Especially as no one saw what had happened. One moment, apparently, he was cleaning the fascia board above the window of an estate agent in St John's Wood – and the next thing he was lying on the pavement. They thought he'd fallen off his ladder and smacked his head on the ground. Slipped, lost his footing, and that was that – a simple accident.

But if karma were true there had to be a cause somewhere – and I couldn't get it out of my mind that if I'd gone to that meeting the night before somehow everything would have come out differently. I didn't know how exactly: it was a stupid idea, born of shock. But I kept thinking that if everything that happens is the sum total of everything we've ever thought and said and done, then maybe if I'd spoken with Geoff on that evening his life would have been different the next day; and he'd still be alive. Maybe he'd have gone to bed a bit later and got up a bit later, and maybe made a slightly different choice about

242

what to clean when; or maybe I'd have said something and he'd have called me to talk about it and not gone up his ladder at that precise moment; or maybe maybe maybe – any one of a hundred, a thousand small causes he'd made leading up to the accident would have been different, and he wouldn't have slipped, fallen . . .

I was confused, of course, not thinking straight. The fact is we don't really know how we affect things. Like how the butterfly flapping its wings in the Amazon can cause a hurricane halfway around the world – except that's obviously bollocks. Or that Frank Capra film, *It's A Wonderful Life*. OK, it's schmaltzy and sentimental, but the central question – what would life be like if we'd never existed? – that's got to be important to all of us. And this *ichinen sanzen* thing had brought it back into play. 'Moment by moment your life both embraces and permeates the entire universe.' That's what Geoff had said. And my life had let him down.

Rationally, I knew it hadn't; but in my gut I felt responsible. Guilty. It tormented me. I knew in my heart how much it meant to him for me to go to that meeting. I was offered 'the meaning of life' versus a possible shag with Angie – and guess what won? We are asked to create meaning for ourselves in each situation – that's what Frankl wrote – and what meaning had I created? Sex. Animality again. I'd even given the book to Angie! Sacrificed it for a tumble I couldn't even rise to. And now I'd have to get it back, because Geoff had given it to Dora *as a present* and she was bound to ask me for it, and I'd have to lie or tell her the sordid truth and neither option made me feel at all good . . . Oh God oh God oh God. I am such a bad person, I thought. Bad bad bad. So what that I'd 'sorted things out' with Angie? What was that against Geoff's life?

243

Dora broke down on the phone when I called her about him. He was a good friend and this was another terrible loss, coming hard on the failure of her business. But through her tears she started to talk about karma and how he'd 'prolonged his life'. Apparently he'd had an accident at work seven years earlier – to the week, practically. That time he'd fallen while cleaning a first-floor window and had been rushed to St Thomas's, where they'd just managed to save him.

'I don't understand,' I said. This sounded too weird for me.

'He was protected,' she sniffled, 'and lived another seven years.'

'So why wasn't he protected now?' I asked.

'I don't know,' she said. 'Look, I'm sorry, Ed,' she continued, 'but I'm going to have to chant. I'll call you back when I feel a bit better.'

I didn't hear from her again for nearly a week.

I felt incredibly lonely. And I missed him. I missed his cheerfulness, his stockiness, his earthiness. The spark in his eyes when he spoke. His gusto, his guts. His hundred-per-cent-ness. The fact that I felt I could tell him anything and he wouldn't be shocked or judge me. Diamond geezer. Diamond bleeding geezer. Dead.

Then the post-mortem revealed that he'd actually had a coronary thrombosis and had died instantly; in the pathologist's opinion he was probably dead before he hit the ground. Which let me off the hook in terms of bearing any responsibility for it but confused me even more.

I found out about the post-mortem from Liz the producer, who called to say she thought I'd done a really good job on the script reports and would I like to do some more – for money this time. She wouldn't be able to pay me much but it would help them clear their backlog and who knows where it might lead? I told her I'd been walking round like a zombie since Geoff's death, which she'd heard about on the Buddhist grapevine, and that was when she dropped the nugget about the heart attack. Anyway, I was more than grateful for the offer of work and the chance to talk to someone who might explain this whole karma thing to me – again. I didn't want to disturb Dora and her chanting, but I needed help to process my thoughts and feelings, to make sense of it all. What I needed most, of course, was to talk to Geoff . . .

***

'God, you look terrible,' Liz said as she opened the door to me.

'Do I? I'm sorry.' I was surprised – well, more disappointed. I'd shaved and everything.

'I didn't realise you and Geoff were such close friends.'

'I'm not sure we were,' I said. 'But I really liked him, respected him. He was becoming a bit of a mentor, I suppose.'

'Well, come in,' she said, laying a concerned hand on my arm. 'Let's talk – about work or whatever.' She led the way to the office. 'Have you been eating?'

'Not a lot.'

'Sleep?'

'Ditto.' I suddenly remembered a dream I'd had that night. I was one of the sabotage team in that stupid script, *Diamonds Are For Eva*, when the mine's flooded and all the workers are drowning. We're OK because we've got our special gear, except the team leader's suddenly in trouble – which doesn't happen in the story. He's struggling and we can't get to him. And then the water closes over him and he's gone. I woke up feeling desolate, and knew straight away who the team leader was, though I never saw his face.

I got up and tried to read, watched some television, then went back to bed and finally fell asleep around four. No wonder I looked like shit – I felt like it, too.

A large, grey-haired man was sitting on the sofa in the office, reading. 'This is my husband Frank,' Liz said. He heaved himself to his feet and stuck out a hand.

'Hi, pleased to meet you,' he said in a soft US accent.

'And you,' I said, though I didn't immediately warm to him. He wasn't anything like I'd imagined. Liz was slim and fit, well put together for a woman in her forties, and I'd pictured her Hollywood producer husband as small and dark and toned – a bit like Al Pacino, I guess. I'm not often right but I'm wrong again, as my mum used to say.

'This is good work,' he said, waving two sheets of paper that I realised were my script reports. 'You've got a good sense of story.'

'Thank you.' I tried to sound enthusiastic but my energy levels were right down.

Liz came to my rescue. 'Ed's finding it hard to make sense of Geoff's death. You know, the whole karma thing.'

Frank looked sympathetic. 'Yeah, it can be tough, especially when it's so sudden.'

This was my cue to ask the question that had been bugging me since breaking the news to Dora. 'What I don't get is what Geoff did to deserve this. He wasn't a bad man, he helped people, he created value. And just saying it was his karma doesn't help me. I mean, could he have avoided it? Or was it predestined, fated, and nothing he or anyone else could have done would have made any difference?'

Frank looked thoughtful. 'Well,' he said after a long pause, 'it definitely was his karma, because we all have effects lying latent in our lives, waiting to be triggered by the right stimulus, if you like. But Booddhism' – which was how he pronounced it – 'talks about two kinds of karma, mutable and immutable; or stuff you can change and stuff you can't. Like the fact that I'm a slob I can change. I know if I go on a diet and haul my fat ass round the block three times a week I'm gonna lose weight, right? But there are certain things in my life I can't change; like when and where I was born, who my parents are, my eye colour and so on. That stuff's the result of causes made in a previous life. And so, says Buddhism, are things like incurable illness and the length of your life span. You make a cause in one life, you get the effect in another.'

I couldn't accept this. 'You're saying Geoff was predestined to have a heart attack as punishment for something he did in a previous life?'

'Two things,' said Frank. 'Punishment is the spin you're putting on this event. Who knows what good might come of it? And second, although the exact circumstances of how his immutable karma manifests itself won't have been predestined, he had a finite life span, for sure.'

'Which it sounds like he prolonged,' chipped in Liz.

'Absolutely,' agreed Frank.

'Hang on,' I objected. 'I thought you just said life span was immutable.'

'Buddhist practice can help you change even immutable karma,' Frank said simply.

Liz could see I was confused. 'It's called lessening karmic retribution,' she said. 'The good causes you make in your present life can lessen or soften the effects of bad causes you made in the past.'

'That's handy,' I said. 'And impossible to prove.'

Frank smiled at my scepticism. 'Sure,' he said. 'But it comes down to how you see things, how you make sense of them. And if you can't believe in the eternity of life – especially your own life – then you can't accept karma. To me it does make sense, both theoretically, and also

247

because there are so many examples of people who practise this Buddhism changing their karma that, well, it's commonplace.' He could see I wasn't convinced. 'OK, a couple of stories, both true, both guys personally known to me.'

I nodded.

'OK, friend of mine, lives just up the road here. Last year one morning he's getting ready to go to work when he gets this severe pain in his neck, almost passes out. He calls his wife and to cut a long story short he's taken into hospital and given an emergency operation because he's had a cranial aneurysm – a bleed just under his skull. He's saved from death's door, makes a full recovery and now he's fitter than he ever was.'

'So?'

'He's fifty-three – and his father died of an aneurysm. At fifty-three.'

'That just means medicine's better than it was in his father's day.'

'His uncle, his dad's brother, also died at fifty-three, though from something else.'

A double punch-line. If it was meant to shut me up it worked.

'To my friend's mind,' said Frank, 'he's survived his family karma to die at fifty-three. He's prolonged his life.' He could see I was struggling to understand.

'OK, try this. Guy I knew out in the States, ex-military. He married a Japanese girl, Buddhist, who taught him to practise. He took to it like he'd been doing it all his life, but there was a problem. He'd served in the Gulf War, the first one, and had killed a lot of folks on the Basra Road – the turkey shoot, remember?'

I did, vaguely.

'Well, it really troubled him, especially the cause and

248

effect thing. How was it going to come back on him? So he went for guidance with a senior Buddhist, and he was told basically that there was nothing he could do to change the past, but if he did everything he could to create the maximum value now, the effects would definitely be lessened one way or another, though the adviser couldn't say exactly how, or when they'd manifest themselves. But my friend was reassured enough to stop worrying about it, and did everything he could to create value for himself, his family, his neighbours, you name it; especially in telling people how they could change their karma through Buddhism.

'Anyway, he had a job as a salesman, travelled all up and down the West Coast, and one day a couple of years later his wife gets a call from the California Highway Patrol. He's been found dead in his car. But the strange thing is it's simply driven in a straight line off the freeway and come to a stop. There's been no collision, nothing, and the body's completely unmarked. Turns out he's had a heart attack, like Geoff, but no one really knows what happened: if he felt pain coming on and pulled over, or died at the wheel and just miraculously came off the freeway without crashing, or what. But again, his wife felt he'd definitely lessened his karmic retribution. And' – seeing me still struggling – 'even in death he created value, because his family to that point had been anti-Japanese and anti-Buddhist, but seeing how his wife faced up to her loss, and overcame her shock and grief, they were so moved they began to support her, and some of them eventually started to practise themselves.'

I let out a deep sigh. 'So basically you're saying that Geoff had the karma to die seven years ago, because . . .?'

Frank shrugged. 'Who knows? "It's impossible to fathom one's karma."'

'Why?'

'Because the memories are too deep. I mean, I can't remember everything I did in this lifetime, let alone past lives.'

'OK,' I said, 'so, for some unknown reason, he had the karma to die seven years ago but because he practised Buddhism he cheated death, only for it to catch up with him now. Is that it?'

'That's not how I'd put it,' said Frank, glancing at Liz for help.

'How would you put it then?' I asked Liz.

'He lessened his karmic retribution and prolonged his life by creating the maximum value he could.'

'Through chanting?'

'Among other things.'

I looked at them both, then shook my head. 'Well, I'm sorry, but it just sounds like a nice theory to me, to make you feel better about something that's random and meaningless. Sorry.'

'Yup. And I'd think that way too, Ed,' he said, 'if I hadn't seen stuff like this time and again.'

Liz nodded her agreement.

'Look at it through the Buddha's eyes and it's not random or meaningless – quite the opposite.'

I had a flash of being with Geoff on the side of that City office block, and him yelling out, 'Life's wonderful, death's wonderful. It's all fucking wonderful!' I told Frank and Liz the story. They smiled.

'Sounds like Geoff,' said Liz.

'Wish I'd known him better,' said Frank.

'He was great,' I said, swallowing hard to stop the sudden emotion. 'Which is why dying like that . . . And I can't see what's so wonderful about death either. You work, you bring up a family, you achieve something –

maybe. And then you die and everything you value is just taken away from you. Everything . . .' I shook my head, bewildered. 'And then, according to you Buddhists, you come back and do it all over again! What for? I mean, really – what *is* the point?'

This was the nub of it for me. I was grieving, sure, but the sudden, abrupt snuffing out of a life of someone from whom I was learning so much and who still seemed to have so much life to live . . . It had shaken me, scared me to the core. I didn't want to think about death, or hear about it, or be anywhere near it. Because I didn't want to be reminded of my own mortality. The thought of extinction – *my* extinction, that great black hole of oblivion . . . it gave me the chills.

The trouble started, I think, when my mother died. My father died first but he was nearly eighty and it seemed fair enough when he went. I was sad, of course, but that was life – so to speak. But my mother was quite a bit younger than him and in good health. Then, a few weeks after his death she suddenly got ill and two days later she was dead. I was shocked. At her funeral I remember them bringing in the coffin on their shoulders and thinking, She's in there. Lying in there. Dead. Just a week earlier she'd been up and about, nagging me to pull my finger out and make something of my life, and now here she was in this box, about to be burned to a crisp. I couldn't get away from the funeral and reception fast enough, and I suppose I buried my fears as quickly as I could, too.

Now here I was again. Someone close to me had died unexpectedly and my sleeping terrors had been awoken. There would be a funeral, of course, but would I go? I'd have to, out of respect if nothing else. But then again, if I didn't who would know? Dora and maybe Piers, and possibly the two people in this room with me now, Liz and

Frank – who was looking at me strangely. He'd asked me a question and I'd been off in another world.

'Sorry? I drifted away for a moment there.'

'He's not been sleeping very well,' Liz explained.

'I said, are you one of those people who thinks that the fact we die renders life meaningless?'

'Absolutely.' Or more precisely, the fact that *I* will die will render *my* life meaningless. And suddenly I got another of those flashes of realisation: that perhaps this was at the root of my lack of focus and direction. Fundamentally, I didn't believe in the worth of anything I did because one day I'd die and it would all be for nothing.

'Well, I believe the exact opposite,' said Frank.

'What?' His statement startled me back to attention.

'I believe it's only because we die that life has meaning.' His expression said he was being serious.

'How do you work that one out?'

'Because we like stories.'

'Eh?'

Liz got up from the arm of the sofa where she'd been sitting. 'I'll make some tea,' she said. 'I've heard this before.'

Frank called after her as she left the room. 'Bring some cookies, honey.'

'No!' she answered with a laugh.

'Women,' Frank sighed. 'They never do anything you tell 'em these days.'

I smiled politely at his joke but didn't want to get sidetracked. 'So what's this thing about stories?' I asked.

'Well,' said Frank, 'have you ever wondered why people are fascinated by stories? And I don't mean experimental narrative or stream of consciousness or the sort of dreamy art-house movie that wins an award at some obscure European film festival. I mean "once upon a time" stuff:

traditional, mainstream, linear narrative.'

'No,' I said. Which was a pretty shameful confession from someone who had pretensions to writing a bestseller, but then I didn't read much either these days – fiction, non-fiction, anything. Which was even more shameful, especially for a literature graduate. 'Why are people fascinated by stories?'

'I actually think you know,' said Frank. 'Deep down.'

I looked blank.

He tried again. 'OK, what do you think is the most important part of any story?'

I shrugged. 'All of it.'

'Sure,' he said. 'In a sense you're completely right. But take these two scripts you just read: what's wrong with them?'

'I put it in the reports.'

'Remind me.'

I took a deep breath. 'Plot holes, poor character development, clichéd dialogue, predictable narrative – or incoherent narrative, lack of tension. Want me to go on?'

Frank glanced at the reports. 'You used one similar phrase for both scripts. You remember what it is?'

I shook my head.

Frank read. '"The ending doesn't make sense." And "The ending seems simply tacked on."'

'So?'

'The one thing that irritates a movie audience more than anything else is a poor ending. Assuming they buy into the characters and the story premise, they want an ending that satisfies, that makes sense in terms of the rest of the story. Consistency from beginning to end, in Buddhist-speak. It's not so important that it's a happy ending. Stick a happy ending on a story that's been full of doom and gloom and the audience smells baloney, because life isn't like that.

Same as ending a comedy with a death – the audience feels offended. "You made us laugh and laugh – and then you give this clown cancer? What's with you guys?" Of course, there're lots of variations in between, but the same rule applies: the end has to be prepared by what goes before. Sudden reversals, or quickly tying up all the story strands because the movie's already over-length and anyway we ran out of budget; or worse still, not reaching any conclusion at all: "You're the audience: you decide." It drives people nuts.'

'So?' I said again.

'So some time ago I started to think about this, about why people are so into stories the world over, and why the ending's so damned important.'

'And your conclusion?'

'My conclusion is that it's because we're all living the story of our own lives – and we don't know the ending.' He let that sit with me for a moment, then continued. 'We want to know how other people's stories turn out because we want to know how *our* story turns out. Someone once said that every story at some level asks the same basic question: what's the best way to live? We read or watch or listen to stories to find out, learn a lesson, maybe reject alternatives – or accept them. Doesn't matter. We're fascinated by different possibilities. Take *Fatal Attraction*. Huge hit. Why? Because who hasn't, at some point, flirted with the idea of sexual infidelity? Maybe only fleetingly, but it's a possibility, an option we could explore. Except Michael Douglas gets the mistress from Hell. Moral – don't go there. *Brief Encounter* – same subject matter but by *not* having an affair the audience sees Trevor Howard and Celia Johnson are denying themselves something: love, life, happiness. Moral – they *should* go there. People see themselves in both situations.'

'Well, that's all very interesting,' I said, 'but what's it got to do with death?'

'Death is the end of our story,' Frank said. 'It's the final curtain. It draws everything to a close, and so it gives a meaning to the life just lived.'

'I don't see that at all.'

'Well, what meaning is there in a never-ending story?' asked Frank. 'It's just one damned thing after another. Like a football match with no final whistle. The score doesn't matter because there's never going to be a result.'

'Life is not like a football match,' I protested.

Frank sucked air through his teeth, disagreeing. 'Well, we could talk about that, too, but maybe not today.'

'OK,' I said, 'three objections. First, according to Buddhism, life *is* a never-ending story, because you keep coming back.'

'Yeah, in one sense you're right. Except it's more a series of self-contained chapters, each complete in itself.'

'Even so,' I countered, 'for the person who died it doesn't make a blind bit of difference how the story ends – because they're dead!'

Frank pulled another face; he didn't agree with that either.

'And third, for the people watching – us, the audience, the survivors – how a person dies is often a problem for exactly the reason you say a film audience gets hacked off. The ending doesn't fit.'

'Well, that's where Buddhism disagrees,' said Frank. 'In terms of cause and effect the ending always fits.'

'So you *are* saying Geoff deserved to have a heart attack up a ladder?'

'How the ending fits may not be obvious at first, but with the passing of time people often come to understand.'

I shook my head. 'I can't see how Geoff's death was

anything other than totally random, without meaning, just ... useless.'

'So how do you think he should have died, then?'

An odd question. 'I don't know,' I said. 'Just not like that.'

'Why not?'

'Because ...' I couldn't think.

'I appreciate you knew him a lot better than I did,' said Frank, 'but it sounds to me he died doing something he really enjoyed.'

Well, that was true.

'And not everyone wants to die at home in bed. There's a woman I know in her seventies who loves hill-walking. She wants to die with her boots on. Guy I know says he can't think of a better way to go than having sex. Some people want to die peacefully, some heroically, some nobly – all sorts of ways. So why shouldn't Geoff die doing a job he loved?'

'But he was only *fifty*.'

'And who's to say how long we should live?'

He had a bloody answer for everything, but he could see I wasn't satisfied.

'Every life lived has a meaning, Ed – I believe. And every death, too. It's just a question of if and when we can see it.'

Liz came in with a tray of mugs and a plate of biscuits. 'Tea,' she said.

Frank spotted the biscuits and grinned.

***

For some reason I didn't leave them feeling any better than when I arrived. This problem of death and karma still gnawed at me. But they had offered twenty quid for each script report I wrote, which seemed pretty easy money, so I'd picked five, again at random. I flicked through them with some trepidation on the way home, dreading more confirmation of my rampant Animality, but they were a mixed bunch: a comedy, a love story, a couple of action flicks and a . . . I wasn't quite sure, to be honest. A domestic tragedy? So that meant either my life state was all over the place, or that I'd been reading more into the first two scripts than was actually there. Perhaps things would become clearer as I settled down to work.

I fully intended to when I got home, but once back in my flat a terrible lethargy descended on me. It was like an invisible cloud that came out of the ceiling and enveloped me, sucking the life from me. I sat on the sofa, unable to move, to lift my arms almost, just staring, while nothing and everything went through my head. Things Geoff had said to me, Frank's crackpot story theory, Angie . . . And none of it seemed to matter. Whatever Frank said, death didn't give anything meaning – it just wiped it all away.

What I didn't see at the time, of course, was that I was slipping rapidly into a deep depression. Another anchor had gone and I was adrift again – adrift and bereft.

That night I had another dream. I saw my father a little distance away. I'm not sure whether it was in the street or somewhere like a park or garden, but there were other people around. He hadn't seen me and I called out to him, but he didn't hear and started to walk away. I tried to reach him but people got in the way. I called again but all I could see was his back as he moved further into the distance. I shouted as loud as I could – and found myself sitting up in bed. In the quiet. In the dark. And tense.

257

Chapter Fifteen

Young people look forward, the middle-aged look around, and old people look back. If that's true, I was becoming positively ancient. I spent most of the next few days in bed, churning over the past. Geoff, Angie, my family, my far from illustrious career: it all swam in and out of my consciousness in a vague, grey soup of thoughts and images, 'what ifs' and 'maybes'. I was back in the state to which I'd sunk when The Bestseller hit the buffers – depressed, apathetic, gloomy. I had no energy and no hope. The future was totally bleak – just more of the same – and despite all the Buddhist theory I'd learned over the months, I felt helpless to change anything. And all the time I had in my stomach a tight, hard knot of anxiety. Something else was going to happen to top losing my girlfriend, my job and then the man who had appeared as my saviour. I didn't know what or when, but it would be equally terrible and maybe, this time, terminal.

When I did manage to drag myself out of bed, perhaps to go to the bathroom, or because hunger finally got the better of my inertia, I'd have a pee or make some toast or whatever, and then slump listlessly in front of daytime TV. Chat shows, quiz shows, cookery programmes – I'd flick blankly round and round the circuit till eventually, in disgust, I'd hit the standby button and sit staring at the little red light. 'I've got to do something,' I'd tell myself. 'Get out of this mood, get out of this flat. Go the doctor, get some pills – Prozac, Valium, Viagra, anything that will kick-start my life again.' With immense effort, I'd lever myself off the sofa and shuffle the few steps it took to reach the hall, then think, What the hell, turn left into the bedroom and fall back into bed.

'What I'd really like to do is direct . . .' That was me. That was what I'd become. A dreamer, unable to make any sustained effort, hiding under the duvet. And knowing all about the oneness of mind and body, and of life and its environment and *ichinen sanzen* and all that only made it worse, because it was as if the key to changing everything, to happiness, was at my fingertips – but I couldn't turn it. Martin had done it, so why couldn't I? I'd meant to ask Dora but had got sidetracked – not for the first time. Plus I'd lacked courage – also not for the first time – because it would have been inviting her to tell me my faults, and I couldn't stand to have my own poor opinion of myself confirmed.

Or should that be MEF's opinion? I could hardly tell any more. He was my constant companion during those dark days following Geoff's death. He was so much in my head that we seemed to merge completely into one entity. He was my nurse, my confidant, my gaoler. And as long as I didn't try to escape, he was nice as pie. 'It's OK here,' he/I'd say. 'You're warm, comfortable. There's food in the fridge and money in the bank for several weeks if you live simply. Don't fight it. This is your life. Let's face the future one day at a time, and if a problem comes – well, we'll get through it. We always have in the past. Let the world go. It's full of crap anyway. So keep your head down, don't make waves and, above all, forget about trying. It'll only end in failure.'

Any thought of picking up the phone, calling Dora or Liz or the doctor, and at once he'd come up with a dozen reasons not to. Dora is chanting; Liz is busy and anyway she's expecting you to write those script reports, not bleat for help. And the doctor? You really want to get hooked on anti-depressants, you pathetic saddo? He even tried to stop me watering Piers's acorn. 'What's the point?' he said. 'It'll never grow into an oak tree; not unless you find somewhere to plant it out and somehow, against all the odds, it's not uprooted by whoever owns the land or vandals don't destroy it or a dog doesn't just dig it up. And even if it does grow, you'll never live to see it, will you? Because it's not love that conquers all. It's death.' And yet, for some reason, I did water it. It was my one, slender, tenuous link to life. Until Dora phoned.

I didn't stir myself to answer, just lay listening to the machine as she left a message. 'Hi, Ed. It's Dora, 11.15 on Tuesday. Just calling to find out how you are and to tell you that Geoff's funeral is the day after tomorrow at the West Chapel, Hoop Lane, at noon. Hope you can make it. Give me a call if you want a chat. Bye.'

She sounded OK – calm, warm, friendly. Whereas I felt agitated, cold and distinctly hostile. MEF kicked in at once. 'Ugh, a funeral. And a Buddhist one at that. Expect a lot of sanctimonious piety about reincarnation and eternal life and—' But for once I shut him up. There was no way I couldn't go.

***

I arrived several minutes late, deliberately, to let everyone get into the chapel. I wanted to pay my respects in anonymity and then slip away. I didn't want to talk to anyone – not even Dora – because I felt such terrible company. I hated myself, I hated the world, and I had no right to inflict this coiled spring of negativity onto anyone. It was only with a supreme effort of will that I was here at all. I'd ironed a shirt, put on a suit and told MEF to go to hell; but it was just a matter of time before he reappeared and started to strut his stuff, dissing everything and everybody. With any luck, though, I'd already be on my way back home by then. Back to sanctuary.

The sky was overcast and grey – just right for a funeral, I thought, as I pushed open the heavy wooden door to the red-brick, Edwardian chapel. It was even gloomier inside – but packed. To my surprise I found myself at the back of a throng of people. In every pew mourners were pressed shoulder to shoulder, and people were even standing in the aisle. Men and women, black and white, Indian, Chinese; what looked like a couple of Arabs; old, young, middle-aged, the conservatively dressed, the flamboyant, the smart, the casual – they were so varied that for a moment I was quite taken aback. Everyone was listening attentively to a tall, middle-aged bloke in a dark suit, who was standing on a low dais at the front, addressing the congregation.

' . . . which consists of simply repeating this phrase over and over again,' he said. 'But if you prefer to offer you own thoughts or prayers for Geoff during this period, which will last for about five minutes, please feel free to do so. We will then end with a short series of silent prayers, after which we will chant three times. This will be followed by three short addresses: two from friends of Geoff and a brief explanation of the Buddhist view of life and death. Then the body will be committed, during which we will chant again. Finally, I'll ring the bell, we'll chant three more times, and that will be the end.'

During all this I was taking my bearings. Geoff's coffin was to his right, at right angles, lined up on the catafalque in front of an opening in the side wall. Behind the speaker was a chair in front of a small table on which stood a wooden cabinet. Hanging inside the cabinet seemed to be a scroll of some sort, covered with what looked like black squiggles: Buddhist writing, I guessed. Sitting on an ornate cushion to the side of the chair was a metal bowl that I realised was the bell to which the speaker had referred. A heavy wooden stick, one half covered in a white material, rested on a stand by the bell.

I scanned the congregation. There must have been about three hundred people crammed into the place. Then I saw Dora. I smiled. She was radiant, in shiny wig and full make-up, and swaddled in a thick fur coat. To my eye she looked dressed more for a wedding than a funeral, but what did I know? Looking around the assembled mourners, as varied a bunch of humanity as I could have imagined, it seemed that anything went at a Buddhist funeral.

The tall bloke turned his back on everyone and sat in the chair in front of the cabinet. Taking a set of prayer beads from his jacket pocket, he nodded to the scroll and picked up the wooden stick. As he did so there was a rustle as prayer beads appeared from the pockets and handbags of the Buddhists in the congregation. And again I was surprised. The elegant, silver-haired matron who looked as if she belonged in some Home Counties vicarage was getting ready to chant, while the middle-aged Chinese bloke sitting next to her clearly had no idea what was going on. It was a contrast seen throughout the chapel. Two black girls in the same pew – one was going to chant, the other not; a wealthy-looking man in a smart suit had beads in his hand, a younger guy in a denim jacket didn't; and so on. There was nothing to distinguish the Buddhists from the non-Buddhists; which I suppose I should have anticipated, considering the fact that Geoff, Dora, Piers, Liz and Frank seemed to have nothing in common except their faith; but in the back of my mind I assumed that once you got a whole bunch of them together the Asians would predominate.

There was a loud clang. My eyes switched back to the front of the chapel and saw that the tall bloke had struck the bell hard with the stick. As its deep, rich tone echoed back and forth between the polished brick walls, he struck it again, then again and again, in a series of diminishing blows that faded to silence. Then he put the stick back on its stand, placed his hands together still clasping the beads, and, focusing on the scroll, chanted a phrase in a language I didn't understand. As he did so, all the Buddhists in the audience joined him, the sound swelling as the voices of male and female, young and old, blended in harmony. They repeated the phrase three times, then suddenly they were off. All the Buddhists together reciting something at breakneck speed; some reading from a small book they held up in front of them, others from memory. And as they did I felt a strange surge of electricity zing up my spine. The hairs stood up on my arms and neck, my scalp tingled. After a minute or so they paused, the bell was rung once more – and then they were off again, all together, rhythmically intoning, eyes fixed on the paper in the box. Then they began slowing down, and suddenly they were chanting that phrase they'd all said at the start. I still couldn't make it out, but again I felt a surge of energy go through my body. Life force. I was washed in the sound, submerged by it, totally absorbed. I don't know how long they chanted, but suddenly the bloke was striking the bell again and everyone was slowing to a halt. More bell ringing, more chants, then a final clang, three chants – and silence. The bloke at the front nodded to the box, stood up and turned to face the congregation. 'Thank you,' he said simply, and sat in a seat to one side, directly opposite the coffin, looking at the hole in the wall into which it would shortly disappear.

I didn't know quite what had hit me. I felt a bit dazed, as if I'd been scoured by a powerful cleanser, the way you see toilet bowls transformed in TV ads by a whoosh of bleach. A slim woman in her mid-fifties came to the front of the chapel, dressed in a dark business suit, holding a sheet of paper in her hand. She stepped onto the dais and turned to address us.

'My name is Barbara Watson,' she said in a plummy voice, like the headmistress of some posh girls' school, 'and I first met Geoff when he started to clean the windows of our legal chambers in Lincoln's Inn. As you know, Geoff was an extremely approachable and friendly man, who loved to talk – especially about Buddhism. And I personally learned much from him about his faith, which I promised him I would definitely embrace – in my next life.'

The audience chuckled.

'I'm rather like Saint Augustine, I'm afraid, who before he converted asked God to give him chastity and continence, but not yet.'

Another collective chuckle.

'Although, to be fair to Geoff, I can only describe his brand of Buddhism as earthy, very human and, as far as I understand it, utterly practical. All epithets I would also apply to Geoff himself. And more – because he was a man with many facets, which surfaced at surprising times. One morning some years ago, for example, when Geoff was cleaning the windows, he asked what I was toiling over. "A plea in mitigation for one of my clients," I said. "Ah, Portia," he said, and then quoted the entirety of her "quality of mercy" speech from *The Merchant of Venice*. When I expressed my admiration he confessed to a love of literature, which led to many enjoyable and vigorous conversations between us on a whole variety of subjects. In fact, I used to look forward very much to his visits so that we might exchange views on everything from politics to poetry, and I'd be terribly disappointed if I missed him. It was my own snobbery, I know, but I was constantly amazed at the range of topics he could engage with, and the depth of his understanding. And when once I asked him how he knew so much he said, with typical simplicity and modesty, "I read a lot, Babs." Though I have to warn you that he was the only person I allowed to call me that.'

More laughter.

'But by that time we had become friends. An unlikely combination perhaps, but one that certainly enriched me – and I hope Geoff, too. So, by way of tribute to Geoff and what I consider to be his extraordinarily wide-ranging "down-to-earthness", I can think of nothing more fitting than these lines from T.S. Eliot.' She put on a small pair of spectacles and read.

> We shall not cease from exploration
> And the end of all our exploring
> Will be to arrive where we started
> And know the place for the first time.

She smiled her thanks at the congregation and sat down, to a round of applause. I was too shaken to join in. For her to quote the very lines of Eliot that had occurred to me during one of my conversations with Geoff – that was spooky. But it also raised again the unanswered question I had about Buddhism: was it all just a way of appreciating the ordinary, or was it about actually changing things?

A second speaker stepped onto the dais. He was in his forties, short and stocky with a large, bushy beard, and seemed ill at ease in a suit and tie. The reason soon became clear.

'Hello,' he said in a loud, London voice. 'I'm Bernie Stevens and I knew Geoff because I used to lay bricks for him when he was a builder. And when that all went pear-shaped I got to know him better because he kipped on my sofa for a few weeks, till I kicked him out. The next time I saw him was nearly two years later and he was unrecognisable from the depressed drunk I'd chucked out. He was focused, together, happy. "I was so impressed I bought the company"' – delivered in a cod US accent – 'meaning when he told me he'd done it by practising Buddhism I decided there and then to give it a go myself. Because I thought if he can do it, so can I. So – thank you, Geoff.' He turned to the coffin, put his hands together in front of his chest and bowed deeply.

A lump suddenly came to my throat. Why? Because sincere emotion cuts the heart.

He produced a sheet of paper from his inside pocket. 'We didn't have intellectual conversations, probably because he realised I'm too thick.'

The audience tittered uncertainly.

'But he did share bits of writing with me that meant something to him – Buddhist stuff and other bits and pieces. And this I know was one of his favourites. It's by a Buddhist writer called Daisaku Ikeda.' He cleared his throat and read.

I feel most deeply I have done something creative when I have thrown myself wholeheartedly into a task and fought it through unstintingly to its conclusion and thus have won a struggle to enlarge myself. It is a

266

matter of sweat and tears. The creative life demands constant effort to improve one's thoughts and actions. Perhaps the dynamism involved in the effort is the important thing.

You will pass through storms, and you may suffer defeat. The essence of the creative life, however, is to persevere in the face of defeat and to follow the rainbow within your heart. Indulgence and indolence are not creative. Complaints and evasions are cowardly, and corrupt life's natural tendency towards creation. The person who gives up the fight for creativeness is headed ultimately for the hell that destroys all life.

My body went rigid. The shock of recognition. The rest of the words I heard as a series of hammer blows, straight to the brain.

You must never slacken in your efforts to build new lives for yourselves. Creativeness means pushing open the heavy door to life. This is not an easy struggle. Indeed, it may be the hardest task in the world. For opening the door to your own life is more difficult than opening the doors to the mysteries of the universe.

But the act of opening your door vindicates your existence as a human being and makes life worth living. No one is lonelier or unhappier than the person who does not know the pure joy of creating a life for himself. To be human is not merely to stand erect and manifest reason and intellect: to be human in the full sense of the word is to lead a creative life.

Bernie folded his paper and looked up at the congregation. 'The fact you're all here I take to be proof

Geoff did live a creative life. Thank you.' He returned to his seat to another burst of applause.

The tall bloke got up again and faced the front. He, too, took a sheet of paper from his suit pocket and started to talk. He explained how the universe is a great ocean of life, and as the ocean 'waves', so the universe 'peoples' – in fact, creates life in all its diverse, myriad forms, in a constantly recurring cycle of life and death. Geoff was in the phase called death but was taking on energy, as we all do when we're asleep, to reappear in a fresh, new form. In life, in death, his life continued. It all sounded logical enough, and I could see a lot of people there believed it, but I was only half listening. My mind was still ringing with echoes from what Bernie had just said. 'Creativeness means pushing open the heavy door to life.' That described my situation exactly. 'This is not an easy struggle.' You can say that again. And all the time the tall bloke was talking my eyes were on Bernie, who was listening intently, arms folded and nodding from time to time.

Then the talking stopped, the tall bloke sat in front of the Buddhist scroll again, and the chanting restarted. After a short pause, the doors in the wall opened up and, with a slight jerk, Geoff's coffin began to slide out of sight. Thirty seconds later the doors closed and it was gone. Three more bangs on the bell, three more chants – and it was all over. The tall bloke got up, thanked us once more, and a pair of heavy doors opened behind him, under the rose window. We started to file out. I was hoping to get a closer look at the scroll but I was at the back of the throng, and by the time I reached the front the cabinet was closed and two ushers were packing things away.

I emerged into daylight with a mission. Everyone was jammed into the colonnade immediately behind the chapel, huddled against a cold wind that was now spitting rain. I pushed through knots of people – friends and family meeting again for the first time in years; or months, days, hours – till I came across Bernie, rolling a cigarette in a quiet corner out of the wind. 'I thought what you said was great,' I said. 'Thank you.'

'Cheers,' he said. 'But it weren't me. I just read it out.'

'Well, I think you did more than that, but what you read was great, too. Do you know where I can get a copy of it?'

He dug into his suit pocket and produced the folded sheet of paper. 'Keep it.'

'You're sure?'

'Yeah. I know it pretty much by heart anyway.'

'Thank you.'

'No problem, mate.' With that he turned to greet a couple of friends, but I didn't mind – I was already unfolding the paper and starting to read. I didn't get far.

'How's the acorn?'

I looked up to see Piers smiling at me. I hadn't seen him in the chapel. 'It's fine. Doing well. How's business?'

'Can't complain. Well, I can but mustn't – according to that.' He took the sheet and scanned it for a second, then read. 'Complaints and evasions are cowardly, and corrupt life's natural tendency towards creation.'

'Pretty uncompromising.'

'Mmm – but true,' Piers said ruefully. 'Cause and effect, you know. Speaking of creation, how's the bestseller coming?'

I pulled a face.

'Bit of a struggle, eh?'

'That's why I grabbed this.' I waved the paper.

'Well, I'm sure it'll be all the better for it.'

I smiled and changed the subject. 'Have you seen Dora?'

'In there.' Piers pointed to the thick of the scrum. 'Talking to Geoff's ex.'

'She's here?'

'Of course. And his daughters.'

For some reason I was surprised, as if Geoff's life before he became a Buddhist belonged somewhere else. 'I want to give my condolences,' I said, and stuck out my hand.

Now Piers looked surprised. 'Aren't you coming to the reception? It's just over the road.'

'Sorry,' I lied, squeezing his hand, 'but I've got a job interview.' Although my spirits had lifted – pretty odd for a funeral – I wasn't feeling sociable and wanted to run away home as soon as I could. I backed away from Piers. 'If ever you need some muscle, though . . .'

'Of course,' Piers said. 'And don't forget to put your acorn outside over winter.'

'Oh?'

'It needs to toughen up.' He smiled, and turned away. I stepped out from under the cover of the colonnade and skirted the crowd, looking for Geoff's family and Dora. A woman in her forties and two blondes in their twenties were standing slightly apart from the others. I decided to chance it. I approached them.

'Mrs Aston?'

The woman looked round blankly.

'I'm a friend of Geoff's,' I said, taking her hand. 'I just want to offer my condolences.'

'Thank you,' the woman murmured.

I could see she was lost, overwhelmed by all these strangers who knew her husband – ex-husband. I felt the need to explain why we were all here. 'Geoff was a great man,' I said.

The younger of the two blondes snorted and looked away. 'He was a window-cleaner,' she said, with such contempt that I caught my breath.

Then a surge of anger burst in me. 'Yes, but a fucking wonderful window-cleaner. And he loved you.'

All three of them looked shocked. I was shocked myself. How could that have come out of my mouth? The younger blonde flushed with anger and embarrassment, but was too rocked to know what to say.

'Sorry,' I mumbled, and hurried away. I saw an archway through to the car park and exit, and headed for it. My only thought now was to leave as quickly as possible. A hand grabbed my arm.

'Aren't you going to say hello?' It was Dora.

'I was, but I've just made a complete prat of myself.'

'How?'

'With Geoff's family,' I said, not daring to look back. 'I swore at his daughter.'

'Well,' she said, glancing their way, 'you're not alone. I've been in her bad books for years.'

'Oh?' This sounded interesting.

'Buy me lunch and I'll tell you the whole story,' she whispered conspiratorially.

I hesitated – home still seemed the safest option.

'I think you owe me,' she said, 'if only for the commission you lost me on that City job.'

How could I refuse? 'You're right,' I said. 'Where?'

'Oh, we'll find somewhere.' She smiled, and slipped her arm through mine.

***

We did – a small Italian restaurant in the Finchley Road, where she confessed over a plate of fettuccine con vongole. She was the other woman.

She'd met Geoff in – of all places – a pub, and had been smitten from the off. 'I'm an instant attraction sort of girl, I'm afraid,' she sighed. 'And he was younger then, of

271

course. More hair, less stomach. And really into his practice, full of energy, fun.'

'Did you know he was married?'

'Pretty soon, but I didn't care – I had different priorities in those days. I was younger too, of course. And his marriage was obviously not going anywhere.'

'What was the age gap?'

'Twelve years. I was twenty-three, he was thirty-five.' She saw me doing some mental arithmetic. 'I'm thirty-eight, darling, if you're counting.'

I smiled. 'So – you got together . . . ?'

Dora smiled wistfully and sipped her glass of wine.

'What went wrong?'

'Well, when his wife chucked him out he changed. Got depressed, especially at not seeing the girls, started to drink heavily, his practice slipped. He was not a happy man to be around.'

'So you chucked him out, too.'

'Eventually, yes – to save my sanity. Though he did leave me the practice, so something good came of it. And we became friends again, later on.'

I watched her fork some pasta into her mouth.

'Do you mind if I make an observation?' I asked.

She fluttered her eyelashes at me and shook her head.

'Well,' I said, 'I can't help noticing how cheerful you seem. When I told you Geoff was dead it sounded like you fell apart.'

'I did.' Mumbled through her fettucine.

'But now it's like you're almost happy.'

'I've done a lot of chanting.'

'That makes it better, does it?'

'Considerably.' She could see I was perplexed. 'Geoff dying was an incredible shock, but you heard what the guy said about the universe being an ocean of life?'

272

I nodded.

'Well, to me that means Geoff's all around us, everywhere. He's not really gone. I'm still connected to him, he's still part of my life. It's like he's gone on an expedition up the Amazon without his mobile. I know he's there somewhere – I just can't reach him.'

'He's dead, Dora.'

'Yes, but his life's not gone.'

I shook my head, lost.

'The guy who wrote the piece about the creative life – Daisaku Ikeda?'

I patted my breast pocket. 'Got it here. Bernie gave it to me.'

'Right. Well, he put it brilliantly once, talking about death. "You can't escape the universe," he said. Your life's got to go somewhere. And that's even according to physics – second law of thermodynamics, I believe.'

I sat there, trying to take it in.

She looked at me enquiringly. 'But how do *you* feel?'

Good question. 'Well, I didn't want to come, to tell the truth. Funerals are . . .' I shuddered. 'And I've been pretty down since – well, since I called you, I suppose.'

'Just Geoff, or still having woman trouble?'

'Ah.' I took a deep breath and told her about Angie – a censored version. No need to go into graphic detail about my manly shortcomings.

Dora listened carefully. 'So it's all over then?'

'Yes,' I sighed. 'Finally, completely, for ever.'

She looked thoughtful.

'So, what with Geoff, and that, and no proper job, coming along today, facing people – it was a real struggle. But the funny thing is I actually felt better coming out of there than going in, which for funerals and me is a first.'

'Do you know why?'

'Well, I thought the chanting was pretty powerful; not at all like I'd imagined. And the stuff Bernie read out – that blew me away. What's the thing in the box, by the way? The scroll thing.'

'That's the Gohonzon,' she said.

'Gohonzon? Any relation?'

She laughed. 'Yes. *Honzon* means object of devotion, and *go* means "worthy of great respect".'

'You worship a piece of paper?'

She laughed again. 'No: what the paper embodies.'

'Which is . . . ?'

'Buddhahood. The life of the Buddha.'

I was confused. 'If it's the Buddha shouldn't you have a statue or something – one of those little golden ones?'

'We're not worshipping the Buddha, a person, a historical figure. We're worshipping the life of the Buddha.'

'Don't get it.'

'You're the Buddha, Ed. I'm the Buddha. This table is the Buddha. Buddha is another name for life itself – all of it. Past, present, future, from this space where we're sitting right out into infinity.'

'And beyond!' In my best Buzz Lightyear.

She grinned. 'That's it. So when you chant to the Gohonzon you're devoting your life to life itself, in its highest condition. Wisdom, courage and compassion.'

'Ah.' The trio from *The Wizard of Oz*.

'And because the Gohonzon embodies Buddhahood, concentrating on it while you chant brings up your own Buddhahood; just like looking at a beautiful picture brings up certain feelings in you. What's outside connects with what's inside.'

'How do you know?'

'I feel it. Not always at once, but always after a time. Like with Geoff's death. When you told me, I was devastated because . . . well, at one time I loved him. And part of me still does. But gradually, through chanting, I've changed this terrible feeling of loss I had into appreciation: for knowing him, loving him. And gratitude that he gave me this fantastic practice. I'm sad, sure, that's natural. But now it's a kind of smiling sadness, rather than gut-wrenching and crying all the time.'

Something suddenly clicked in me. 'Are you saying you can actually change your mood through chanting?'

'Of course!' She laughed.

'At will? Consciously?'

'That's the whole point!' She sounded amazed I hadn't got it. 'You generate life force, hope – it washes everything, transforms it. You see things differently, start again, don't give up . . .'

I thought for a moment. Perhaps I'd been extraordinarily dense, but for some reason this sounded worth exploring further. 'So what is it you chant exactly?'

She sat back in her chair and gazed at me, then suddenly leaned across the table and kissed me – on the lips. 'I thought you'd never ask,' she smiled.

Chapter Sixteen

One thing leads to another, and Dora and I became an item; then we were together; and now, after several months, I think you could say we're on the verge of becoming a couple; we've been discussing if I should move in with her, or she with me, or if we should both sell up and buy somewhere together. All scary stuff and MEF, bless him, is having a field day – especially about the fact that she's a few years older than me, and black. Except Dora manages to put him back in his box whenever I allow him airtime, which, unlike Angie, she actually encourages. 'You can't fight an enemy you can't see,' she says, before giving him a verbal going-over.

The spooky thing, though, is that the more I've got to know her, the more I see how like Angie she is. Feisty, argumentative, won't take any crap – certainly not from me. The difference is this chanting thing. We have a spat, she goes and chants, she comes back, her mood's changed and somehow we sort things out. Or she comes back and her mood *hasn't* changed and she puts me on the bloody spot. Which is when I've got to chant to seriously take on board what she's saying.

Like when she found out I'd given her copy of Frankl to Angie. I thought she might be all philosophical and

276

Buddhist about it, but she was really upset and insisted I get it back. Now, I really didn't want to call Angie, and Dora pointing out that, 'If you haven't got the balls to do this how the hell do you expect to get anywhere in life?' didn't exactly help. Well, it did, actually, as it forced me to chant about the cowardly lion in me. But – miracle – the very next morning a small, brown Jiffy bag plopped onto the mat containing – tra-la – the book. No note or anything, just the book, so I don't know if Angie had actually read it, but at least it was back. I was amazed.

Dora was a lot less excited. 'Just means you'll have to develop your courage some other way,' she sniffed.

'Sticking with you, perhaps?' I suggested, at which point she threw something at me – only a tea towel, but I got the message.

Still, she was really pleased to have the book back and later showed she'd forgiven me in the nicest possible way – which possibly answers my question about Buddhahood and sex . . . I'm not sure.

Now she's urging me to chant about this idea of living together, so that I 'make the decision from the right life state'. I'm dragging my feet, to be honest, but she's done loads of chanting about it; and she did loads about me after we first met, apparently, which is quite flattering really. Anyway, the point is we seem to have this tool for reaching decisions or mediating disputes, and so far – fingers crossed – it seems to have worked.

So, as you can see, I've succumbed to Buddhism. Not just because Dora's my girlfriend, and not a hundred per cent. Chanting twice a day, morning and evening, can be a real test; but then, I suppose that's the same for making any effort on a consistent basis. But when I do manage it consistently for a week or so I feel great. Dora says it's like PT for the human spirit. You get fit through doing it over a period of time, and then keep at it to maintain your level of fitness. Often you don't see the difference until a crisis hits: like the difference between having to run for a bus when you're fit and when you're not. And I have to say that gradually my outlook on life is changing. My black moods, for example. They used to be a regular feature: once a month, at least, life was pointless, hopeless, bleak. I had one the other day and it came as a real shock because I realised I hadn't felt like this for weeks. And the incredible thing was that, after some extra chanting, within twenty-four hours it was gone. It used to hang around for days.

I've had other realisations, too – about Geoff, for example. According to Dora and other friends of his I've met, he wasn't just active in the Buddhist organisation but was a Samaritan, supported several charities, and worked with the local council on various multicultural projects, like a huge international food fair they put on a few years ago. And to everyone he talked about Buddhism – some directly, some just through encouraging them to believe in themselves. Hearing all this, it gradually dawned on me that he really did spend his time helping people to see at every level. He hadn't misled me at all.

That's one reason I decided to junk The Bestseller and write this instead – to say thank you. Buddhism's got a nice term for it: repaying debts of gratitude. I'm still reading scripts for Liz and Frank, and supplementing that as a freelance proof-reader – not glamorous but it pays the bills. The writing's been a struggle, but Dora's been there to crack the whip whenever I've flagged, and, as you can see, I've nearly finished. I just hope someone might read it and find it interesting; maybe helpful, even. But even if no one does, I've tried my best, I feel, to repay my debt to Geoff, because meeting him was the most significant thing that has ever happened to me.

Talking of which, I now realise that the sentence I started this book with is completely wrong. *Everything* prepares you for the moment when your life changes. That's the whole point. It might be unexpected on one level, but somewhere deep down you're looking for something, otherwise you wouldn't recognise it when the moment comes. If I'd been totally happy and satisfied, nothing Geoff could have said or done in The Three Crowns would have had any effect on me.

Another realisation – two realisations, actually, both about that manhole cover in the Gents. I was thinking about Geoff and WCC – wisdom, courage and compassion – and I realised that in sticking his arm into all that sewage he'd shown all three. The wisdom to know what to do, the courage to do it, and the compassion that through his action everyone in the pub would benefit. The Buddha in the bog . . . But Buddhahood's not some airy-fairy mental thing, I've come to realise, or about sitting on a mountaintop somewhere being 'enlightened'. It's about getting your hands dirty and actually changing things for the better.

The other realisation's more personal, because I've come to see that there's a big, heavy manhole cover over my life, too. There's been a stink coming from it for years, but I've been too squeamish to lift the lid and investigate, let alone plunge my arm in and clear it out. Too scared, basically. There's a Buddhist quote I came across recently that really hit home: 'To discard the shallow and seek the profound requires courage.' It keeps coming back to the same pair, for me at least – fear and courage. But I know now that if I don't challenge this part of me, if I just let the cover drop back into place with a clang, the stink's not going to go away. It's going to get worse. And who wants to live with a cesspit? Angie didn't, and I don't blame her.

And I don't suppose Dora will if I don't change. It's like Freud said: we all find the smell of shit repulsive, except our own.

But even shit has a function, I've realised – which brings me to My Evil Friend. A fascinating development here. I said just now that Dora's all for me letting him speak up so that she can take him on. Well, one consequence of this is that I've become oddly protective of him. He is a *friend*, after all. And increasingly, instead of just relaying what he's been muttering to me, I've taken to chanting about his pessimism, and his Cassandra-like prophecies of doom and gloom, and his cynical sniping about life in general. And what I've realised is that quite often floating around in his sea of negativity are pearls of genuine wisdom and insight. The challenge is to fish them out before they're totally swamped by the waves of rubbish he generates. It all comes down to how you look at it. And that comes down to life state.

Dora explained it one day in a way that even I could finally begin to understand. I'd asked her about *ichinen sanzen* and said I could see how I affected my environment and my environment affected me, but I just couldn't see how they were 'one', different aspects of the same thing, or how there was a true continuity from what went on inside me to the world 'out there', as far as the distant reaches of the universe.

'OK,' said Dora. 'Imagine you've gone to a party and the room's full of people – all different types, all different backgrounds. How you experience it depends on your life condition, the Ten Worlds. If you're in Hell you'll probably not want to talk to anyone, and no one will want to talk to you. If you're in Hunger you might move from person to person but never really stop long enough to talk to anyone properly. If you're in Animality you might be

280

looking to chat someone up to get them into bed. In Anger you might have an argument. In Humanity you'll have a nice enough time, but forgettable perhaps. In Rapture you'll dance the night away. In Learning you'll pick someone's brains. In Realisation you'll observe everyone and maybe draw some conclusion about some aspect of human behaviour. In Bodhisattva you'll be the shoulder the person in Hell cries on, and in Buddhahood you might tell them about how chanting can change their situation.'

'So?'

'So the point is, exactly the same physical and social environment will look quite different to you, and offer you very different possibilities, entirely depending on the condition of your life. You'll approach different people, attract different people, talk to different people – according to your life state. And what results from that will also be different according to your life state. You'll get drunk, make a vital contact, save someone's life – all according to your life state. And so the course of your life, moment to moment, is shaped by which of the Ten Worlds is strongest in you. It controls how you see things, how you think, the decisions you make. Buddhism even says it determines the environment into which you're born; which is a bit like saying which party you're invited to in the first place.'

I liked that: life as a party to which we're all invited. Sounded fun. I also like what Dora said next – but then, I like a lot of things about Dora. Anyway, here's what she said.

'Geoff once told me that the future is like a vacuum, waiting to be filled with reality. That reality will be determined by the strongest input, and if you don't make it, someone or something else will. Cause and effect. So the key question is who or what makes the most powerful cause – and, crucially, can it be you? Geoff said the most powerful cause he knew is chanting, and I agree with him, because it means that gradually, little by little, you're filling your life with Buddhahood, until eventually it's dominated by Buddhahood. You live in Buddhahood now, your future's shaped by your Buddhahood, and your environment – especially the people – is touched and influenced by your Buddhahood. I think it's a fantastic way to live.'

That did it for me. I might not understand the theory, though it's coming slowly, bit by bit; but there's something about the way Dora talks, the way she thinks, that just makes me feel great, and that life's worth living. Geoff had it, Piers has it – in fact, a lot of the Buddhists I've met have it. Not all of them, since quite a few really seem to struggle, but I'm assured that they were even more confused before they started to chant. And the amazing thing is it all comes down to chanting a few Chinese and Sanskrit characters, which translate into a phrase of just sixteen letters. It's hidden in this book if you want to look for it, and when you find it I hope you'll give it a go.

So here we are – at the end. And in my end is my beginning, just like the acorn Piers gave me. I put it outside over winter like he said, and all the leaves shrivelled up and died and dropped off, and there was basically this dead twig sticking out of the pot for a few months. But then – behold – buds appeared, then leaves; three, then five, then six, seven, and at the last count, eight. Winter always turns to spring, according to Buddhism. Which is another statement of the bleeding obvious, from one viewpoint, but which now I think incredibly profound. Because if I've learned one thing from Geoff, it's that when you start to change your mind, you start to change everything.

A Note About the Author

Edward Canfor-Dumas was educated at New College, Oxford, where he started writing and directing. He is well known for his TV work, which includes *Not the Nine O'Clock News*, *The Bill*, *Kavanagh QC*, *Tough Love*, *Pompeii: The Last Day* and *Supervolcano*. He is, with Richard Causton, the author of *The Buddha in Daily Life* (also published by Rider). He lives with his wife and two teenage children in Hertfordshire.